T0281888

By K. L. Cerra

Under Her Spell

Such Pretty Flowers

UNDER HER SPELL

UNDER HER SPELL

A NOVEL

K. L. CERRA

BANTAM
NEW YORK

Under Her Spell is a work of fiction. Names, characters, places, and incidents are either the products of the author's imagination or are used fictitiously. Any resemblance to actual persons, living or dead, events, or locales is entirely coincidental.

A Bantam Trade Paperback Original

Copyright © 2024 by K. L. Cerra

All rights reserved.

Published in the United States by Bantam Books, an imprint of Random House, a division of Penguin Random House LLC, New York.

BANTAM & B colophon is a registered trademark of Penguin Random House LLC.

LIBRARY OF CONGRESS CATALOGING-IN-PUBLICATION DATA
Names: Cerra, K. L., author.
Title: Under her spell: a novel / K. L. Cerra.
Description: New York: Bantam Dell, 2024.
Identifiers: LCCN 2024010716 (print) | LCCN 2024010717 (ebook)
| ISBN 9780593500279 (trade paperback) | ISBN 9780593500286 (ebook)
Subjects: LCSH: Missing persons—Fiction. | LCGFT: Thrillers (Fiction) | Psychological fiction. | Novels.
Classification: LCC PS3603.E7475 U53 2024 (print) | LCC PS3603.E7475 (ebook) | DDC 813/.6—dc23/eng/20240315
LC record available at https://lccn.loc.gov/2024010716
LC ebook record available at https://lccn.loc.gov/2024010717

Printed in the United States of America on acid-free paper

randomhousebooks.com

2 4 6 8 9 7 5 3 1

Book design by Susan Turner

To Andy, my best decision yet

UNDER HER SPELL

1

NOW

MY FIANCÉ WAS STANDING TOO CLOSE TO THE TRAIN
tracks.

I'd only stepped away for a minute to toss my
empty water bottle and then there he was, the toes of his
dress shoes on that pimpled yellow stripe. I could tell from
the set of his back and neck that he was scrolling through
emails. A subtle line of fuzz edged his neck below his neat
haircut. Glimpsing that vulnerable part of him made emotion well inside me.

It would be so easy to push him.

A gangly stranger jostled me in the crowd, stumbling a
bit before righting himself. It was enough to snap me out of
my bad thoughts.

"Careful!" I snatched Noah's hand and pulled him
away from the tracks, unsure if the warning was for him or
for me.

Noah moved toward me obediently, eyes still on his phone screen. A beat later, he looked up, and his crinkled gray eyes made my heart plummet. With my opposite hand, I rotated the ring I wore on my right index finger—the one I'd designed to look like a spiny bird's nest out of wire—and pressed the pad of my thumb into its sharp edges.

Bad Liv.

Noah smirked, reaching for my hand. "You're cute when you get all mother-hen on me, you know that?"

I smiled through a tide of anxiety. Anxiety, yes—that must be why I was having these unwelcome thoughts again. I felt for the heart-shaped outline of Sam's letter in my pocket, itching to unfold the worn piece of notebook paper right there in the terminal and read it for the umpteenth time. No use in telling Noah how on-edge I felt—he'd never understand why a letter from my childhood best friend was freaking me out. I'd breezily told him I was taking the train into Guilford for an impromptu get-together and he hadn't asked for any more details. This wasn't quite a lie. It *was* an impromptu get-together. It just happened to be with someone who'd been ignoring my pleas to reconnect for eight years.

With a shriek, the train materialized in the dark, glowing headlights like insect eyes. Noah squeezed my hand and I gave two quick squeezes back. It was our secret code we'd developed freshman year of college. *Love you. Love you, too.* Noah was a Midwestern brand of cute with a heartrendingly shy smile; the moment his broad shoulders cut into the doorway of the dorm common room I'd had a singular thought: *Mine.* My suitemates had groaned about what a disgustingly cute couple we made, but I didn't miss the glint of envy in their eyes. I knew they could scarcely believe I'd somehow—on a campus swarming with entitled man-children fixated on getting into as many girls' pants as possible—locked down our dorm's most eligible bachelor. Sometimes, I had trouble believing it myself, even after all this time.

Noah drew me into a kiss and I leaned into it, hoping to blot out my unease. Then I forced myself to be the first to break away and slipped onto the train, sending him a little wave from the door. I'd woken that morning with dread pulsing through me, in that weird way you can sometimes feel your heartbeat in your muscles. Just thinking about winding below the dark canopies on West Lake Avenue toward Sam's house set my blood simmering.

What could she possibly want to tell me?

I chose a seat by the window and settled against the fabric headrest, wrapping one leg around the other twice like a vine. I spotted Noah on the platform, watching a family wrangling two small children into their double stroller. It was something he'd started showing more of an interest in since we'd gotten engaged. *Don't get any ideas,* I warned the first time I'd seen his eyes go soft and wistful watching a toddler chasing a gaggle of pigeons. We'd both laughed off the sharpness in my voice. Yes, I was insanely lucky to have Noah, but sometimes he needed to be reminded to pump the brakes. I wasn't even twenty-seven; I wasn't even used to the term *fiancé* yet. On good days, it raised my heart rate in a not-entirely-unpleasant way; on bad days, it made my whole body stiffen, like a cobra preparing to strike.

Across the aisle of the train now, a forty-something man folded an empty wax paper bag in half, eyes flickering away from me. The train jerked to life and slid from the platform. It was only once we'd built speed that I turned my hands palms-up on my thighs, studying the pad of my thumb I'd pressed into my ring. Dark blood clamored under the skin.

Good.

Once, over happy hour, a coworker had grabbed my hand at the wrong angle. Her wine-stained lips had cinched tight with shock as she recoiled. *Jesus, Liv. Was that your ring? Do I need to get a tetanus shot now?* Later she'd joked about how brilliant I'd been to design jewelry that doubled as a weapon out in the city. I didn't have the heart to tell her I'd only ever turn it against myself.

I slipped Sam's note from my pocket. She'd folded it in the same heart configuration we'd used for countless notes to each other senior year of high school. I shivered, smoothing the worn paper against my thigh. I could still remember the little thrill I'd feel after noticing the bulge on the outside compartment of my backpack: my best friend was stealthy, and had always insisted on dispensing her notes in secret. I'd make myself wait for the most mind-numbing of classes—U.S. history—to unfold and savor them. And they never disappointed. Sam's notes would spill outside the confines of the page, crawling up into the margins like ants. They were always in metallic gel ink, and filled with her signature scathing commentary of our peers that made me alternately fight down snorts of laughter and thank my lucky stars to be on her good side. The memories made this note, penned in clotted ballpoint ink, all the more chilling:

Liv,
I know it's been a while, but I need to talk to you.
I need help and don't know who else to turn to

I'd studied those words for what felt like hours. Two stark lines. No period or sign-off. It was almost as if Sam had written this in the midst of fleeing. Was she being stalked? Running from a vengeful ex? Of course, I'd gone straight to social media to contact her. Our "correspondence" was a string of my own desperate attempts to break her silence, dating back to the summer after our high school graduation. They'd tapered to about once a year by now, all unanswered.

Found that set of stacked rings you made in my old jewelry box! How're you doing?

Omg, did you see who just got engaged from GHS??

Thinking about you. Let me know if you ever want to catch up.

But this time, every one of Sam's accounts had gone dark. I tried texting the old number I had, but—no surprise—my text bounced back as undeliverable. On the outer envelope she'd sent me, there'd been no return address, just the zip code. There was something ominous about those stark five numbers, staring up at me.

Yes, my relationship with Sam had been complicated, but weren't all teen-girl friendships? It had taken me well into college to recognize that what we'd had was special.

Sam's ferocious loyalty, our shared passion for jewelry making: I probably wasn't going to find that a second time around. Leave it to me to have ruined it all. What could have possibly compelled Sam to reach out to me, after what I'd done?

MOM PICKED ME UP IN the same gray Corolla she drove when I was in high school. There were new dents on the passenger side. When her eyes picked me out in the dark, she made a move to exit the driver's seat and help me with my suitcase, but I waved at her to stay inside. I could handle the luggage. Plus, I wasn't prepared to see how frail she'd gotten. The last time I was home—months ago now—I'd been blindsided by the knobbiness of her knees poking out from her burlap dress, transparent skin giving way to the blue neon of her veins.

I threw my suitcase in the trunk and climbed into the passenger seat. The semi-darkness of the train station carved deep hollows under Mom's eyes. She'd always been slender, but it hadn't been until Dad moved out that she started looking gaunt. It seemed she still hadn't recovered.

"Hiya," she said, leaning over to wrap her arms around me.

The smell of sandalwood essential oil came with the embrace. I pressed my face into Mom's shoulder. Guilford was one of the last places I'd wanted to be these past eight years, but by seeking refuge in Boston, I probably hadn't helped Mom any.

"Thanks for picking me up."

"Don't be silly. I got us a big vat of pad thai but I ended up caving and having a plate before you got in. The rest is waiting in the fridge for you. Sorry."

"Mom, it's past nine. Don't apologize."

A smile quirked over her lips. "Okay, then. I won't."

Mom nosed the Corolla out of the train station and onto Old Whitfield Street. I looked out the window, a knot tightening in my chest. How had I ever been accustomed to all this hulking greenery? Massive oaks choked the narrow roads, colonial homes with their neat painted shutters peeking from behind. They grew steadily more impressive as we approached the town Green, crisscrossed with dark ribbons of pathways and flanked by imposing, pillared churches. Then the memories bludgeoned me. Breath misting as we clutched paper cups of hot cocoa waiting for the lights on the town Christmas tree to come to life. That unmistakable musty-cellar smell that hit the moment you jangled the door open to Page Hardware. Sam and I had dug through refrigerator magnets in the front of the store and fished out matching ones: TRUE FRIENDS DON'T JUDGE EACH OTHER. THEY JUDGE OTHER PEOPLE TOGETHER.

I gulped down a mouthful of car air and cracked my window.

Mom glanced over at me. "Warm?"

"I'm okay."

We were past the Green now, turning onto Boston Post Road, then past Bishop's Orchards and its giant red apple sculpture out front. Past the expanse of Strawberry Hollow Farm and the lipstick-colored cottage set close to the road, which opened Labor Day every year selling gourds, pumpkins, and bittersweet wreaths. As we wound down into the dark network of roads off Route 1, the knot in my chest slid up into my throat.

Minutes later, we pulled into the gravel drive outside the house I'd lived in senior year of high school. As I followed Mom inside, dragging my suitcase, I wondered how it felt to live here alone. The door slammed shut behind us, moths flapping up against the screen.

Mom was at the refrigerator. "Let me warm up that pad thai."

Despite skipping dinner, my stomach was an anvil. "Actually, do you think I could save it for tomorrow? I'm kind of exhausted."

"Of course." Mom shut the fridge. Her face looked like she was running calculations.

"Thanks for getting it for me, though."

"You don't have to thank me." There was a hint of frustration in her voice.

Something twisted deep inside me. Mom and I were dancing around each other like strangers. It didn't use to be like this. Especially in the throes of Dad's rages, I'd felt closer to Mom than I'd felt to my own sister—after all, Penny had the good fortune of graduating three years before me, leaving Mom and me to weather it alone. I'd hide in my bedroom as Dad thundered a floor below, trembling and clutching my phone. Eventually, Mom would text me an update.

All fine. He's in the shower now.
That should be all for tonight.
Try to get some rest, sweetheart.

At the base of the stairs now, I couldn't resist peeking into Dad's old office. His sturdy mahogany desk had been removed, a white triangle on the wall where he'd hung his Northwestern Law pennant. Mom had shifted some things around to fill up the space—her old Singer sewing machine, an ugly squat filing cabinet—but it only seemed to highlight what had been removed.

Up the stairs on the second floor, I braced myself in the entry of my old bedroom. Thanks to our family's move from Denver the summer before my senior year, I'd only lived in Guilford one year before leaving for college, and my room had always been sparse. Still, I dreaded seeing what relic might have bubbled up from my closet or nightstand. I tiptoed inside and felt the crush of the lavender walls immediately.

I lay face up on my bed. A pointed corner caught my eye from the bedside table. It was a framed photo of Sam and me, ruddy-cheeked, in our ice skates.

I sat up sharply. Part of me was tempted to take Mom's car now and drive straight to Sam's parents' house. But it would be rude to swing by unannounced after nine P.M. It would have to wait until first thing tomorrow.

I snatched my phone and tapped out a text to Noah.

Arrived in one piece!

My blood sang through me as I scrolled the text message chains on my phone. After college graduation, I'd had a solid group of girlfriends over to our apartment for Thursday game nights. But somewhere around our twenty-fifth birthdays, the group began to dwindle. One girlfriend got married and bought a house in Rhode Island with her new husband; another two moved out of the city, citing skyrocketing rent. For a precarious few weeks, it was just me and Noah drinking cabernet and playing Scattergories in the living room, until we mutually decided it was kind of silly playing with just two people and never mentioned it again.

My childhood room felt so suffocating that I actually started typing out a message to the dormant group chat. But then I deleted it and laid back against my bank of pillows. Out of habit, I searched Sam's name—I'd been checking incessantly since receiving her note to see if any of her social media had reappeared.

I froze. Had I neglected to check this particular site? Not only was the page live, a photo had been posted: Sam's oversized smile, her face ghostly in the flash of a phone camera. It had already amassed over a hundred comments.

A headline blared across the top of the image.

26-YEAR-OLD GUILFORD WOMAN MISSING

2

THEN

"LET'S TAKE A LOOK AT YOUR SCHEDULE."

The guidance counselor—whose name I'd already forgotten—spread the sheet on her desk. The smell of fresh ink wafted up from the paper, turning my stomach. That single forkful of scrambled eggs I'd managed for breakfast half an hour ago still felt like a block of cement.

"Okay, for your first period, physics, did you see the trophy case when you walked in the front door? You'll want to hang a left at the end of it, take the hallway down the stairs, and your classroom will be the first one on the right."

"Okay, thanks." Under the table, I fiddled with the strings hanging from my cut-off skirt. I could feel the bristling energy of students coalescing in the hallway outside. Gathering in front of lockers and stairwells, bumping hips and shoulders, helping one another fill in the blanks of summer vacation. Every now and then, an elated shriek punctured the stillness of the administrative office. And me? I was stuck in the snow globe of this grim, adult world: all humming fluorescent lights, clacking keyboards, and my paunchy guidance counselor dressed in beige, squinting at my schedule. The first bell hadn't even rung, and already I felt left out.

"Where did you say you moved from, again?"

"Denver."

"Colorado, wow." The counselor pushed back from her desk a bit. "You're far from home."

Her sympathy was lacerating. *Please stop*, I thought.

But of course, she kept going. "Goodness. I can't even imagine—twelfth grade, being ripped out of school and forced to come to a new one. You'd think your parents could have held off moving for a year, until after you'd gradu-ated."

"You'd think."

A low whistle. "You poor thing."

"Well," I managed. "My dad got a job offer he couldn't turn down. So." I swiped at my schedule. "Thanks for this."

Then I trudged out of her office before she could make me feel even worse.

In the hallway outside, I flipped the hood of my sweat-shirt over my hair and let myself be swallowed in the sea of students. At 5:45 that morning, I'd put on my sparkly-appliqué shirt and black denim skirt and revved my courage in the mirror. This would be a good day. It would be a good year. A chance to reinvent myself into someone more . . . alluring. I'd had a few loyal friends back in Denver, but maybe this year, I could have more. Maybe, because of my new-girl allure, I'd even edge closer to that pulsing center of popularity.

But as soon as I spilled out of the guidance counselor's office, my predawn optimism deserted me. My schedule stuck damp in my hands. The counselor's pitying voice rang back at me.

I can't even imagine—twelfth grade, being ripped out of school and forced to come to a new one.

You poor thing.

Who was I kidding? This was going to suck.

First period at Guilford High started at an eye-watering 7:28 A.M. The next several hours were a blur of unfamiliar faces and syllabi. Dire warnings from one teacher after the next that I was embarking on the most rigorous academic endeavor of my high school career. Finally, unable to stand the torture another moment, I nabbed the clunky bathroom pass from the front of the classroom. The nearest girls' restroom was mercifully empty. I locked myself in the far stall and finally indulged in the sting of tears, even though I knew it would wreck my makeup. The guidance counselor was right: Why *had* Mom and Dad made me do this? And why hadn't I even tried fighting back? It was the kind of thing they wouldn't have dared pull on Penny.

The bathroom door opened suddenly. I held my breath. Under the stall door, I saw chunky combat boots plod over the bathroom tiles. A beat later, the brisk swish of a paper towel pulled from the dispenser. I sniffed, wiping my face with the backs of my hands.

"Hey," someone said.

My heart jolted. I hadn't thought my sniff was loud enough to hear over the crunching of the paper.

To my horror, the chunky boots marched to stand directly outside my stall. "Are you okay?"

"Yep." I reached for some toilet paper to blot my face and turned to flush the toilet.

Another beat of silence, during which this girl must have peered under my stall door. "I recognize your high-tops from English class. Not everyone can pull off that lime-green, so props! Anyway, I know you're the new girl. Just open up."

I stared at the metal door in disbelief. WHORE was scratched in bone-white lettering near the latch.

"I'm serious. Crying alone is just going to make you feel even shittier."

I waited a second to see if the girl would go away. She didn't. Defeated, I unlatched the door and stepped outside. The owner of the combat boots stood assessing me with her hands on her hips. She was petite and curvy, clad in ripped fishnets, with a thick plait of dark hair slung over one shoulder.

"So they didn't even give you a buddy or anything?" she asked, lifting her chin at me.

"A buddy?"

"Yeah. For the first day of school. Since you don't know anyone."

I shook my head, swiping at my bottom lash line. "No buddy."

"Unreal. Well, at least now you know someone. I'm Sam."

I gave her a weak smile. "Liv."

"I know." She pulled another sheet of paper towel from the dispenser, moistened it with water from the tap, and handed it to me.

"Thanks." I dared to look in the mirror, horrified by the spidery mess of mascara clotting my face.

"Bad first day?" Sam asked.

"It's just a lot, I guess."

"No shit. Bet it sucks."

In contrast to the guidance counselor's saccharine sympathy, Sam's straightforwardness was refreshing. "Yeah. It kind of does."

"Are you thirsty?"

I blinked.

"Whenever I cry, I get really thirsty," Sam clarified.

Now that she mentioned it, the back of my throat was achy and parched. "Maybe just a little. Is there a water fountain nearby?"

"Yeah, and it tastes like cat piss. I'll grab you a Coke from the vending machine."

Warmth flowed through me. I never would have expected a stranger to go out of their way like this for me. "Won't you get in trouble for being out of class too long?"

Sam flapped a hand at me. "The first day doesn't count. Teachers are too busy scaring the shit out of students to care."

I smirked, starting to dig around in my purse. "I noticed that, too. Let me get you some change for the soda . . ."

"Oh, stop. I want an excuse to wander anyway. Clean yourself up and I'll be back in a minute."

With Sam gone, I could focus my full attention on wiping down my face in the mirror. A makeup wipe was what I really needed—the paper towel was coarse, catching on my skin and reddening my cheeks. I looked so terrible in the mirror I almost laughed at myself. It'd been a tumultuous day and it wasn't even lunchtime yet.

The restroom door swished open again and a couple of girls drifted in, chatting and laughing. I hid behind my paper towel but I needn't have—I was invisible to them. One locked herself in the stall while the other fixed her hair in the mirror, avoiding my eyes. For a split second, I worried that Sam might decide not to return, and that the gesture of kindness would turn out to be an empty one.

Eventually, the two girls left the bathroom and a third swept in. She was undeniably striking, wearing a pair of shredded jeans and a tiny ribbed top she'd torn along the neckline and ruched with giant safety pins. She pulled a pot of lip gloss from a slouchy black bag and began to apply it with a fingertip. A strip of tanned, flat abdomen flashed each time she touched her upper lip. I couldn't help staring at her face in the mirror. She had a sheet of white-blond hair that fell down her back, and incongruous, nearly black, peaked eyebrows. The small bump on the bridge of her nose kept her face from being conventionally attractive, but even so, there was something intriguing about it.

Her eyes veered to mine in the mirror suddenly. "Oh, chickadee," she said. Her voice was coarse as gravel. "You're a mess."

I retreated behind my hair, cheeks flaming.

"Come here," she said.

The directive terrified me. What would she do if I re-fused? It didn't seem like an option. Even so, I was para-lyzed.

The girl closed the distance between us, pushing my hair behind my ears. Then her fingertips drifted to cup the base of my skull and I flinched, looking down at the bath-room tiles. They were the color and shape of stained front teeth. The girl was so close to me, I could smell her cinna-mon lip gloss. Why was she gripping me like that? It was bizarre.

"Look at you," she said.

"I know." Fresh tears swelled inside me. "I'm such an ugly crier."

"No such thing," she said. Then she released me, pulled a fluffy makeup brush from her bag and swiped it over the bridge of my nose twice. I stood stock-still under the fluo-rescent lights; eventually, I glanced up at the mirror in con-fusion.

My face peered back at me, smooth and luminous. No more red eyes, not a hint of mascara on my cheeks. In fact, I couldn't remember the last time I looked this pretty. But there was something strange about my eyes: they'd gone white, as if covered by a film or an opaque contact lens. I blinked and the effect went away.

"I—" I staggered closer to the mirror to assess myself. It had to be the lighting. My pupils had reappeared, but I still looked as fresh-faced as ever. How had this girl managed to get all the mascara off my face with only a couple swipes of her brush? I hadn't even seen her dip the brush in any powder. Somehow, I must have misjudged how badly I'd smeared my makeup in the stall—

"Do me a favor." It wasn't a question. The girl smoothed down her bright hair on her way out of the restroom. She looked back over her shoulder at me. "Never call yourself ugly again."

EVENTUALLY, SAM DID RETURN TO the bathroom with two bottles of Coke in tow. If she was surprised by my fresh face, she didn't say it. Instead, she asked to see my schedule and perused it as I palpated the pillowy skin beneath my eyes. I was still in shock. Where had the mascara streaks gone? And how had my skin turned so luminous? I thought about saying something to Sam about the strange blond girl, but worried that she wouldn't believe me.

The electronic tone of the bell sounded.

"We both have free period next," Sam said. "Want me to show you around this shithole?"

There was, in fact, nothing I wanted more.

Sam was a confident tour guide, sweeping through the hallways and voicing over the highlights. Art wing (where she spent most of her time), English wing, band room. An area by the stairwell I should be wary of, as it tended to attract entangled couples. On our way through the cafeteria, she stopped to introduce me to a handful of girls whose names I promptly forgot. It didn't matter—I'd found my safe haven with Sam. Thanks to her, I wouldn't have to tromp through this mazelike high school on my own. I tightened my grip on my backpack straps to hide the way my hands were shaking with relief.

Sam chattered to me about her summer break, which she spent working as a counselor at a local handicrafts summer camp. "At least I got to spend my days surrounded by art," she said. She cast a look around with a sharp squint. "Unlike here." I listened to her with half my attention, smiling and laughing at what I hoped were the right times. I couldn't stop touching my face, though, wondering what that blond girl had done to me in the bathroom.

Sam led me outside and into a small grassy area by the edge of the athletic field. "Not much to see out here. People smoke there." She indicated a sheltered area farther out. "The junior and senior lots are over there. Is that where you parked this morning?"

"Tragically, I don't have my license yet."

"Oh. That *is* tragic, Liv."

We were approaching what looked like a white gazebo at the edge of the grassy area. Leafy tree canopies arced above the structure, shrouding it in shadow. From between the slats in the wood, I could just make out the back of a ribbed top, a sheet of white-blond hair. An electric feeling streaked through me. It was the girl from the bathroom, sitting cross-legged with a couple of friends. They seemed to be gathered around something on the ground.

"Hey," I said, gesturing at the gazebo. "What're they doing in there?"

Sam grabbed my arm suddenly and yanked me in the opposite direction.

"What're you doing?"

But Sam wouldn't provide an explanation until we were safely back inside the cafeteria, the din of conversation settling around us. "Okay," she said, in a low voice. "That area is kind of off-limits."

"Why?"

"Because it's been claimed. Did you see those three girls in there?"

"Yeah. Who are they?"

Sam bit her lip. It was the first time since I'd met her that she looked unsteady. "Well, the blond one, Eden, is like the ringleader. The one with the long hair is Cora and the tall one is Avery."

"Okay . . ."

She rolled her eyes. "They call themselves The Sisterhood."

I bit back a laugh. "You can't be serious."

"Hey. I couldn't make this shit up if I tried."

With the invocation of the blond from the bathroom, Sam had my full attention now. "Okay," I said, "first of all, who makes a name for themselves like that? Do they have their own TV show or something? And what were they doing in that gazebo?"

"I don't know. Probably playing with their tarot cards and crystals."

I scoffed. "So what? They're witches?" But even as I responded, I flashed back to the way the blond had taken my face in her hands, how she changed the way I saw myself in the mirror. A heavy, unsettled feeling began to seep through the pit of my stomach.

Sam leaned up against the wall, crossing her arms.

"They don't really . . . play well with others. The popular kids think they're full of themselves and that they're weird. Avery collects animal skulls—I saw one of them hanging from the rearview mirror in her car. Maybe it was a squirrel? And Eden has a tattoo of a black stag on her bikini line."

"Wait a second. An actual tattoo? Have you seen it?"

A frown from Sam. "Well . . . no. But anyway, then there are the guys. They're scared shitless of The Sisterhood, especially after a rumor went around that Eden hexed her ex-boyfriend. Pretty messed up, right?"

Sam's description startled me. What kind of girls wanted boys to be afraid of them? The popular girls at my old school drew their power from the fact that they were never unattended by their male counterparts. In Assembly, they squirmed over guys' laps, laughing and snatching away their baseball hats. Their lockers were full of photographic evidence of their boyfriends and the other guys who followed in their glittery wake.

My own friend group had never been alluring enough to attract a single guy. I opened my mouth to tell Sam about the incident in the restroom that morning, but my courage deserted me at the last moment. Here was a promising new friend—did I really want to endanger the possibility by telling Sam a story that would have her doubting my sanity?

My thoughts were drowned in the drone of the bell. Free period was over.

Sam nudged me with her elbow, shattering my thoughts. "Wanna split a bag of Swedish Fish for the road?"

3

NOW

N THE RECEPTION AREA OF THE GUILFORD POLICE STATION,
a fluorescent light whined, one of its panels darkened. I
clutched Sam's note, folded back into its original heart-
shaped configuration and tucked inside its envelope as if to
keep its secrets safe. My sweat was dampening one of the
edges and I released it into my lap. Sam's note had been
disturbing enough—after all, it'd spurred my impromptu
train ride to Guilford—but coupled with the announcement of Sam's disappearance, it felt like I was cradling a
grenade. In the empty reception area, I tapped my foot
impatiently. The young woman who'd greeted me twenty
minutes earlier had disappeared, leaving me to stare at the
shallow dish of Dum-Dums at the desk. Only the worst
flavors languished at the bottom: grape and mystery. This
struck me as immensely sad, the idea of offering lollipops

to people with problems large enough to warrant a trip to the police station.

Sam had loved cracking the candied shells of Blow Pops (cherry) with her molars, the better to access the soft wad of gum inside. It was a vice that had driven her step-mother up the wall.

Regardless, Sam wouldn't have been caught dead with a grape or mystery Dum-Dum.

Eventually, the young paper-pusher returned and invited me behind the reception desk to a sterile conference room. She looked meaningfully at me, as if I should know what to do, until I deposited myself in a pebbly plastic chair at the table in the center of the room and pulled my purse into my lap. Then she gave me a curt nod and left.

A vent behind me sputtered to life, spewing icy air across my lap. Goosebumps reared up on my bare thighs. Was this an interrogation room? I'd never even been inside a police station before, but it tracked with what I'd seen on TV: a bare-faced clock on the wall, a single box of sandpapery tissues in the center of the table. I stared at the closed door, waiting. Finally, a man entered the room. He looked distracted, scrubbing a palm over his silver buzzcut and glancing backward into the hallway.

"Detective Patterson," he said, offering his hand. "Hannah tells me you received some kind of communication from Sam Mendez?"

"Yes." I drew out the envelope and placed it on the table between us. "I got this in the mail three days ago. Sam

and I haven't talked since high school, so I thought it was"—
I gulped—"odd."

The detective sat down across from me and slipped on
a pair of gloves. "No return address," he said, peering down
at the envelope.

"I know. Just the zip code."

He was already opening the letter. The notebook paper
heart looked so ridiculous in his meaty hands that I had the
sudden urge to cry. He wasn't the one who was supposed to
be handling this. "Sam and I used to write each other notes
in high school folded like that," I blurted out. Patterson only
gave me a strange look and moved his thumb under the fold
until the heart sprang open like an accordion. I watched his
eyes flit back and forth over the scant two lines I'd long since
memorized. *No period, no sign-off.*

"How do you even know this is from Sam?" he asked
finally.

Hot embarrassment seeped through me. "It is. It has to
be. I remember her handwriting and—I mean—who else
would have sent me this? Folded into a heart like that?"

"Okay," Patterson said gently. I had the sense I was failing some test. "Thank you for bringing this in."

"Of course. Do you guys have any leads in the case
at all?"

Patterson frowned. "We're in touch with the family regarding the investigation. Forensics has Sam's devices, we're
looking into phone records, and continuing to conduct in-
terviews with family and acquaintances."

That would mean no. "Okay. Thanks. I'll let you know if I
come across anything else."

"Please do." Patterson handed me a business card and stood, indicating I should do the same.

I made my way back through the reception area. My pocket felt empty without Sam's note. While handing it off to the police had been necessary, it didn't seem fair that I had to part with the first overture from Sam in eight years. Mere feet from the door to the station, I doubled back and pocketed a mystery-flavored Dum-Dum. Even a shitty lollipop was better than nothing.

NOTHING BUT MUSCLE MEMORY GUIDED me through the winding, canopied roads to Sam's house. It was exactly as I remembered it: dark green siding, large windows that opened to the woods on either side. These days, if I closed my eyes, I could still see the layout of her living room and kitchen—everything down to the bowl of seashells her stepmom had curated in the first-floor bathroom. I cut the engine and wrestled against my raging heartbeat.

I never would've imagined I'd be back here.

Sam's stepmother came to the door when I knocked. Her bob had lightened a few shades so it was almost platinum now, and the lines around her mouth may have grown deeper, but she looked so like I remembered, it was jarring.

It took her a few moments to place me. "Liv?"

And then I was spilling my guts to her, standing there on her pineapple doormat. "Sam wrote to me, so I took the train out to meet her, but on my way over, I saw the news—"

Her face softened with sympathy. "Come in," she said quietly.

On watery legs, I followed her to the living room. This, too, was exactly as I'd remembered—hulking sofa with crisp, overstuffed pillows. It'd never been comfortable, but even back them, I'd appreciated how expensive it must have been. I wedged myself into a corner of the couch and crossed my arms tightly over myself. Sam's stepmother sat on the opposite couch and was watching me, concern bright in her eyes.

"I'm guessing there have been no updates," I said weakly.

She shook her head. "Tom just left for the station now to follow up. It's been . . ." She passed a hand over her face. "It's been quite the week."

"I'm so sorry." Words I'd been wanting to express to Sam's family for years now, but they weren't nearly enough. I stared at the grille over the fireplace until I was sure the image was imprinted on my retinas.

Sam's stepmom crossed her legs. She had a scarlet pedicure and wore a metallic sandal with some interlocking brand insignia on it. "We're very lucky to have such a supportive community. Sam's roommates organized yesterday's search party, and it felt like all of Guilford showed up. One of Sam's friends, Maddie, even set up the 'Find Sam' hashtag. I'm not sure if you've seen it online?"

"Good." I let out a breath. "I haven't seen it, but I'm so glad people are stepping up." I felt a twinge of guilt: of course I'd missed the search party.

"Some of her friends seem to think Sam was burnt out and was looking into a trip to Europe. Admittedly, we hadn't been talking much after Sam moved out, but it seems unlike her to drop everything on a whim. Plus, going to Europe is a big deal! I just can't believe she wouldn't think to tell us."

My head swam with the influx of information. A trip to Europe? That sounded . . . hopeful. But then I remembered the note I'd just dropped off at the police station. I swallowed and reached for my phone. "Would you like to see the note she wrote to me?"

"Please."

"I just dropped the original off with the police, but I have a picture here." I pulled it up, pinched apart the screen to zoom in. Sam's stepmom fairly snatched it out of my hand. I felt a sinking sensation as I watched her eyes skate over the screen, its square of white reflected in her pupils. I thought of the words she was taking in. *I need to talk to you. I need help and don't know who else to turn to.* It was the very last thing you'd want to read from your recently disappeared daughter.

Sam's stepmom looked up, visibly shaken. "She didn't sign it. It was almost like she . . ."

"Was rushed. I know. But I'm sure it's Sam because she used to write me notes like this all the time in high school. She'd folded it up to look like a heart and everything."

Her stepmom wouldn't look at me as she handed back my phone.

"I'm sorry," I said again. It seemed the only appropriate sentiment.

"Don't be." I could tell she was trying hard to compose herself, sitting back against the couch cushions and jiggling her foot. "I'm glad you came here to share this with me, and with the police. Thank you."

"Of course." I hesitated. "Do you have any idea what

Sam could have been talking about, when she said she needed help?"

"No. Not at all." Her eyes were on her pant legs now, which she smoothed with her red nails. "Sam has been a bit distant from Tom and me these past few months. From Everett, too."

Sam's twin's name sent a bolt down my spine. "Oh? Where is Everett these days? Do you think he'd be willing to talk with me?"

Sam's stepmom gestured out toward the back of the house. "He lives in our guesthouse out back. I'd say you could drop by now, but it doesn't look like his car is in the drive." She lowered her voice, even though we were the only ones in the house. "Truthfully, Everett's been taking this whole thing extremely hard—harder than Sam's father, I think."

I felt a deep pang of sympathy—for Everett, and the entire Mendez family. They'd been dealt an atrocious hand within the past decade or so. "I'm so sorry."

"Yes, well." Sam's stepmother's gaze went far away for a moment before snapping back into focus. "Anyway, what I was saying: Sam dropped out of our family group text back in May and even called me around that time to let me know she was getting really busy with her jewelry making and wasn't going to be able to visit as often as usual."

A cold sensation crept down my forearms. "I noticed her social media accounts went dark, too."

"Mmhmm." Sam's stepmom traced her bottom lip with a finger.

"I'm just curious—was Sam dating anyone?"

"No, not that we know of."

We both slipped into a buzzing silence. My mind whirred. If Sam were really feeling afraid or in danger, booking a last-minute trip to Europe might have been her solution. But why wouldn't she have reached out to her family if she were feeling that desperate? Had she really been busy with jewelry making? Or had that been an excuse for something else, something darker she found herself swallowed up in?

"I want to show you something," Sam's stepmom said suddenly.

I followed her across the living room, down the hallway, past the seashell bathroom, and into Sam's bedroom. The memories walloped me the second we set foot inside. There it was, that same bed with its bark-brown comforter we'd both splayed across sorting beads and bending wire. Sam had me sit there when she did my makeup before dances; it was there she'd once inadvertently clamped my eyelid while trying to curl my lashes. When it came to friendships between girls, some bruising was always inevitable, wasn't it?

Sam's mother lifted a lacquered jewelry box off the dresser. She opened it, exposing a pile of the leathery mermaid purses that Sam used to collect as a kid. But there was something else beneath them, something pale.

"Hearts," Sam's stepmom said, lifting out the familiar, folded ruled papers. She gave me a sad smile. "When you were telling me about the note, I connected the dots in my head. Did you know Sam had been keeping all of yours?"

The punch of sadness and guilt nearly knocked the wind out of me. I swayed for a moment on unsteady legs. What had I done with Sam's notes? Shoved them in the bottom of some gritty backpack? I lifted a finger and thumbed the edge of a folded heart as my insides twisted. "I had no idea."

There was another item at the bottom of the jewelry box. Sam's stepmom scooped it out so we could both study it: a round ceramic tile with a wide blue eye upon it.

She frowned, turning it over. "Any idea what this is?"

"No." But even as I said it, the eye niggled at me like a pesky cuticle. Where the hell had I seen that before?

"Ah, well." Sam's mom returned the tile to the bottom of the box. "You know what one of the hardest parts of this investigation is? Besides the fact that Sam is missing, of course."

"Hmm?"

She closed the jewelry box gently. "I've just had to accept that there are some things about my daughter I'll never understand."

4

THEN

TWO WEEKS AFTER THE START OF SCHOOL, I HUNCHED over my workstation with a pair of round-nosed pliers. Moving boxes sat around the perimeter of my room. I hadn't gotten around to them; something about the syrupy East Coast heat, coupled with my mounting dread as the school year crept ever closer, had rendered me paralyzed. But I'd intentionally packed my jewelry-making supplies in a separate box to be unpacked on Day One. I wouldn't have made it this far into the summer without it.

My bracelet was almost done. It was a wide cuff, its delicate swirls inlaid with iridescent beads. Although it hadn't been my intention while designing it, something about the chaos of the stacked spirals made me think of Medusa. The harder I concentrated on manipulating the copper wire into perfect spirals, the less Dad's roars, one floor below, edged into my consciousness.

"—the fuck do you think I mean?"

This time I flinched, dropping the pliers. The rubber-ized grips bounced against the tabletop.

Mom's shrill voice fired back, something unintelligible.

Breathe, I instructed myself. *You're okay.*

I picked up the pliers again to add a final bead to my cuff. Before Penny had left for college, she'd invented ways for us to distract ourselves during the worst of the fights. Sometimes she'd hand me one white earbud and we'd slip together into the electronic heartbeat of her music. Some-times she'd come into my room and flop on my bed with theatrics of her own. The day she left Denver for Yale, I hadn't cried. I kept my eyes dry to telegraph the message to her: *How could you do this to me?*

My phone screen illuminated on my worktable—a text from Mom.

Meet me outside in 5

A shard of fear lodged in my throat. It must be bad if Mom was fleeing the house. Had he hurt her again? Most of the time, Dad's lashings were strictly verbal, but I'd never forget the night he sent Mom sailing across the kitchen, cracking the back of her head against the cabinets. She pre-tended that since her hair hid the lump that rose hours later, it didn't count.

I fastened the final bead on the cuff and forced it over the knobby bones of my wrist. The bracelet had heft, shunt-ing to either side as I rotated my arm. It made me feel se-cure, like I was wearing a piece of armor.

I crept down the stairs with my shoes in my hand and slipped out the front door. Mom was already in the driver's seat of her car, the air-conditioning set to full blast. I opened the passenger side and climbed in next to her.

"Are you okay?" I asked as the gravel ground beneath the tires.

"Sure, yeah." She sounded breathless and her cheeks were pink.

I stared at my lap as we wound up our street, looming trees blurring past my window. "This is the second time this week, isn't it?"

Mom set her mouth. She didn't look over at me.

It was getting worse. Once, I'd had the courage to ask Mom when "it"—that's the term we used—had all started, since I couldn't remember a time unmarred by their fighting. Mom had looked only vaguely uneasy before telling me, *The day after our wedding.*

"Have you heard of the Wythers House?" Mom said suddenly, in an overly bright voice.

I fiddled with my beaded cuff in my lap. "No. What's that?"

"This gorgeous historic home off the Guilford Green. They have tours all weekend and we're going on one now."

I ran my tongue over the ridges on the roof of my mouth. Even though it was Mom's style to avoid, it still frustrated me that we weren't having the conversation we needed to have. Mom and I had just fled from our own house to escape my father's wrath, and here we were, making plans to visit some stupid colonial shack.

"Okay," I said. "But maybe we should—"

"We're going on the tour," Mom said firmly. She kept her gaze on the road. "And we're going to have a great time."

THE WYTHERS HOUSE WAS EVEN more underwhelming than I feared. It was cream-colored and shaped funny, its roof slanting sharply downward on one side. The women who greeted us in the dark living room explained that this style of house was called a "saltbox."

"Even back in the 1600s, larger homes were taxed more heavily," she explained, leading us through the gloom to sign in. "If a man could reach up and touch the roof, the home would be taxed at a lower rate. Some very crafty individual designed a two-story home that allowed a man to touch the roof—but only on one side. They'd get the best of both worlds: two floors and lower taxes."

"Very crafty," Mom agreed.

I looked around the space, my eyes adjusting to the darkness. A wide harvest table ran down the length of the room, bare except for a metal can of wildflowers. Immediately behind, a deep soot-stained fireplace yawned, big as a closet, a cauldron hanging from an iron hook over a stack of firewood. Narrow windows crisscrossed with metal latticework ushered in shocking diamonds of light. The room smelled like pine and woodsmoke.

"Liv." Mom nudged me gently in the side. "Want to sign in for us?"

I approached the writing desk in the back of the room. But as I drew closer, I noticed the figure sitting behind it wasn't some woman like the one who had led us inside.

It was the blond from the bathroom at Guilford High. Eden.

Warmth leaped through me. Here was Eden, making money on the clock—like a real adult—while I'd officially been caught, as if with my pants down, spending my weekend bounding after my mom. And of all the kids to have spotted me out in the wild like this, Eden had to be the worst.

"Sign in here." Eden indicated a clipboard, barely looking at me.

Heart racing, I printed our names on the ledger. Sam's voice echoed in my head. *They call themselves The Sisterhood.* I dared a surreptitious glance through my hair. Eden was working her jaw, pulling little cherry-shaped candies from a white paper bag, despite the framed No Food or Drink, Please placard next to the sign-in sheet.

I scrawled the last of my name in one wobbly ribbon. As I put the pen down, my bracelet clomped against the clipboard.

Eden had half a cherry candy on her index finger. "Nice bracelet."

"Thanks."

Languidly, she bit the piece of candy off her finger and reached out to touch the copper whorls on my cuff. Then her eyes went wide, dark brows snapping together. "Where did you get this?"

"I-I made it."

Her mouth opened, the insides of her lips stained candy-red. "Wait a second. I remember you . . ."

I was just taking a breath to respond—to confirm or

deny, I hadn't yet decided—when Mom's voice rang out across the room. "Liv? They're willing to start a tour with just us two. Ready?"

I nodded once at Eden with my own lips pressed together before joining my mother.

Our guide, Tabitha, snaked us through the shadowy interior. A "keeping room" with massive, dark wood built-ins and windows crowded with sharp leaves from the garden. A parlor with faded stencils along the tops of the walls that looked like blazing suns. Tabitha walked through the spaces as if in a daze, long gauzy dress drifting behind her.

"Oliver and Harriett Wythers purchased this home as newlyweds in 1657," she said, coming to stand beneath a framed square of needlepoint on the wall.

I squinted. The pattern looked almost like an enlarged human eye.

"Oliver passed away in 1660 from brutal gastrointestinal complications, and Harriett tended to the home until her own passing thirty-three years later. Though she had no shortage of interested suitors, Harriett never did remarry. This was unusual at that point in time—more than enough to get the town talking."

I could have sworn I saw Mom's jaw sharpen next to me.

"Likely," Tabitha went on, "it was one of her embittered castoffs that started the rumor that Harriett poisoned her husband."

I turned at a flash of movement behind me. At first, I thought it was Eden, but it was her petite friend I'd spotted

with her in the gazebo on that first day of school. I caught
a glimpse of a tapered gray eye before she left the room.

"Of course," Tabitha continued, sweeping us out of
the parlor and toward the staircase to the second floor,
"there were whispers of witchcraft, as well."

Witchcraft, Mom mouthed to me, with a dangerous
smile. I knew she was trying to spice up the tour because she
felt bad for dragging me there, felt bad that her fight with
Dad had ruined the day.

I quirked my lips right back at her. *Please,* I thought,
hard. *It's not your fault.*

Up the stairs and to the right was a bedroom with a
four-poster bed and a mannequin wearing a frilled, high-
neck dress, yellowed with age. Tabitha was telling us more
about Harriett and all the steps she'd taken to care for the
house, but I tuned out, listening to the whispers and giggles
of the two girls at the foot of the stairs. Were they laughing
about me, on a tour with my mom? They had to be.

Suddenly, I felt a telltale warmth under my dress.

Could it . . . ? No.

My period wasn't due for another few days. I crossed
one leg over the other, felt it again. The second hot gush was
undeniable.

Frantically, I unzipped my purse, feeling around for a
tampon. My fingers closed around the crinkly plastic.

Hallelujah.

"Sorry, um." My words landed like lead on the floorboards, cutting Tabitha's monologue short. "Can I use the
bathroom?"

"Of course," Tabitha said after a beat. Then she turned to call down the stairs. "Cora?"

Presently, the girl with the tapered gray eyes entered the room.

"Do me a favor and show this young lady to the outhouse, will you?"

Cora ducked her head. It struck me as an appropriately old-fashioned gesture: she was clearly in character.

I thought of Eden gnawing cherry candies off her fingertips in the living room. *She* evidently wasn't.

Cora didn't try to speak to me as she took me downstairs, out the front door, and across the lawn to the outhouse. I felt more relaxed with her, none of the bristling energy I'd felt with Eden. Still, I caught myself studying Cora as she cut through the wet grass. I wanted to ask her what she'd been doing with her friends in the gazebo that first day of school—maybe it would help to explain what Eden had done to me in the bathroom. I even started piecing some of the words together in preparation. *Were those tarot cards I saw you looking at the other day? My friend mentioned you were into crystals?* But I didn't have the nerve to spit them out.

"Here you go," Cora said, stopping short of the outhouse. "The door locks from the inside, but you don't have to worry about anyone bothering you out here."

"Thanks." Then I scuttled inside, locking the door behind me.

There were no windows. Should there have been? I flipped the light on—a bare bulb in the center of the ceiling—and tore off a clod of toilet paper to clean myself up. This was not what I would have expected from the interior of an outhouse: crown molding at the ceiling and wainscoting along the floor, a vase of dusky roses on the pedestal sink. The lack of windows, however, made my chest tighten. Was Cora still standing outside? I hadn't heard her swish back through the grass toward the main house and for some reason, this bothered me immensely.

Afterward, I washed my hands, peering at my reflection in the mirror. Unfamiliar shadows ringed my eyes; in this light, my blue eyes looked so dark they appeared almost black. I put a wet hand to my clavicle. My skin was blazing.

A clang at the door made me jump. Was someone trying to get in? Cora assured me I wouldn't have to deal with any competition for the outhouse. Besides, I'd just been inside the main house—I was sure Mom and I had been the only visitors.

"Just a minute," I said, my voice high.

I touched wet fingertips to my hairline, which cooled my body considerably. With no windows to crack, the air inside the structure was thick with summer heat.

After drying my hands, I reached to unlock the door. But even after I'd flipped back the lock, the door wouldn't budge.

"What the hell." This was exactly the kind of thing that would happen to me—getting locked inside a seventeenth-century outhouse. I jiggled the heavy iron knob.

Had the door mechanism simply gotten stuck? Expanded in the heat? I switched to using two hands, wresting the metal knob back and forth with all my might.

"Cora?" I called.

Silence. Then—I could have sworn I heard it—a snatch of laughter. The same breathy giggle I'd heard at the foot of the stairs in the main house.

I rapped on the inside of the door. "Hey, if you can hear me, can you come here?"

My bracelet jumped off my wrist, clattering to the floor. Immediately, panic washed over me.

"Shit!" I snatched my bracelet off the floor and staggered to the center of the outhouse. Hands shaking, I unzipped my purse and grappled for my phone. Five ghosts of bars taunted me from the left-hand corner of my screen: no reception.

I reached for the doorknob again as my head began to tilt with hysteria. How long before Mom or Tabitha realized I'd been gone for a concerning amount of time? What if, by then, I'd devoured every last mouthful of humid air in this tiny space?

Something tickled my fingertips and I reared back. A beetle with a shellacked black body was edging its way out of the keyhole, antennae probing the air. It was about the length of a standard, rectangular pink eraser. I watched, horrified, as it jerked onto the panel of the door and stood there, swaying on slick filament legs. Looking straight at me.

Those inky beads sent a chill through my limbs. But that wasn't the worst part: on the beetle's back was a distinct white-and-blue pattern that could only be a wide, unblinking human eye.

The next few seconds were a crush of panic—swiping with my purse at the eerie insect, another desperate attempt at the doorknob, and somehow, miraculously, spilling out into the dewy lawn.

I doubled over, sucking down fresh air.

I was free.

When I glanced up, I saw a fringe of blond hair whip around a hedge before disappearing from view.

5

NOW

MOM WANTED TO SURPRISE ME WITH A SPONTANEOUS outing the following morning. I'd gotten little sleep, my mind a hive of anxiety, but the excitement on her face pushed me to drag my exhausted body back into the passenger seat of her Corolla. Mom put classic rock on the radio, humming under her breath, and drove us back in the direction of the Green.

"How was Sam's stepmom holding up?" she asked at a stoplight.

"Like you would imagine. It was so weird being back in that house without Sam there." I thought about telling her about the pile of heart-shaped notes I'd seen in Sam's jewelry box, but even the thought of describing them made me miserable.

"Well," Mom said. "All the more reason to get you out of the house today for something fun!" Her shoulders jumped to her ears, her signature display of excitement. "I have a feeling you're really going to like this."

She was driving us past the Green now, into the grid of colonial homes—the historic heart of Guilford. White clap-boards, dark shutters, and that unending swath of foliage. We approached a tall, narrow Victorian home with scal-loped siding the color of cotton candy and elaborate, swirled finials along the roofline. A Pegasus weathervane swiveled on the roof; weeping willows like arcing fireworks obscured the dark windows. One façade of the house was choked by a trellis full of clambering ivy.

A woman in a flowered dress stood in the driveway, watching us with one hand shielding her eyes.

"Um, *surprise?*" she said, as we got out of the car.

I blinked at her. "Oh my God. Penny!"

"That's more like it!" My sister grabbed and hugged me fiercely and I laughed against her. But something felt . . . off. I dared to study Penny as I pulled away. This sallow-faced woman hardly resembled the girl who'd turned heads at my college graduation in her electric-blue minidress and with the sun trapped in her striking copper mane—a per-fect nod to her name. Now, I couldn't quite tell, but her body seemed lumpy under the unfamiliar billow of her dress. There were purplish crescents under her eyes. I didn't recall her looking this haggard when I'd last seen her a cou-ple of months ago.

I tried my best to mask my alarm with happy disbelief. "What are you doing here? I was going to come out to visit this weekend—"

"Mom thought we should surprise you. She found us a

sitter for the day and I wasn't going to turn down that offer. Plus, I did not want to miss this. I don't know what strings Mom pulled to get you an appointment—these girls have a year-and-a-half-long waitlist!" She considered. "The feature in *Glamour* probably had something to do with it."

"Shhh," Mom hissed to Penny, elbowing her in the side. "I haven't told Liv anything. Don't ruin the surprise."

The three of us tromped up a hollow-sounding porch. A glossy green door beckoned, adorned with a bittersweet wreath. I reached a tentative finger toward the translucent orange casing of a bud. The edge was startlingly sharp and I drew back, half expecting to see blood on the pad of my finger.

Penny rang the doorbell. A mournful tone resonated through the house, calling to mind an organ, or a church bell.

"Get ready," Penny said, nudging me.

There was a scrabbling sound on the other side of the door. The hinges groaned as the door opened to reveal a twenty-something girl dressed all in black.

"Welcome to Beloved," she said.

Mom squeezed my arm.

We were ushered through a foyer of dark wood into a room with petal-colored walls and crisp crown molding that mirrored the finials on the exterior of the house. Its sparse elegance made my breath catch in my throat. In front: a seating area with three spotless white upholstered chairs, a glass table with a sculptural display of dark flowers, and a small, tasteful chandelier overhead. Beyond, a full-length oval mirror stood by a pedestal. But my eyes were pulled more urgently to the two lithe mannequins beyond the seating area. They each wore couture wedding gowns whose sweeping lines, dramatic trains, and immaculate beading made it clear why this place had garnered a year-and-a-half-long waitlist.

"Champagne?" The black-clad shopgirl offered me a crystal flute from a tray.

"Sure, thanks." The bubbles felt like bites on my tongue.

"You are *so* lucky," the girl whispered to me, as Penny and Mom chattered amongst themselves. "I commissioned my wedding dress from Beloved a year ago, and it honestly changed my life."

"Wow." I took another jerky sip of champagne.

The clack of heels sounded in the foyer.

"Oh," the shopgirl said, pulling away. "Eden's here. I'll leave you girls to it."

Wait a second . . .

"Liv Edwards." The gravelly tone was unmistakable, even after so many years. "It's been a minute."

My head snapped up to follow the voice. The sculptural face peering down at me elicited a dull jab of recognition. Lacquered lips spread over bared teeth, slashes of black brows over oil-slick eyes.

Eden Holloway was welcoming me into her shop.

HERE WAS A SCENARIO I never would've imagined. Eden and I had exchanged only a handful of words over the course of our time together at Guilford High, the majority of them that very first day in the girls' bathroom. After that

I'd tracked the way The Sisterhood cut through the hallways like a school of predatory fish, loath to admit—even to myself—the way these girls simultaneously unsettled and mesmerized me.

Mom began gushing to Eden the moment she entered the room. "You have no idea how grateful I am that you opened up an appointment for us today. I didn't think there was even a chance we'd get in—"

Eden settled herself in one of the white chairs. She wore a chic, sage-colored romper and chunky nude peep-toes. Admittedly, this is not where I would have pictured her landing post-graduation. A wedding shop owner? I remembered Eden's talon-like hands at the base of my skull that first day of school. All of this around me now—the flowers and the chandelier and the gowned mannequins—it all seemed so . . . sweet.

"Please," Eden was saying to my mother. "When I saw Liv's name, I recognized it immediately from high school." She winked at me. "Class of 2011 needs to look out for each other, right?"

I felt transported back to the Wythers House as an insecure seventeen-year-old. Once again, Eden was the paragon of maturity and sophistication—her own bridal boutique, profiled in *Glamour*!—and here I was, a kid trailing after her mom.

"Cupcake?" A second antique-looking silver tray appeared under my nose. Instead of champagne flutes, this one boasted a diamond-shaped configuration of miniature cupcakes, the exact cotton-candy shade of the shop's exterior. The tops of the cupcakes were studded with what looked like pearls arranged in intricate whorls. Exquisite, just like Eden's couture.

I glanced up at whoever was proffering the tray, and my ribs tightened in surprise. Cora stood smiling down at me, clad in a smoke-colored sheath dress, those distinctive, guileless eyes fringed with inky lashes. She and Eden had stayed friends, all this time? Cora couldn't possibly remember me—the two of us had probably exchanged less than a sentence throughout my entire year at GHS.

"Oh my gosh, *Liv*." It was almost impossible not to soften at the warmth in her voice. "It's amazing to see you again!" Where Eden's voice was gravelly and no-nonsense, Cora's was effusive and sweet as syrup.

"You, too." Though amazing? Maybe a bit of an overstatement. "These are pretty." I picked up a cupcake gingerly, afraid I'd mar the intricate design. A delicate bite revealed a blood-red interior that melted on my tongue—less sweet than I'd expected—with hints of something botanical, like rose.

"Oh, you're too sweet! If you particularly like the design or the flavor, let me know, and I'll remember when designing your wedding cake." At my look of surprise, she pointed toward the end of the studio. "My bakery is over in the next room."

Ah, so Eden and Cora had figured out how to run a joint venture. That part made sense—the choice of industry, however, was still throwing me for a loop.

"No Avery?" I asked, craning my neck to look in the direction of Cora's domain.

Cora shook her head. "Sadly, we fell out of touch after

high school. But I'm so lucky to have this one around every day!" She bent down to give Eden a little side-hug, who rolled her eyes playfully in response.

"Alright," Eden said, squirming out of Cora's grip and uncovering an iPad on her lap. "Let's get down to business." She passed me a dark matte business card, tapped out something with black nails on her screen, and then fixed me with a sudden and disarming smile. "When's the big day?"

And with that, I was slammed back to reality: we were here because of *me* and my upcoming wedding. Noah had been pushing me to lock down a date, but every time he proposed a venue or even a season, something seemed wrong about it. Summers in Boston were brutal. Did I really want to be sweating through a wedding gown? But spring threatened rain, and that didn't seem like a good omen, either.

"We haven't nailed down a date yet, but we're thinking spring or summer of next year," I said.

"Nice. We have some flexibility, then." Eden went back to tapping on the iPad. "You're going to have to fill out the bridal questionnaire after this consultation. Generally, I have brides do that ahead of time, but given the short notice, I wanted to get you in today with no issue. Your fiancé will also have to come in for a couple's interview."

"I—really?" Eden needed to talk to Noah? What kind of bridal boutique was this?

Eden nodded. "Yep. It's a bit unconventional, I know, but we're best able to meet your needs when we get a full three-sixty-degree picture of not just the bride, but of the relationship as a whole. To be honest, the bridal questionnaire and couple's interview are usually screening criteria—"

"We're *very* selective about the brides we take on," Cora cut in.

"We are." A bland smile from Eden. "But since we're having you jump the line, Liv, it'll be more of a formality in this case." She turned to Cora. "You have that three P.M. tasting ready to go?"

Cora visibly deflated, her chin touching down to her breastbone. But to her credit, she corrected herself quickly, straightening her shoulders with a purposeful grin. "On it!"

Once she'd left, Eden turned back to me. "As I was saying—the couple's interview. Is your fiancé local?"

I hesitated. Scratched my clavicle, which had suddenly erupted with pin-like itchiness. "He's in Boston, but I'm sure I could convince him to come out for a weekend."

"Excellent."

"Thank you," Mom said, clasping her hands under her chin. "I can't thank you enough for being so accommodating."

"It's the least I can do for a fellow classmate."

I dared a glance over at Penny.

You lucky bitch, she mouthed to me.

"Okay," Eden said, smoothing the fabric of her romper across her thighs, "talk to me, Liv. What's your wedding inspiration? Any gown silhouettes you have in mind?"

My head spun. "I . . ." *Shit.* I hadn't even been able to commit to a date—how could I possibly have a wedding inspiration? And silhouettes? I didn't know a sheath from a mermaid. An ugly metallic flavor seeped out from underneath my tongue. It reminded me of the night Noah had proposed. He had a waiter bury the diamond in my chocolate mousse; the prongs had clicked against my teeth and I'd spit the ring out, thinking, inexplicably, that I'd almost swallowed a thumbtack.

Without realizing, my hand had navigated to my spined ring. Once I managed to surface from my frothing mind, I realized that Penny, Mom, and Eden were studying me with avid concern.

"You okay?" Penny asked me, under her breath.

Eden's dark eyes were fastened on my right hand. "Wowza, what a ring. Actually, can I see that?" She reached over and something like foreboding streaked through my bloodstream. I didn't want to show Eden my ring. It was sacred, private. Privy to all my darkest thoughts and inclinations that it snuffed out with its painful teeth. But part of me was—after all these years—still afraid to defy her, just as I'd been on that first day of school.

To my surprise, she reached out and splayed my fist open with firm fingers. Then she touched the pad of her index finger to the spiny bird's nest.

"You made this, didn't you?"

I snatched my hand away.

Eden's eyes were burning when they met mine. "It reminds me of something Sam would make."

I looked up at her, stunned. "Sam? Do you mean Sam Mendez?" Had Cora or Eden ever spoken a word to her?

"Of course. We all have Sam on the brain these days. Surely, you've heard the news."

"What news?" Penny said sharply.

I turned to my sister, fighting down my irritation. "Sam is missing. Wait—" I turned back to Eden. "What do you guys know? You haven't seen her since high school, either, right?"

"Sam works with us," Eden said. "And lives with us. We're still riding the shockwaves of this whole horrible week."

Eden and Cora were Sam's roommates? How was that even possible? Eden, Cora, and Avery had been so odd, yet so untouchable. Rejected by our classmates—or maybe *feared* was a more apt term—and yet the subject of so many rumors and whispers. A dark fascination had bubbled around The Sisterhood at a magnitude the school's popular clique never could have commanded. I couldn't imagine Sam actually being drawn into their fold.

That's a nasty thought to have about a missing girl. I ground the pad of my index finger into my spined ring as punishment.

When I glanced up, Eden was frowning at my hands—she'd caught me in the act. "Sam designs jewelry for the boutique," she offered, after a moment. "She's brilliant."

"But you guys weren't friends in high school. How did you even . . ."

"Cora took an art class with Sam over the summer. They hit it off . . . and turns out Sam was exactly the kind of girl we needed on staff at Beloved."

My mind was blank with shock. Sam's stepmother's words rang in my ears: *I've just had to accept that there are some things about my daughter I'll never understand.*

"And as far as what we know about Sam going MIA," Eden continued, "not much. We're really concerned. Sure, she'd talked about wanting to go to Ireland someday, but we don't buy that's what happened."

The pink cupcake was growing sticky in my hand, but my stomach was too stuffed with anxiety to even contemplate another bite. I thought back to my conversation with Sam's stepmother. "You and Cora organized the search party, didn't you?"

"Of course. And we've been in and out of the police station all week."

"I met with a detective, too," I said, breathlessly. "Sam sent me a note a couple days ago asking to talk, saying she was afraid of something. So I gave it to them—"

"A note?" Eden asked. Her eyebrows had flown to her hairline.

"Yeah. Do you have any idea what she could have been referencing? I mean, you live with her. Did she seem . . . scared at all? Upset?"

"Liv." Penny put a hand on my thigh. It took the pressure of her skin on mine to make me realize how quickly I was talking, a rock careening down a cliffside. "I'm really sorry to hear about your high school friend. But don't you think you should leave these kinds of questions to the detectives?" She gave Eden an apologetic smile. "We only have twenty minutes left."

Eden was silent for a beat, recrossed her legs. When she finally spoke, it was me she addressed, rather than Penny: "To answer your question, Sam didn't seem out of the ordinary before she disappeared." She paused. "But your sister is right—I'd hate for this to monopolize your appointment. Let's find some time to get together, just the three of us, to trade notes? My cell number is on the back of my card."

I nodded, thumbing the matte black business card in my lap. Accordingly, the conversation turned back to details of Eden's design process and what I was looking for in a dress. More tapping on the iPad with those dark nails, interjections from Mom and Penny. But I must have navigated the remaining twenty minutes on autopilot. Once Sam's name came up, my mind had gone as blank as the mannequin faces staring back at me.

6

NOW

THE MOMENT WE ARRIVED BACK AT MOM'S HOUSE, I BOLTED to my room to check the #FINDSAM thread. I still couldn't believe Sam had been living and working alongside Eden and Cora; I was desperate for my next revelation.

Unfortunately, besides the old announcement about the search party and the upcoming candlelight vigil, there were no updates. Just a piling up of trite concerns. *Praying for you, Sam. Hope you're okay.* I clicked on the user who posted the latest update. Maddie Scroggins, a girl with a sharp chin and corkscrew curls. Undoubtedly the same Maddie that Sam's stepmother had mentioned. As I studied her profile picture, a memory sprang to mind: Maddie, toting a large black instrument case—bassoon?—through the halls of Guilford High. I typed out a hasty message to her:

Hi Maddie! It's been a while—not sure if you remember me from GHS. I'm back in Guilford now and Sam's stepmom mentioned you'd been supporting the investigation. I'd love to help. Is there any chance you'd be willing to talk with me sometime soon?

There was a light rap at my door. "Liv?"

I clapped my laptop shut on my bed. "Come in!"

In the meager lighting of my room, Penny looked even more haggard than she had at the boutique.

"Hey," I said, sitting up. "Are you okay?"

Penny slid onto the edge of my mattress, putting her head in her hands. "I'm so exhausted I can't even think straight."

I rubbed a little circle on her back. "I'm sorry. I'll come downstairs now. I just wanted to check on things with Sam . . ."

To my surprise, she pulled away from under my hand and sighed. "Hasn't it been . . . like eight years since you've spoken to this girl?"

I bristled. "What do you mean? Sam was my best friend, Pen. And she's *missing*."

"And that's scary! But it seems like you're obsessing over something you can't control. When the subject came up at your appointment today, you got really intense. Like you didn't want to talk about anything else. Honestly, it came off as a little . . ."

"A little what?"

She grimaced. "I don't know. Ungrateful?"

Hot anger surged through me. I wasn't the one who

made the appointment at the bridal boutique. I'd been ambushed by Mom and Penny—and went along with it because I knew it came from a place of love. But if it were up to me? I wouldn't be having conversations about illusion necklines and trains when there were clearly more important things at stake.

Like Sam's life.

"I'm not ungrateful," I finally choked out. "I'm worried about my friend. I'm overwhelmed and I'm scared for her. Apologies if I wasn't in the mood for wedding dress shopping."

Penny scowled at my sarcasm. "I don't know anyone who's snagged an appointment at Beloved. Brides will put themselves on the waitlist before they're even officially engaged, in hopes of doing what you got to do today. That was a big deal. For you, and honestly, for me, too."

I blinked. "For you? But you're already married."

"Who cares? Liv, this was the first time I've gotten out of the house since the twins were born. Mom booked a sitter and everything."

Her first time away from her children in a *year*? How was I just now hearing about this? "Why—"

"Because it's expensive and makes me feel guilty as shit. Even though I know I should be enjoying the break, it just feels . . . illicit to be away from them. Indulgent."

My anger was softening into concern now. "Pen, you hired a babysitter to help your sister look at wedding dresses. You're allowed to do that."

My sister shook her head, tightening her topknot. "You wouldn't get it."

A ribbon of dread ran through me. I'd taken the train to see Penny's twin boys when they were born, shocked by the alien-like scrunch of their faces and those impossibly tiny fingers. I hadn't been blind to the ways in which my sister had changed since then. Once the prolific texter, Penny took weeks now to respond to a single question. They weren't even questions that required deep introspection: Are we still wearing skinny jeans or nah? And I've decided folding a fitted sheet by yourself should qualify as an Olympic event—thoughts?

"Give her a break, she's a mom now," my friends told me when I shared my concern, as if Penny's new role had edged out her ability to continue being my sister. After my initial spritz of irritation, I felt stupid and ashamed. My sister had brought two new lives into this world and was busy sustaining them around the clock. And me? I was texting her about skinny jeans and folding laundry, getting miffed when she didn't reply right away.

Maybe I truly couldn't understand.

"Try me," I said.

A weak laugh. She picked at a stretched-out elastic on her wrist. "No, you're not a mom, so you're not going to understand. It's like every second I do anything that isn't explicitly for my children—even if it's just taking a shower for the first time in a week—I'm positively drowning in guilt. Sometimes I feel so overwhelmed, so . . . alone . . . that I have to take a few minutes to sit in my closet and cry."

Was she serious? Penny hadn't mentioned this any of the times I'd come to visit. I readjusted so I was sitting on the bed directly facing her. "Pen, you should be able to take a guilt-free shower—and preferably every day, not once a week."

"Ha!" Now it was Penny's turn to laugh, head thrown back, in an ugly way. "I'd like to see you try wrangling two thirteen-month-olds through the shower door."

I could feel my shoulders turtling up toward my ears. Maybe Penny was right; maybe I couldn't understand her because I wasn't a mom. Maybe Penny had severed our ability to relate to each other by procreating. Bam—bun in the oven, she'd fundamentally become someone else. Someone who existed on a wildly different plane than the rest of us.

"Can't Carter watch the boys sometimes?"

"Carter! Oh, please. The guy can't even put together a bottle."

I thought of Carter, the slight, gentle architect with his square-rimmed glasses and one dimple. He always deferred to my sister's whims. I'd never been sure exactly what motivated this: his enormous love for her or just flat-out apathy. "Why? Aren't these his kids, too?"

"Liv." She said my name through a strangled laugh. "That's not how these things work. Carter got, like, one week of paternity leave. It wasn't enough time for him to learn how to do anything. I'm the one who quit my job to take care of the kids. This is my job. My *one* job."

"Did you . . . want that job?"

"It was just assumed that I'd be the one to take the step back professionally. Carter makes so much more; my salary wouldn't have even covered childcare."

I chewed my lip. Penny had been wild about her job

as a docent at an art museum in Hartford. She'd actually cried tears of happiness when she secured the position—something she'd been warned was close to impossible in the field of art history. I'd just assumed she'd approach motherhood with the same gusto, that she'd wanted to quit her job to dedicate her life to her children.

"Sometimes . . ." Penny trailed off, locked eyes with her pale reflection.

"Sometimes what?"

She shook her head, dislodging a piece of hair. "Sometimes I look in the mirror and I don't even recognize myself anymore. I just feel like . . . a shell of who I used to be."

That itchiness from the bridal salon reared along my spine again, with a new vengeance.

"Seriously. I love my children, but they ruined my body. I don't sleep more than two hours in a row, and don't see how I ever will again. I used to write twenty-page papers on Klimt. On Van Gogh. Now I don't have the brain power—let alone the time—to read more than a headline in a tabloid."

Why hadn't anyone told me Penny had been suffering like this? I felt embarrassingly naïve, as if I'd been tripping along in my own petty, parallel reality when all the while my sister had been drowning in the black hole of motherhood.

Not to mention, her diatribe wasn't exactly making me calmer about my own upcoming nuptials.

"Is there anything I can do to help?" I asked quietly.

"No," Penny scoffed, turning away from me a bit. "No. This is just the way things are."

I scratched at my collarbone with a ragged nail. Scrolled

through my head for a suitable remark. I'd been looking forward to visiting the twins during my stay in Guilford, but this seemed like a bad time to mention it. Eventually, I decided: generic was best. "I hope," I said cautiously, "that despite all the hard parts of being a mom, you find some redeeming moments, too."

An eerie, blank smile ghosted across my sister's face. It was so unlike Penny, whose facial expressions claimed her every feature—eyebrows flying to her hairline, crinkles of laughter gathering around her eye. But this odd smile didn't touch her eyes.

Penny's empty face met mine, a glass drained of water. "Being a wife and mother is the greatest sacrifice," she said. And then, in a monotone: "But don't worry. It's worth it."

EVENTUALLY, PENNY AND I HEADED downstairs to join Mom for a game of Scrabble at the kitchen table. We joked amongst ourselves and caught up on everything we'd missed, but a prickliness persisted between my sister and me. Why the hell had no one told me what a hard time Penny was having? Did Mom even know?

After about an hour, Penny had to leave to start the hour-long trek back to Hartford. I retired to my room and called Noah to fill him in. I'd been in such a tailspin since arriving in Guilford that I hadn't even told him about Sam's disappearance.

"There she is," he said, by means of a greeting. Just hearing his voice sent relief billowing through me. Noah listened raptly to my news, as I knew he would. He'd listened patiently as I agonized about my soul-sucking job as a paralegal, too, until I'd finally been laid off and was spared having to make a decision myself. His brand of unwavering emotional support was nothing to sneeze at. Three weeks after our engagement, Noah's brother had died from an aneurysm, and I found myself on the other end of the equation in the most extreme way. I'd hugged a sobbing Noah, ropes of saliva dropping from the corners of his mouth to soak my jeans, terrified by my own blank helplessness. What exactly was I supposed to do here? What was there even to say?

"God," Noah said, when I finished explaining. "That's really freaky. Especially after that letter she sent you."

A heaviness in my stomach. "I know."

"How long do you think you're going to end up staying?"

"No idea. I feel bad that I missed the search party, so I'm just hoping"—my voice broke—"that I can help in some other way. They're having a candlelight vigil this weekend, so there's that."

"Of course," Noah said, voice low and soothing.

I thought about telling Noah how overwhelmed I felt and that I couldn't get Sam and her note out of my head. I thought about telling him about today's outing to the boutique—how the wedding was the furthest thing from my concerns and my sister had called me *ungrateful* for failing to engage in the process. But I stopped myself just in time. Would Noah be hurt if I admitted I saw our wedding as a stressor?

"Hey," Noah said, shattering my thoughts. "How about

I come out to Guilford and join you this weekend? So you're not all alone out there."

I smiled against the phone.

"Is that a 'yes'?"

"I'm smiling."

"Good. Mission accomplished, then."

I twisted the engagement ring on my finger. In moments like this, I hated myself for those bizarre flashes of terror I sometimes got when I imagined walking down the aisle, maybe starting a family in a few years. This was Noah, after all, not some faceless man I was sacrificing myself to at the altar. We'd been together since freshman year of college. What could possibly leap out of the shadows to surprise me at this point?

"This is actually a great idea." Noah's voice was gathering conviction. "We'll go to the vigil together. I'll get to see your mom, put in some face time. And we should definitely stop by to see your sister and the kids. They've gotten so big in her pictures! How long has it been since you've seen them?"

A pinch of guilt, exacerbated by my recent conversation with Penny. "Too long, you're right."

"Great. I'll get the Amtrak tickets tonight."

After hanging up a few minutes later, I sank back against my pillows, feeling fizzy with gratitude. I was lucky to have Noah. I knew I still had a lot to figure out. What to do after getting laid off (was law school really what I wanted?), jump-starting my stale friendships—at least for those who'd remained in state and stood a chance of being salvaged. But unlike my sister, I had a supportive partner to lean on, and for this I was exceedingly fortunate.

Soon, I dozed off, and my head clotted with weird imagery.

In my dream, I walked along the Green. A bite was in the air; I pulled my knit wrap tighter around my shoulders to ward off the chill and sped my pace. Past the coffee shop, past Page Hardware and the Village Chocolatier, to a familiar tall, narrow Victorian, cream on the bottom, its peak covered in pink scallops.

I reached for the door and opened it as if this were my home. But the entrance looked nothing like it had on my visit to Beloved. Sunlight pooled on wide planks in the entryway. Beyond it, the peek of old-fashioned black-and-white kitchen tiles and a red teapot on the countertop. I went straight for the narrow, creaking staircase and followed it up and up. Past a landing with a reading nook nestled full of pillows and a semicircle of stained glass—a swollen, thorny rose—and into a bedroom off the hallway, the second on the left. Someone had stoked a fire in the fireplace, leaving red embers crackling in the grate. Kicking off my boots, I nuzzled under the duvet of the iron four-poster.

Home, I thought, distinctly. *I'm home.*

In my dream, I sank into the warm mattress, curling my toes under the blankets. Then I noticed a dark spot on the pristine duvet. It was black and oblong, and crawling toward me. The beetle from the outhouse so many years ago. Yes, I remembered the lurch and sway of those filament legs. As it approached my pillow, I saw the blue-and-white eye on its back, wide and lidless. But this time I felt no fear or revulsion.

"Come here," I said, beckoning with my hand.

The beetle surged toward me, clambering over the divots in the down comforter. Closer, closer, until I felt the tickle of its feelers on my neck.

"It's okay," I said, and the beetle crawled onto my face, tapping its little feet over my chin. It gave my lips an affectionate nudge before slipping between them. Its body felt like warm licorice on my tongue.

I woke gasping and sputtering. Frantic, I swiped at my mouth, digging a finger under my tongue and around my lips. The dream had felt real—too real. I could still feel the skittery tracks of the beetle on my skin, and was still trembling when I finally slid back under the covers minutes later.

If last night was any indication, it appeared sleep wouldn't be coming easily in Guilford.

7

THEN

WATCHED SAM TURN THE STEERING WHEEL, HAND-OVER-hand, into the parking lot at Jacob's Beach. It was such an adult gesture, the same way my mom handled the steering wheel in her own car, and I wondered with a pang when I'd ever get to do the same. As I'd alluded to Sam, moving had thrown a wrench in my plans to get a license. I'd attended a few driver's ed classes back in Denver, but neither Mom nor Dad had really committed to driving around the neighborhood with me as the move loomed over us all.

"I really need to get my license," I sighed, slumping against the passenger-side door.

"No shit." Sam jerked the gearshift into Park. Then she reached for a scarf from the back seat. I hadn't understood why she wanted to come to the beach in September, but Sam had insisted, claiming it was one of her favorite places to "clear her head." The phrase made her sound like an old lady and I told her as much. We'd started hanging out ever since that very first day of school; as a result, Sam was growing more accustomed to my snark, and even seemed to appreciate it from time to time. She told me it kept her on her toes.

Earlier that day, Sam had come over and asked to see my jewelry-making supplies. She'd turned over the implements with something close to reverence and asked me to show her how I'd made my cuff bracelet. In school and during outings, Sam was always the one calling the shots. It was refreshing to see her take the back seat as I began to demonstrate how to manipulate wire, the various tools I had and their different purposes. She seemed enthralled by it all. Before we knew it, the sun had set outside my bedroom windows. Sam and I had looked at each other in bewilderment: three hours, gone in a flash.

Now, as we exited the car at Jacob's Beach, a violent wind stung my cheeks. I followed Sam onto the packed gray sand. We trailed close to the water, watching the ribbon of pocked froth recede and reappear.

"The best thing about having my license," Sam said, smudging the sand with the toe of her combat boot, "is that I can escape whenever I want. School—at least during free period. Home. It all gets to be so suffocating sometimes, you know?"

"Hear, hear." I paused, deliberating whether or not to get into the details of my own home life. I'd been hanging out with Sam for a solid month now; though she talked openly about her frustrations with her brother ("fucking golden child") and her critical stepmother ("she asked me today if I wanted to get Invisalign before college"), I hadn't dredged the courage to start being vulnerable myself. The only reason I'd let her come over today was because I knew my dad was away on a business trip and wouldn't be starting any fights.

Sam glanced up at me. "For you, too?"

I kicked a piece of driftwood. "I guess you could say that."

Uncharacteristically, Sam was silent, and I realized she was holding space for me to elaborate. The gesture simultaneously warmed and terrified me. "Well," I said, haltingly. "The usual, you know. Moving sucks. My parents at each other's throats. Metaphorically."

Metaphorically?

Sam nodded, swiping dark hair out of her eyes. "That sucks. I've never moved in my life. And for all that I bitch about my stepmom, she and my dad hardly fight. Actually, they're so lovey-dovey it makes me want to puke."

A bark of laughter from me. "Gross."

"What do your parents fight about?" Sam asked.

I hesitated. "I try not to listen. Yesterday my dad flipped out because he saw the balance on my mom's credit card. Then my mom has this way of escalating things, like really screaming at the top of her lungs . . . and it gets ugly fast."

"That's messed up," Sam said.

"Yeah." It felt good to be able to tell someone about what was going on at home. Most of my friends from Denver had known better than to ask. For a moment, I wanted so badly to spill the tale of Dad flinging Mom across the kitchen, but I quickly lost my nerve. That was too much, too soon.

"So they fight about money?" Sam prompted gently. "That happens with my parents, too, sometimes."

I shook my head. "It's more than that. For my dad, it's a respect thing." Whenever I heard that word, goosebumps coasted along my arms: it was a sure sign there was going to be trouble. Like the other day, when Dad exploded because my mom was acting too "friendly" with a male waiter. I wasn't ready to tell Sam about that one, either. But I had a hard time forgetting the words he'd spit at her during that interminable car ride home.

Sam grimaced. "No offense, but your dad sounds super controlling."

That's when the conversation stopped feeling good. Sam was right—so why did her words make me feel like shit? "Yeah," I mumbled, kicking the sand. "I'm not saying my mom is perfect or anything. But she's given up so much for him. And none of it seems to matter."

Sam bumped up against my shoulder with her own. "Ugh, I'm sorry. You know, if you ever need to get away from the screaming, the fighting, whatever, you can text me. I have a car, 'member?"

"Sure, thanks." I bumped her back, smiling. Our family's surprise cross-country move had been far from ideal, but in times like these, I realized it could have been a hell of a lot worse.

"Actually, you should come by my house tomorrow

after school," Sam said. "I kind of want to try making a bracelet myself. You'll help me?"

"Of course." The idea of losing time to another joint jewelry-making session with Sam made me grin.

"Hey." Sam dropped to a crouch in the sand. Then she lifted something black, looking victorious. "A mermaid's purse!"

"A what now?" I leaned over to study the object on Sam's palm: a square-shaped, leathery sac with four antenna-like barbs at each corner.

"A mermaid's purse. It's like, some kind of egg case. Oh my God, don't tell me you've never seen one of these before."

"Girl, I grew up in Colorado. Never." I squinted at it. "Actually, if I'm being honest, it's kind of creepy-looking."

Sam wrenched her palm away. "Is not! It's adorable. Every time I see one of these, I imagine a little mermaid holding it like a clutch as she runs off to some fabulous underwater ball." As if to demonstrate, Sam lifted the brittle pouch beneath her chin and took little mincing steps across the sand.

"Ha," I said. "You're ridiculous."

"I've been collecting mermaid purses since I was a little girl. I have a whole jewelry box filled with them."

"And think of all those poor, purse-less mermaids out there. Where are they supposed to stash their tampons?"

"Here." Sam held out her hand, presenting the scraggly pouch.

I shook my head, smiling. "You're the one who collects them."

"I have plenty. A whole box, like I said." Sam pressed the brittle black cushion into my palm. An air pocket, it felt deceptively light.

I looked up. For some reason, Sam's hopeful smile made my eyes sting. I thought back to that first day of school, when she'd lured me out of the bathroom stall and gone to buy me a Coke. Sam had her quirks, but she had to be one of the most generous humans I'd ever met. Without her, who knows where I'd be.

"Thanks," I whispered.

My hand closed over the mermaid purse, even as its barbs bit into my skin.

8

NOW

MADDIE MESSAGED ME BACK SOON AFTER PENNY'S DE-
parture.

> Hi Liv! Of course I remember you. I'll be working at the Marketplace
> Mon-Thurs this week. Want to stop by?

The next day, I borrowed Mom's car to meet Maddie.
The shops lining the Green were decked out for the Halloween season—coppery leaf garlands and gourds nestled
in window displays, wide-mouthed ghosts and jack-o'-
lanterns hand-painted on the glass. Inside the Marketplace,
it smelled like cinnamon and cloves. A milk-frother shrieked
from the café side of the store. Gourmet pasta and sauces
lined the market side; clusters of small tables and copper-
colored chairs crowded the interior.

Maddie was waving to me from behind the glass case of muffins and cookies. She looked exactly the same as her profile picture.

"Thanks for coming by to meet me, Liv!"

"Are you kidding? Thanks for responding to my message." I shot a look behind the counter. There, a lanky college-aged boy was pouring a steaming drink into a paper cup. "Is now a good time to talk?"

"Yep! Let me just clock out for my break. We can take a walk around the Green if you want?"

That's how I ended up strolling along the decorated storefronts with Maddie. She was making small talk about all the changes this part of town had experienced since we were in high school, and I listened with half my attention, anxious to bring up Sam.

"So how do you know Sam?" I interjected finally. "You two weren't friends in high school, were you?"

"Nope, we met a few years ago. Sam has been a regular at the Marketplace and the two of us just started chatting. Eventually, we started hanging out outside the café."

"That's cool. Do you know if there have been any updates on the investigation? Beyond what's been in the news, obviously." Of course, I'd set a Google alert on my phone so I'd be notified each time there was a development in Sam's case.

Maddie shrugged. "Well, you probably heard about the search party. There's a vigil coming up, but apart from that, there really hasn't been any news."

"Okay. I'm just—I'm really worried about her. I got this disturbing letter from her in the mail . . ."

Maddie's eyebrows cinched together sharply. "Disturbing letter?"

"Yeah. She said something about needing my help, wanting to talk. And then, two days later, she was declared missing."

Maddie tore at some skin near the base of her thumbnail. I noticed her hands were chapped and red, flaking skin visible along the knuckles. "Did you tell the police about this?"

"Of course." I couldn't help the rash of defensiveness in my voice. Why would I have kept such critical intel to myself?

"Okay, good." Her shoulders sagged. "I've talked to them, too. It seems so out of character for her to up and leave like this. It has us all feeling . . . not so great."

That drumming of dread along the insides of my stomach. We turned onto the pathway bisecting the Green. A bunch of local businesses had set up Halloween décor to advertise their services: T-shaped scarecrows with stitched faces and flannel shirts, a whimsical witch with a lopsided smile and impossibly tall hat.

"What was she like?" I asked. "Right before this happened?"

"I don't know. I would've told you she was happy. She loved her job at the boutique. She had a house with super cool roommates she talked about all the time. What was there to be upset about?"

"She didn't seem . . . stressed at all?" I swallowed. "Afraid?"

"No." Maddie frowned. "I mean—and I told this to the

police—the last couple times she came in to buy a coffee, she was so preoccupied checking her phone she barely spoke to me. Which was out of character—Sam would often stay for twenty minutes or so just to chat. When I teased her about it, pretended to crane my neck to look at her phone and made some joke about her swiping on dating sites, she got super defensive and wouldn't let me see the screen."

I chewed on this for a minute. Who could Sam have been communicating with? Was that the person who had made her want to go to Ireland?

"Sam's stepmom said she didn't think Sam had been dating anyone . . ."

"Nope," Maddie confirmed. "I would know."

"Did she have any, like, jealous exes or anything?"

"No! She just didn't seem interested in dating. That's why I thought my Tinder joke was so funny."

Except Sam hadn't agreed. I scuffed my Converse in the dirt. A sudden thought occurred to me. "Did Sam ever mention to you why she'd been pulling back from her step-mom?"

"What do you mean?" Maddie's eyes were squinched in confusion.

"When I spoke to Sam's stepmom, she told me Sam had been increasingly distant. She'd even warned her step-mom she wouldn't be coming around as often because she was going to be so busy with her jewelry making."

"Hmm." Maddie nibbled at the side of her thumb. "She *was* spending a lot of time making those pieces. But she never mentioned anything about wanting pull back from her family."

"She dropped out of a family text chain, apparently? Wasn't talking much to her brother, either."

"Really." Maddie blinked. "That part surprises me, to be honest. I'm not clear on Sam's relationship with her step-mom, but she and Everett were really close, ever since . . . well, if you know her from high school, you probably know about her accident."

My heart flipped about in my chest cavity. I funneled every ounce of my energy into making my face a mask. "I do."

"Everett took care of her through her recovery, helped her get back on her feet. That's why it's so strange to me to hear she'd been icing him out, after that."

"Really strange," I agreed, feeling for the tines of my spiny ring with my thumb.

"You should try to talk to him," Maddie said.

"I'm planning to. He wasn't in when I stopped by the Mendezes' house."

"Great. And in the meantime, let me give you my number."

We'd made it back to the Marketplace by now. Maddie handed my phone back and grimaced, nodding toward the door. "Sorry. My break is up—duty calls."

I shot her an understanding smile and pocketed my phone. Then I pressed my finger to the cold metal fangs of my ring; they sank into the whorls of my fingerprint with a delicious zing of pain.

· · ·

I WAS EXHAUSTED BY THE time I arrived home. The music filtering from the back of the house indicated that Mom was tucked in the spare room she used for her pottery. I made myself a cup of tea and sat at the kitchen table, the brick floor cold through the heels of my socks. Outside, light was draining from the sky, leaving a sliver of anemic moon. A couple of raggedy moths flung themselves against the glass of the front door. I studied my bruised fingertip as the facts I'd gleaned that day rattled in my head.

Sam was living with Eden and Cora, making jewelry for their wedding boutique. Sam had been distancing herself from her family and texting with someone she didn't want her friends to know about. But something about the theory wasn't nesting right. Sam had never been private about anything. She'd been the kind of person to crow about her accomplishments (a 96 on a calc exam; her acceptance to RISD) and bitch about her screwups (backing her car into a pole on her way out of the Friendly's parking lot). On one hand, her lack of filter was wildly refreshing: I knew my best friend was always being real. But it also meant I couldn't trust her with any meaningful secret.

"You're home!" Mom breezed into the kitchen, carrying a mug of her own. "How'd it go?"

I shrugged. "The more I learn, the more confused I get."

She joined at me at the table, studying me with sympathy. "You know it isn't your job to figure this out, right, Liv?"

My hands curled into fists on the tabletop. I knew she was speaking from a place of concern, but the way she brushed any accountability of mine under the rug made my blood hot. There were some things Mom just didn't know.

In the spiky silence that followed, she changed tack. "I meant to thank you for humoring Penny and me. I know you weren't quite ready to start dress shopping, but your sister really enjoyed seeing you. And, frankly, having an excuse to get out of the house."

Penny. With a start, I remembered the pain she unleashed to me after the appointment. I'd been so consumed chasing down leads that I hadn't had a minute to dwell on her words.

"About that," I said, sitting up in my chair. "I didn't realize Penny was having such a hard time."

Mom cocked her head at me. "What do you mean?"

"After our appointment at Beloved, she was telling me some pretty worrying stuff. She said that since she's home all day taking care of the boys, she only gets to shower, like, once a week. And . . ." I lowered my voice, as if I were about to utter a curse, "that she feels like a shell of who she used to be."

Mom's mouth pressed into a line. "Well," she said. "I mean, she's a new mom of twins."

And did that make it okay? "I didn't realize she hadn't wanted to quit her job. She told me it was just assumed that she'd be the one to step back from her career since Carter—"

"You haven't experienced it yet, Liv, but once you and Noah get married and have kids, you'll understand."

My mouth filled with that bloodlike metallic flavor again. Self-sacrifice, overwhelm, and a steady draining away of my own identity—is that really what I had to look forward to on the other side?

"You know I closed up my pottery shop when you were born. It was important to your father that I stay home with you; that's how he was raised."

"I know." Once, when I was very young, I'd fingered one of the glazed bowls shoved in the back of our kitchen cabinet and asked Mom where she'd gotten it. The veined pattern reminded me of a butterfly's wing. I'd been so confused to see the wave of sadness that crossed my mother's face before she snuffed it out with a forced smile. Years later, Mom would point out the studio she had once rented—the back, she explained, had been a paint-spattered space with a pottery wheel and kiln, while the front was all polished wood and glass artfully exhibiting her wares. She'd given up the lease to stay home full-time with my sister and me. The spot had turned over to a dog groomer with a poodle-shaped sign out front that said TOOTSIE PAWS.

"Everything changes when you have a family," Mom said. "And I mean *everything*."

"Well, obviously." And yet, why did it have to sound like such a bad omen? The snake in my gut tensed again.

"After marriage and children, your life . . . well, it doesn't belong to you anymore."

I ran a tongue over dry lips. "Are you speaking from experience?"

Silence. "Well. I wouldn't trade it for the world."

Under the table, I scratched at a mosquito bite on my

calf. I thought of Mom sailing across the kitchen in slow-motion after Dad struck her, smashing up against the turquoise cabinets with the tender underside of her head.

My next thought startled me in its vehemence.

Sure, you wouldn't.

9

NOW

I SLEPT RESTLESSLY THAT NIGHT, LOOPING THROUGH ALL THE conversations I'd had since arriving in Guilford. Detective Patterson, Sam's stepmom. Penny and Eden and Cora and Maddie. Their words tangled together in the dark recesses of sleep. *Forensics has Sam's devices . . . burnt out and was looking into a trip to Europe . . . Sometimes I feel so overwhelmed, so . . . alone . . .*

Eventually, I woke twisted in damp ropes of sheets and grabbed my phone. It was time to follow up with Eden and compare notes about Sam. I dug out the matte black business card that Eden had handed me. It was minimalist, designed with an artist's eye, and manufactured with high-quality material. I ran a fingertip over the silken blackness. The silver cursive raised slightly off the cardstock, like a scar:

Beloved
A bridal boutique
You deserve your happily ever after

I texted the number indicated on the back.

Hey Eden! It's Liv Edwards. Any chance you'd want to get together
and finish our conversation from the other day?

As I waited for Eden to respond, I tried—unsuccessfully—
to distract myself by skimming law school applications online. Mom didn't own a printer, so I forced myself to take
notes on what I was absorbing, which wasn't much. Hours
later, a single line stared back at me on my notepad, wavery
like my penmanship got whenever I felt insecure about what
I was writing.

Motivation behind pursuit of legal education?

A single thought flashed like a panic signal: Why was I
doing this? My days at the law firm had scraped at me, hour
by excruciating hour, like rugburn. Sliding behind my desk
in the morning, I'd fairly feel my soul begin to liquefy and
dribble down my pant leg as my Outlook pane filled. I'd
spend much of the day clicking aimlessly on my desktop—
adjusting the brightness, scrolling forward and backward
through my calendar. Getting laid off had felt like a godsend.

I stared back at my pathetic note. Why was I setting
myself up for a lifetime of this?

I spent the afternoon toggling between law school applications and the #FindSam thread. Refresh, refresh: nothing new.

EVENTUALLY, I DRIFTED DOWNSTAIRS TO hang out with Mom, periodically checking my phone for updates. It wasn't until after seven P.M. that my phone finally illuminated with a text from Eden.

Yes, please. Come by the shop whenever

It was all the invitation I needed. I rushed back to my room and threw on a pale blue dress with cap sleeves. Warm dusk slid in through the open window, thick with the scent of wet soil and pollen. When I glanced in the mirror, I barely recognized myself. My cheeks were stung red, eyes glassy and feverish. The lavender walls of my childhood bedroom—with all their generic teenage fixings—seemed to be marching toward the center of the room. Crushing me.

I had to get out.

I slid through the darkening house easily, too easily. Swiped Mom's car keys from the hook by the front door and tripped into the embrace of evening air. With the windows down, it streaked my face, kicked up my loose hair. Mom's car took me through the serpentine roads behind Route 1. I hadn't yet acclimated to Guilford's dark nights. No smear of high-rises here to sully the sky. I wondered if the streetlights were even enough to light my way.

Soon, I was pulling up to the scalloped pink Victorian. It looked like a dollhouse sitting there in the night, waiting for its child to come play again come morning. After parking and getting out, I paused for a moment on the front porch, looking up at the oak canopy stretching above. It shuddered a little in the wind as stars blinked in and out of view. Standing there, looking up at that pointy pink house, I felt myself settling back into my dream from the night before.

The door swung opened soundlessly. Eden stood there, resplendent in a blood-red dress, with a pendant festooned with cameos dangling along the deep V-neck. The pieces of hair around her face were shot through with soft light.

"Welcome back," she said.

This time, she led me to a back entrance. Instead of walking into the petal-colored boutique, I found myself in a different entryway with wide, honey-colored wooden planks. A narrow staircase ascended to the second floor; a black-and-white tiled kitchen peeked from behind a dark doorframe.

"Wait," I said, pushing past Eden into the kitchen.

On the counter was the red teapot from my dream.

I pressed my fingertips to the sudden blooming of a headache between my eyes. "I've been here before," I said faintly.

Eden laughed. "Of course you have. Come on, let's have a drink."

Like in the Wythers House, the rooms were narrow and dark. But it smelled homey, like garlic and slightly burnt wood. Soon we were in a dining room, the carved mantel over the fireplace covered in flickering candles. Cora stood at the scarred harvest table, pouring purple liquid from a narrow glass bottle. Tonight, she wore a silver barrette in her long hair; gold eyeliner glinted on her bottom lash line.

"Sweet violet gin," she said, handing a faceted glass goblet to me. "It's the absolute best!"

"Thanks." Something clanked in my goblet: twin sticks of ice, minuscule wildflowers embedded in their depths. Frozen flowers? I dared a sip. It tasted like a garden.

"So." Eden met my eyes over her drink.

"I want to hear what you know about Sam," I said.

"Ugh. I wish I had more I could tell you," Eden said. "The police came in here to search for evidence the day after we reported her missing. Since then, Cora and I have been over and over the weeks leading up to it all—with detectives, and with each other. We honestly saw no signs of this coming, and we're really worried. But you said she'd written you a letter?"

I pulled up the image of Sam's note on my phone and passed it to Eden and Cora across the tabletop. Eden's eyebrows cinched together severely; when Cora tried to manipulate the image with her fingertips, Eden pushed her hand away.

"This scares me," Cora said finally, looking up. Her face was bloodless.

"Me too," I said. "I mean, I haven't spoken to her in quite some time"—I avoided Eden's eyes—"but from what I remember, this is not how Sam typically sounds." No quips, no text crowding like ants into the margins. Just naked desperation. *I need help and don't know who else to turn to.*

"Yeah, this looks really bad. I feel sick just looking at it."
Eden pushed my phone back to me over the table. "By the
way, no offense, but why would she have sent this to you?
Cora and I have been here all along. Sam knew she could
rely on us."

I tried not to let on how deeply Eden's question wounded
me. It was one I'd been asking myself ad nauseum.

"The three of us are like sisters," Cora added, and her
eyes filled.

"I have no idea," I whispered. I took another sip of violet gin; watching me, Eden reached over to top off my goblet.

"Are you sure there wasn't anyone in Sam's life that she
was feeling threatened by?" I asked.

Cora dragged bone-white nails over the scratches in the
table. "There was this road-rage situation," she said slowly.
"I told the cops about it, but I'm not sure if it holds any
water."

"Sam flipped someone off on I-95 and they followed
her off the highway," Eden clarified.

"All the way to some gas station where she pulled over
and called us," Cora added.

Maybe Sam hadn't changed so much in eight years,
after all. "Who was it?"

"No idea. She never even saw their face. We told her to
report the license plate to the police, but I doubt she ever
did."

I frowned. It was definitely a theory, but one that didn't
strike me as substantial enough. "Sam's stepmom said she
didn't know of Sam dating anyone. Did you?"

"No," Eden said, shaking her head. "Definitely not."

The three of us returned to contemplating the table. A stony silence closed in around us. I could feel it—Sam's note wasn't sitting well with any of us.

"Maybe we should have something to eat," Cora ventured, finally.

I was expecting her and Eden to rustle up a bowl of chips—maybe some hummus if I was lucky—so I was shocked when Cora left the dining room and returned with platter after platter of cookbook-worthy spreads.

"Need help with anything?" I asked, on her second trip back to the table.

"Nope!" Cora pushed her hair behind her ears and darted back into the kitchen. I snuck a surreptitious look at Eden. She hadn't moved from her seat at the head of the table, where she was scrolling on her phone.

Eventually, the entire tabletop was covered. Cora pointed to each item as she named it. "Wild garlic and walnut bread. Here's some rose honey to drizzle on top—the combination is just heavenly. Wild mushroom soup. Goat cheese and pomegranate salad. Be warned: the arugula is especially spicy tonight!"

I stared at the steaming arrangement; its divine smells made my stomach growl. "Did you make all this?"

Cora glowed with pride. "Of course! We like making things in this house." Then she started spooning food on my plate like I was a child: drizzling the rose honey on top of the bread, then reaching for my bowl to ladle mushroom soup inside.

When she placed the plate in front of me, it struck me

how hungry I was. I pulled a bit of bread off with my fingers and popped it in my mouth. A sigh escaped me. It was an explosion of spices and flavors, the crust sharp against my palette. I couldn't get enough of the soup, woodsy and dark; a forkful of salad and I felt as though I were sinking into a forest, the pomegranate seeds tiny, tart pillows bursting between my molars.

After a time, I looked up. The girls hadn't even touched their food. They watched me, amusement tugging at their lips.

"You like it?" Cora asked.

My spoon clattered against the bowl as I reached for more bread. "Hate it. Clearly."

That made them laugh. Then they started eating their own meals, delicately.

Eden reached for a bottle of red wine. "Can you get—" she started, then said, "Never mind." She took something from her side, slicing into the foil around the cork.

I paused in my rabid consumption to assess what she'd placed on the table next to her plate. It looked like a small dagger, its blade narrowing to a startling point. The handle was studded with gemstones that glinted in the scant light from the candles. They were milk-colored, with bright blue centers.

"What is that?" I said, gesturing toward the blade.

Eden gave me a sheepish smile. "A girl's got to be prepared to open wine bottles at a moment's notice, right?" She poured me a hasty glass, the liquid dark and glugging. "Drink up, girlie," she said, passing it to me.

I took a sip. Silk on my tongue, the deep flavor melding

seamlessly with the rest of my meal. After another pull, I realized I was well on my way to getting tipsy, my head helium-light. My eyes fell across that dagger again. It struck me suddenly where I'd seen that pattern before: on the tile inside Sam's jewelry box.

"What are those gemstones? They're so distinctive."

Eden smirked. "No idea. Sometimes we find ourselves inspired by the most unexpected things, don't we?"

It should be illegal to make something dangerous so pretty. For a fleeting moment, I imagined lifting it off the table—curling my hand around the hilt, feeling its heft—and plunging it into the heart of an enemy.

Not again.

Under the table, I pressed my finger to my spiny ring.

Bad Liv.

"How's your sister doing?" Cora asked suddenly.

It was so far afield from any of our previous topics of conversation that my mind emptied like a pail of water. "What?"

"I noticed her lock screen had two little babies on it." Cora was assembling a forkful of salad on her plate, teasing the tiny gemstones of pomegranate seeds onto the tines. "Is she a new mom?"

"She is. Good eye."

"How's she holding up?" Eden asked.

I shrugged. "Fine."

"I only ask because my sister is married with two little kids," Cora said. "I know it can be super hard."

"Such a sacrifice," Eden intoned drily.

I crunched on a piece of bread. How honest to be with these girls I hardly knew? My first instinct was to hold back, to shield Penny's privacy. But something about Eden and Cora's patient expressions, the comfort of this delicious meal and the firelight playing over the mantel, coaxed an admission from me. "I don't know . . . she kind of freaked me out, honestly. She just kept talking about how she'd given up so much—her job, her body, her time, her sleep— and it bothered me because it didn't really sound like it was affecting her husband the same way at all."

Eden shrugged. "Sadly, I think that's just the reality for women."

Cora nodded gravely. "I watched my sister go off the deep end after getting married. It started so innocuously— her husband wasn't 'good' at cleaning or doing laundry, so she just did it for him. She was one frazzled mess trying to juggle corporate real estate with breastfeeding, with keeping her husband fed and her house clean. By the time the second kid came along?" Cora looked up at me with an ugly grimace. "There was no hope."

Surreptitiously, I used my thumb to swivel my engagement ring so the gem was facing my palm. I'd heard similar horror stories, but I knew it wouldn't apply to Noah and me. We were different. Whenever we cooked a meal, he always helped me clean. He was particular about his laundry settings; surely, he wouldn't abdicate that responsibility to me.

"I mean, there are exceptions," Eden said, as if reading my mind. "My cousin married another woman, and they have the split of domestic responsibilities down pat. But they're still moms at the end of the day, still expected to bleed themselves dry for their children while working jobs with ten days' vacation per year, so . . ." She gave me an exaggerated shrug. "What can you do?"

The stony silence from before descended back over the table. I thought, suddenly, of Noah beaming at the double stroller in the train station and my stomach tightened.

"You know what I think we need?" Eden said suddenly. "A good run in the woods."

I snorted into my wineglass. But to my amazement, she and Cora sprang to their feet and raced out of the dining room, pounding across the floorboards. I looked around the empty space in disbelief. These girls couldn't be serious. Running through the woods? Now?

A rap on the window across the table made me jump. It was Eden, already outside. "Come on!" she shouted through the glass.

I balked.

Another knock on the window, and she was gone. I stared at the yawning night behind the glass. Dazed, I let my feet carry me back through the heart of the house and out the front door. It smelled of earth and leaves. Above me hung a fragile moon. The closest neighbor was only a peek of gray clapboard, a good fifty yards away. Cora and Eden's backs were to me, long hair flying, as they dashed in the direction of the dark fringe of the woods that beckoned at the edge of the property. One of them let out a delighted cry in the crystalline air.

Eden turned around to face me. Her face was a ghostly smudge of white. "Come on," she called again.

The wet grass gave way to a blanket of rot beneath the tree canopy. As I plunged into the woods, clawlike branches tore at my shoulders and thighs. A stitch was opening up in my side. When was the last time I ran like this? I stopped, panting, to brush some sweat from my upper lip.

Suddenly, a nudge at my elbow: "Take this." Some kind of stick thrust into my hand.

I willed my eyes to adjust to the darkness to see who was speaking to me. But before I could peel back the night to see, the stick in my hand burst into a flaming purple dandelion head.

"Whoa." I'd never seen a sparkler this powerful, and certainly never in this rapturous shade of violet. I lifted it like a beacon.

The voice was far away, but the words were unmistakable: "Run, Liv!"

The purple dandelion on the end of my sparkler turned . . . red. And then green. I stared, transfixed. Did sparklers even do that?

I heard a snatch of laughter. And then—was that my name?

"Liv!" It was. A distant echo.

I looked back at my sparkler, hissing and spitting in brilliant fuchsia. Then I broke into a run and my heart lifted. Everything around me—knobbed bark, groping branches, rocks and moss and sticks—was reduced to rushing darkness. My breath came faster and faster until I was laughing giddily, drunk on my own elation. Damn, it felt magnificent to be outrunning everything that had plagued me of late. My anxiety about Sam, about law school and my engagement. My guilt. Something knotted and calcified inside me cracked open; I was free. Laughing wildly and gulping down the night.

At last, I happened across Eden and Cora in a clearing. They were piled over each other in the grass, spread-eagle, as if making snow angels in the fallen leaves.

"You found us!" Cora chirped.

Without thinking, I tumbled onto the dew-soaked grass beside them. My heart was beating fast in my chest, like a small animal's. The scent of moss filled my nostrils; one of their hairs tickled my face and I laughed again, more wildly, perhaps, than the moment merited.

Eden emitted a sudden quiet squeak, her chest rising sharply.

I sat up. "What was that?"

"Oh," Cora said, dissolving into laughter. "That was Eden's daily hiccup."

"It's nothing," Eden said, turning over in the grass.

"Wait a second—what? A daily hiccup?"

"Ever since I've known Eden, she gets a single hiccup every day." I could see Cora's grin in the dark; she tugged a piece of Eden's hair affectionately. "Never multiple hiccups, and she never skips a day. Honestly, it's pretty adorable."

"Shut up," Eden muttered, but there was a tinge of playfulness in her voice.

I couldn't believe it. The darkly mysterious Eden Holloway was plagued by chronic hiccups? I wished I'd been privy to this insider information back in high school. I'd never seen Eden as more of an approachable human as I did now, lying beside her on the forest floor after hearing her involuntary squeak. And what was more? She seemed . . . embarrassed.

"Hey." I frowned down at the extinguished sparkler in my hands. "It blew out."

"No, it didn't." Eden raised her own naked sparkler in the dark. "Bring it here."

I tried handing it to her, but she forced the stick back into my fist. Lazily, Cora extended her own extinguished stick so all three of our sparklers were touching. A zap ran through my bones. Then a plume of white fire tore up into the night, tinsel-like, so high it nearly grazed the dark tree canopy above.

"What the hell?" I dropped my sparkler stick, rubbing my wrist. It still stung from the shock of electricity that had torn through it. In the jangly aftermath, I felt like dissolving into more frantic laughter. What had just happened? One of the sparklers must have still been lit and reignited the other two at once. Whatever the cause, I'd been filled—just for a moment—with a voltage so powerful it left me light-headed.

Eden and Cora were giggling at my reaction. After the blast of white against my retinas, their features looked splotchy and half-formed. Sudden iciness filtered into my body, eclipsing the giddiness.

For a second, I could have sworn I saw a third face laughing at me in the dark.

10

THEN

SAM AND I SOON SETTLED INTO A ROUTINE, HANGING OUT on a near daily basis. She was ravenous to learn more about jewelry making, and soon procured her own supplies, which she'd spread out over the floor of her bedroom where we worked after school. Sam picked up techniques with astonishing speed—so quickly and easily, in fact, that I had to fight down a flicker of jealousy. Her first bracelet was only marginally clumsy; the next was nearly flawless. After that she moved on to crafting earrings—something I'd never covered with her—scanning examples she found online.

The experience of making jewelry alongside Sam was . . . odd. I was no stranger to losing track of time while working on my own pieces, but to do so in tandem with Sam felt very different. Sometimes, when reaching for a set of pliers or a spool of wire, I would feel the air between us thicken, charged and humming like an electric fence. It made the little hairs on the back of my neck stand up. I'd thought about mentioning it to Sam to see if she'd ever picked up on it, but I always lost my nerve—although something told me she was experiencing it, too.

Since Sam and I were spending so much time together, when rumblings of the Guilford Fair started up, a critical social event for us high schoolers, it seemed a natural conclusion we'd go together. The fair was allegedly a vestige from the 1850s, when four Guilford farmers organized the first event to parade livestock and harvest in front of the town. These days, of course, there was more than livestock and crops. From what I could glean, my classmates seemed most interested in the carnival rides and who was going with whom.

There was only one problem: Sam wanted to get ready at my house.

"My brother is having friends over," she whined. "My house is going to be overflowing with smelly lacrosse guys."

I didn't know how to tell Sam she'd be walking into a minefield. "My room is a mess," I said. "I'm not even finished unpacking."

"I already saw your room! It's fine. Besides—have you seen all the empty soda cans in mine?"

In the end, Sam arrived at my house the day of the fair with her makeup bag and flat iron. She divided my hair into sections and straightened it for me, the damp strands hissing inside the clamp. I sat tense on my bed, listening through the walls for signs of a fight. Mom was chopping onions in the kitchen and Dad was buried in his office. As long as the steady metronome of her knife against the cutting board continued, we would be okay.

"Oops," Sam said, reading my body language. "Did I burn you?"

"Nope. All good."

"Okay, phew." She unclipped another section of my hair and began brushing it out, chattering about a craft fair she wanted us to attend to get inspiration for our jewelry. I was only half-listening: the sound of mom's knife against wood had suddenly stopped.

"—this video about soldering," Sam was saying. "Have you ever seen anyone do it before?"

"I . . ." *Oh shit.* Through the floor, I could distinctly hear my father's voice threading through my mother's. He'd entered the kitchen; they were starting to talk.

"I think the kits are kind of expensive."

Then—a slam downstairs, like a sandbag hitting the floor. The shrill crescendo of my mother's voice: "You have got to be shitting me!"

The flat iron sprang open in Sam's hand. "Was that—?"

It was, and I wanted to crawl into a ball and disintegrate. Another night of my parents' fighting was bad enough. But to have my new friend here to witness it all? The thought was absolutely unbearable.

Realization dawned on Sam's face. "Oh my God. This is what you were telling me about, isn't it? Your parents—"

I turned away from her, just as my father began to roar.

"Hey," Sam said, jumping off the bed and coming to squat in front of me. "Hey, it's okay. We'll just—we'll just bounce early. We can do our makeup in the car."

My dad shouted again; had I been in the battlefield of the kitchen, I was sure I'd see the cords standing out on his neck. I could just make out the words *ungrateful bitch*.

I flinched.

"Okay," Sam said, throwing the claw-clips into her makeup bag. "Let's go."

Sam held my hand tightly down the stairs and out the back door. She drove us to Friendly's, where she cajoled me into ordering a Shirley Temple and Monster Mash sundae to match hers, the mint-chip monster faces replete with jagged Reese's Peanut Butter Cups horns. Her chatter filled our little booth until my leg stopped shaking under the table. While she had lots to say about the fair—preparing me for the best rides and exhibits, along with the lamest ones—Sam didn't utter a word about my parents' explosion. She'd read it in my body and my face: the topic was off-limits. Later, she did my makeup in the Friendly's bathroom, her eye pencil gentler than normal on my waterline.

"Gorgeous," she pronounced, after she finished.

I turned away from her, feeling the traitorous burn of tears. "I'm really sorry, Sam."

"What are you talking about." It wasn't even a question; Sam was re-capping her eye pencil brusquely.

"Earlier. At my house. I'm so embarrassed—"

"There's nothing to apologize for." Sam stowed the pencil and gently adjusted a couple strands of my hair to frame my face. Suddenly, I was overwhelmed by this girl's care for me. Sure, my friends had been supportive back in Denver, but they'd never witnessed such rawness between my parents and been there to soften the blow. Tough as she was on the outside, Sam had a soft core, just like the bubblegum-centered lollipops she loved. How many others had gotten the privilege of experiencing this side of her? How had I gotten so lucky?

I pressed my lips together to rein in the rush of emotion. "You're such a good a friend."

"Oh God." Sam stood, zippering her makeup case. "That's your Shirley Temple talking now."

The sky was just darkening when we turned into the swarming fairground. The sharp elbows of the fair jutted above the crowd: white tent tops and the light-studded steel of the Ferris wheel and Pirate Ship. As soon as we'd parked and hopped out of the car, Sam looped her arm through mine.

"Okay, let's get cotton candy!"

I didn't even have time to dwell on what had happened back at the house. Sam ushered us from one stomach-plummeting ride to the next. The cotton candy and ice cream in my stomach turned to a brick on the Tilt-A-Whirl; then I really had to question Sam's order of operations. But any lingering upset was eclipsed by a wheeling happiness to be sharing the moment with Sam—this bold, often-ridiculous girl who made earrings and necklaces alongside me was quickly growing to be my best friend. I glanced over at her on the ride. She had a giant open-mouthed smile, dark hair snarling across her face. Sam shrieked and so did I.

After the Tilt-A-Whirl was the livestock competition. The smell of animal hit me as soon as we entered the tent: straw and manure and musk. A midnight-black Netherland Dwarf had snagged first place in the rabbit competition and sat munching hay in the corner of its cage. Its eyes, positioned on either side of its head, swiveled to take us in. Quickly, it dismissed us.

"Look at this one!" Sam crouched next to a lop-eared rabbit. It had dark fur around its eyes like a bandit's mask. "It's like a little robber."

A hushed giggle made me spin. Eden, Avery, and Cora stood huddled around a cage not twenty feet from us, peering at the animal inside. My heart jolted. For weeks I'd watched these three girls slice a path through the hallways of Guilford High, wondering what made them so captivating. It wasn't their clothes—they wore odd, mismatched outfits that looked pulled from thrift stores, Eden's especially torn up and stitched back together in jarring ways. It wasn't beauty, either. Cora was the only conventionally attractive member of the group—Eden had a face so severe it was slightly terrifying, and one could say Avery's height made her gawky. Finally, it'd dawned on me that Sam had been right: The Sisterhood truly didn't give a shit about what anyone else thought. Other girls, teachers, even boys—they were impervious to them all. The Sisterhood were one another's entire universe; they didn't need anyone or anything else. In fact, the way they whispered and moved seemed perfectly orchestrated to shut out the rest of the world.

I couldn't very well blame The Sisterhood for that. If I were one of them, I wouldn't want to let in anyone else, either.

Tonight, the crowd had dispersed around the girls as well, forming a buffer of space around them. Eden wore a gauzy black floor-length dress—it looked as though she'd taken scissors to the waistline, creating artful cut-outs that exposed a mosaic of tanned skin. She'd swiped on thick winged liner that matched her eyebrows and was sticking a finger into the gaps of the rabbit cage. For whatever reason, this made the other girls explode into laughter. I frowned, trying to figure out what Eden could be doing that was so damn funny.

She straightened suddenly, gave me a little wave. "Hey, Liv."

A comet of shock streaked through me. I hoped my face didn't show it.

"Hi," I said.

The girls trailed out of the tent soon thereafter, but my heart was still beating hard, long after their bodies had dissolved into the crowd.

Beside me, Sam's jaw hung wide open. "What the hell was that?"

I looked back at her blankly, unprepared for her sneer.

"You mean to tell me you and Eden Holloway are besties now?"

I scratched my shoulder, startled by my friend's sudden venom.

"Hey, Sam! I think you should consider entering the rabbit contest next year."

A boy our age had appeared beside us in the tent. He was elbowing Sam in the side and this surprised me—I'd never seen her interact with a guy. Especially not guys with this lacrosse-player musculature, all sinew and liquid smile and mussed hair, and all too aware of the effect of it all.

The guy clamped Chiclets-white teeth over his bottom

lip. "Just watch. We'll get you a little carrot and you'll be right at home."

Sam's face contorted; she shoved him away. "Fuck you."

I wanted to shake her. What was she doing? Even if this kid was making fun of Sam's slightly yellow overbite—that had to be what he meant by the comment—he was giving her attention. And he was *hot*. The dark-haired boy caught me staring at him and my body flushed in sudden heat. I glanced away quickly, but not before catching the tail end of a rakish grin, directed straight at me.

"Hi," the guy said. I couldn't help it—I had to look at him again. To my delight, his attention was no longer on Sam, but instead on my body, lingering on the strip of skin between my shirt and the waistband of my jeans. He took his time assessing the rest of me before thumbing his full bottom lip, shooting me one last smirk, and sauntering away.

Flushed, I watched him disappear from the tent. That lazy yet deliberate once-over had made me shiver in such a delicious way.

Sam stood gripping her elbows over her chest. She glanced over at me quickly, as if it pained her. "Don't even think about it."

"What are you talking about?"

"Don't give in to his little fuckboy charms. It won't end well. It never does." Then, to my surprise, she stomped out of the tent, leaving me stranded in a sea of livestock.

• • •

TURNS OUT, THE GUILFORD FAIR was a very unfriendly place to be alone. I tried running after Sam, but she had rounded the corner and disappeared into the throng of fairgoers just as The Sisterhood had. Panicked, I dug in my pocket for my phone and texted her.

Where did you go???

The block of cotton candy turned over in my stomach. I was tempted to call Mom to pick me up, but it seemed such a depressing waste of the night. Instead, I began to wander, feeling increasingly ill at ease. What had Sam been thinking, abandoning me like that?

Eventually, I found myself at the mouth of a fun house, a rotating plastic tunnel encircled by neon green lights. *Why not?* Walking through a fun house, it'd be harder for onlookers to see I was alone. Abandoned. Besides, I had nothing better to do.

I texted Sam one last time.

Going into fun house. If I don't make it out, my blood will be on your hands.

My Converse slid against the roiling floor, palms screeching for purchase on the shifting walls. Had I really raced through these kinds of fun houses as a kid? This one had to be more intense than normal.

Soon, I faced a shuddering platform obscured by fog. Slowly, I placed a foot on the black sandpaper treads, spreading my arms wide for balance. The vapor from the smoke machine had a distinctive chemical scent, pressing along with the heat of the night against my face and throat.

It's only weirding me out because I'm doing this alone. Because not only had Sam left me, there was a curious lack of fairgoers inside the structure. This didn't make any sense—crowds of families and teens had permeated every other attraction. Maybe it was common knowledge this fun house sucked; maybe every Guilford native already knew this. Had Sam warned me about this in Friendly's? I pushed aside a series of hanging sandbags with my elbows. They obscured my vision; I couldn't see what came next.

And then, suddenly, I could see—over and over again. I stood in a narrow corridor of mirrors, my own darkened figure reflected back to me infinitely. I shifted on one foot, and the hundred Liv-reflections feinted in a coordinated dance. I drew closer, studying my face in the glass: the thin upper lip that didn't match the full bottom one, my sleepy-looking eyes turned down at the corners. The hundred other Livs touched their faces, too, feeling their asymmetry in the dark. There was a cascading rhythm to our movements, like rippling centipede legs.

I looked down at my sneakers. The white toes had turned purple in the black light. When I peered up again, there was a second face in the mirror. Sam. I felt a burst of relief; she'd found me. Sam tipped her head back, looking like she was about to speak. But something strange was happening with the bottom half of her body. Her legs began to refract at the knees, her shins rotating forward, the opposite direction as they should. I was horrified; I couldn't look away. Sam's legs continued to contort, jutting at that impossible angle like a deformed crab or spider until—snap!—her very skeleton seemed to fracture in the glass.

Someone grabbed my wrist and I screamed.

"Gotcha." Sam—the real Sam—grinned in my face.

I was breathing hard. The horror of Sam's contorted limbs felt seared into the inside of my skull.

"W-where did you go?" My voice was shaking, to my immense embarrassment.

"Sorry. I needed a minute."

My heart rate was finally coming down. Anger snuck in to replace fear. "You ditched me!"

"I know, and I'm sorry! Really. I shouldn't have done it. Please forgive me?" Sam pouted exaggeratedly behind clasped hands.

I laughed, against my will. The relief was apparent on my face in the mirrors. "Why'd you do it, though?"

Sam looked down at the scuffed fun house floor. "Everett just likes to push my buttons. The lecherous douchebag."

Everett, Everett. The name was so familiar . . .

"My twin," Sam said, casting a dirty look in the mirror.

I thought of the perfect architecture of the face I'd just seen, those vivid lips and brows.

"Oh." My neck felt hot. But of course—I'd known Everett existed, but I'd never actually seen him at Sam's house because he had lacrosse practice every day after school.

"For your information," Sam said, "he's a man-whore. He goes after anything with lips and tits—no offense."

"None taken." I twisted my hair up on top of my head. A few scrawny middle schoolers pushed past us in the fun house, but Sam and I remained rooted in place.

"And the reason I freaked out . . . he's gone after one of my friends before. Last year. Her name was Sarah—she moved away, so you wouldn't know her. But we were close. Until Everett got his talons in her, that is. They only lasted like two weeks—which was probably a personal best for my brother, honestly—but Sarah didn't want to hang out with me after that. Shocker."

I looked at Sam in the fun house mirror. One of her eyes bulged like a deranged fish in the wavy glass, and it gave me a pang of sympathy. Poor Sam—abandoned by her friend, made a fool by her dashing twin.

"Promise me you won't stoop to taking his bait," Sam said, extending a pinky in my direction. "I don't want to lose another friend." She gave me an exaggerated frown. "I don't want to lose my Liv."

My Liv. Even my family had never employed such affection; the words made my heart swell. I grinned, linking pinkies with Sam. The motion caused my own cheekbone to warp and sharpen severely in the fun house mirror. Sam and I made quite a pair: one deranged fish, one maniacal cartoon villain.

We both laughed at our ridiculous reflections.

"Promise," I said.

11

NOW

WE DIDN'T MAKE IT BACK TO THE HOUSE UNTIL 1:30 A.M. Eden said I could crash with them and I agreed; I was feeling so dizzy from the alcohol and my romp through the woods that I scarcely trusted myself to get behind the wheel.

Eden yawned noisily as she trod up the narrow staircase to her bedroom. Cora and I followed behind. The rest of the house unfolded, dreamlike: that familiar landing with its reading nook stuffed with pillows and the rose sealed inside the stained-glass ring. How did I know this house so intimately without ever having seen this part of it? I opened my mouth to say something, but Cora had moved ahead to rummage in a giant hall closet.

"Here you go." She handed me a neat pile of items: a soft nightgown with ribbon straps, a toothbrush still in its crinkly plastic wrapper, a travel-sized tube of Crest, and a plastic cup. "Need anything else?"

"No, thank you." From my dream, I was certain I knew the room she'd be showing me to, the second off the hallway on the left-hand side. I raised my chin in its direction. "Is that—?"

"Sam's room. Yeah." Cora led me inside. I shivered, despite the fact that my blood still felt molten after our run through the woods. It was exactly as I'd dreamed it, with the addition of Sam's essence, trapped and lingering: in the overflowing patent leather makeup bag on the dresser, the discarded black tank top that had missed the rolling wicker hamper and lodged instead in the corner of the room. A miniature glass toucan sat in a tiny cage on the corner of her desk, calling to mind the extensive collection of glass animals she'd had back in high school. But whereas Sam's high school bedroom had been plastered with photos— Sam with her summer camp friends, with her family, with me—these walls were completely bare.

Cora grimaced. "Sorry. I didn't think how weird it would be for you to sleep in here, given everything that's been going on."

"No, it's okay. I appreciate it." I deposited my toiletry items on the bed. Then I glanced over to where I knew I'd see a fireplace: directly across from the bed, its grille seared into my memory.

I pressed my eyes shut. Reopened them.

Cora studied my face. "Are you okay?"

"Yeah, just tired. Thanks again." I forced a tight smile;

the euphoria from out in the woods had all but drained away by now.

"Anytime." Cora hesitated before turning away from me. "Sleep tight." Then she shut me softly inside.

Alone, I paced the length of the room. My shoes sounded hollow on the wide, honey-colored floorboards. Like much of the old house, they were slightly warped, creaking underfoot. Lavender filled my nostrils. I picked up the caged toucan and turned it over in my hands, staring at its beady black eyes. With the exception of these small details and the absence of a fire in the fireplace, the room was the same as my dream. Did this mean there was a beetle waiting for me in the sheets, about to crawl inside my mouth? I shuddered, dragging a hand through my hair. No; this had to be an especially persistent case of déjà vu. That was all.

I ran a hand over the uneven cream walls. Pulled aside the curtains to peer into the darkness outside, the leaves edged in light from the gas lamps. There was a heavy trunk in the corner of the room. Once I'd figured out how to depress the locking mechanism, I heaved the chest open. The smell of must and mothballs flew at me. Inside were stacks of folded blankets and sweaters, ostensibly stowed for colder months.

I crossed to the opposite side of the room to the closet. It groaned open on stubborn hinges. The rickety rod was packed with clothes. How much had Sam even taken on her trip? Did Eden or Cora know her wardrobe well enough to identify missing articles of clothing?

I shut the door and emptied Sam's makeup bag onto

the bed. I smiled to myself, seeing that Sam still favored bold colors: deep purple and electric blue eyeshadow that I'd never have the guts to wear myself. I snapped open and closed her eyelash curler, gummy with mascara. I wished she were here so I could tease her about bruising my eyelid back in high school. *You kept squeezing, even when I screamed! Who does that?*

Gently, I began packing the makeup back inside the patent leather bag. I wondered what the police had made of Sam's room when they searched it. Did they search everything? A bright red tube of lipstick rolled off the bed and popped open on the floor. Great—Cora had probably heard the sound down the hallway; I was sure she wouldn't appreciate me digging through her missing roommate's things. When I bent to retrieve the lipstick, shock tore through me.

Instead of a stick of pigment in the base, a hooked blade glinted.

A miniature dagger disguised as lipstick? I snatched it up to study more carefully. Why would Sam have something like this? I thought of the clotted letters of her note—*I need help and don't know who else to turn to*—and goosebumps popped on my forearms.

"Who was scaring you, Sam?" I whispered.

The empty room swallowed my words, mocking me. Outside, the wind scraped a couple of pointy leaves against the glass and the crickets shrieked. Impulsively, I shoved the lipstick dagger in my clutch—I'd have to bring it in to Detective Patterson first thing the next morning. Then I dumped the rest of Sam's makeup in her patent leather bag, flipped the lights, and climbed fully clothed into bed.

. . .

I woke to a scrabbling sound in the walls, or maybe the leaves scratching at the window again. *Tiska-tisk-tisk.* A mouse? The skittery sound pulled my body from sleep. I surfaced slowly, as if from the bottom of a murky lake.

Sam's room was bright. A headache pressed from behind my eye sockets. When I reached for my phone, shame crashed over me: my lock screen was stacked with texts from Noah from the night before, and it was already past eleven. I'd been so absorbed in my night with Eden and Cora—and later my investigation of Sam's room— that I hadn't even noticed Noah's texts come in. What had happened last night? Had I really run through the woods, shrieking, with Eden and Cora? Laid in a dew-soaked meadow with them, lighting colored sparklers? There'd been something almost enchanting about the entire night, starting with the way the night air had curled into my childhood bedroom and drawn me out into the car. Looking up at the Victorian façade of 128 Whitfield Street—and then moving through the strangely familiar spaces—had felt like a fever dream.

It was probably this damn house that made it impossible to wake up.

Suddenly, the door to my room flew open. I rocketed upright in bed.

Eden stood in the doorway, eyes wide with panic. She held something glittery in one hand. "Liv," she said, without prelude, "I hope you can help us."

Thank goodness I'd slept in my clothes. I rolled out of bed and joined Eden by the door, adrenaline pumping. "What's going on?"

Closer now, I saw she held what looked like a bridal tiara, all silver swoops and iridescent gemstones. Eden uncurled her left hand, exposing a couple of naked gems in her palm. "Our bride accidentally stepped on her tiara just now during her fitting—there was this crunching sound and then the gemstones came right out. I tried sticking them back in, but they don't fit anymore."

Gently, I took the tiara from Eden. There were two gaping bezels where the gemstones had clearly once nested, misshapen now from the abuse. "Yeah," I said. "These bezels need to be opened and then reformed around the stones."

"What the hell does that mean?"

"See these little metal wells soldered to the tiara here? There's a special tool to manipulate them. Sam probably has one."

Eden looked at me helplessly.

I sighed. "Where does she keep her tools?"

Eden was wringing her hands now. It was odd to see her normal composure so shot. "In the studio. I'm sorry, Liv— I'd say it could wait, but the bride was hoping to take her dress and accessories home today . . ."

"It's okay." I needed to get my day started, anyway. I handed the tiara back to Eden. "Show me where the studio is?"

I hadn't even noticed the stand-alone structure behind

the house last night when I'd slipped outside. It looked a bit ramshackle from the outside, one faded façade blanketed with climbing honeysuckle. Eden jiggled a dark bronze knob. It looked as though it had a face carved into it—a gargoyle? An angry owl? Finally, with a defeated shuddering noise like a sigh, the Dutch door to the studio let us in.

Inside smelled of warmth—of hearth and hot cocoa and sun-warmed floorboards. There were two stations filling the space, one in each back corner of the room. Eden's caught my eye first with its hulking bolts of fabric—lace and silk and taffeta in pure white, bone, and blush—all lined up like ghostly soldiers in the studio's sizeable built-ins. A large square of wood on the wall, covered in pegs, held rows of different implements: at least seven different scissors of varying sizes and colored handles, skeins of tape measures, and a shelf packed full of thread ranging from pale pink to snowy white, and every shade in between. A Singer sewing machine, the star of the show, sat on a cork work surface; beside it, a headless white mannequin with panels of diaphanous fabric pinned into the beginnings of a delicately boned bodice.

Sam's workstation—that's what it had to be—was no less impressive. Beside a vase of white calla lilies sat a giant teal trunk. I found my feet carrying me toward it of their own accord. Then, without invitation, I began opening the rows of velvet-lined drawers. They were filled to the brim with every jewelry-making material I could possibly imagine: drawers and drawers of high-quality beads, gems, pendants, and glass drops sorted by color. Coils of wire in every gauge. A magnetic metal bar running the length of the worktable boasted an assemblage of files, pliers, tweezers, and soldering picks.

When I looked up, Eden was watching my exploration of the workstation with a tiny smile. "What do you think?"

My cheeks went hot, chagrined to have been caught greedily thumbing through Sam's stuff. It felt dirty, like pilfering money from a corpse—even if Eden didn't seem to mind.

"It's really nice," I muttered.

"Do you see the tool you were looking for?"

"Give me a minute." It didn't take me long to locate the bezel pusher, nestled in a drawer toward the bottom of the teal trunk. Eden watched anxiously as I coaxed the bezels back open, used a set of tweezers to set the gemstones inside, and crimped the metal frame back around them, using techniques I'd taught myself back in high school by watching videos online. It'd been a while since I'd picked up tools like these, but my hands were sparked by muscle memory; it made my heart lift to see how capable my body was after so many years.

"Amazing." Eden all but snatched the tiara out of my hands the moment I set down Sam's tools. She studied the repair, pressed a fingertip to the secured gemstones. "You really saved our asses today, Liv. Thank you."

Such effusiveness from Eden was a rare treat. "No problem. I'm glad something good came from my hangover."

"Come grab a slice of wedding cake before you go. Cora just made a new batch of red velvet for a tasting."

I hesitated. I needed to get to the police station to drop off the lipstick dagger I'd found in Sam's room.

"Come on," Eden said. "It'll only take a second."

Cora's bakery was in the space adjacent to Eden's bridal salon, separated by a set of dark walnut pocket doors. She'd set up a couple of circular tables featuring scrolling ironwork on the legs and beneath the glass tops, cluttered now with plates of wedding cake. The bride dug the tines of her fork into a slice with a shocking pink interior. She was giggling—giddy, I assumed, in the midst of such elegance and attention. Cora hovered in the wings, topping off the couple's champagne. The groom looked somewhat less pleased, scratching at the regrowth of hair on his neck. He kept peering over at the bridal salon. Hoping to sneak a forbidden glimpse of his fiancée's dress, perhaps? At the next table over, two women—one with a black bob, the other with a waterfall of turquoise hair—clanged forks accidentally over the same sliver of yellow cake and burst into laughter.

Eden whispered something in Cora's ear—presumably about the piece of cake she'd promised me—then led me into the bridal gown portion of the boutique. Suddenly, I felt shy, reduced to my role of tongue-tied bride-to-be. A petite redhead stood smoothing down the sides of her tailored gown on the pedestal. Like the women sampling cake on the other side of the room, she radiated good cheer, grinning at her reflection in the oval mirror. An open row of tiny, white satin buttons ran down her back, exposing a sliver of pale skin—that distinctive brand of button a bride has no chance of fastening by herself.

"Great news, Christina," Eden said, coming around behind the bride. Eden adjusted Christina's train over the edge of the pedestal. Then she drew the repaired tiara out from behind her back, brandishing it like she'd done a magic trick. "A little birdie helped me fix the gemstones on your tiara."

Christina locked eyes with herself in the mirror and began to clap with joy. "Oh, thank God!"

I stood by, feeling conflicted. Part of me wanted to melt into the background of this beautiful boutique that still made me feel like a fish out of water; another yearned to be called out, to be recognized for the work I'd just done.

A little birdie? Is that all I was, in Eden's eyes?

Gently, Eden nestled the tiara in Christina's dark red hair and affixed a veil. Then she began to fasten the trail of satin buttons in a confident, unhurried manner. Christina didn't take her eyes off her reflection. I blinked, feeling a crease chisel between my brows. There was something unusual about the raptness with which this bride was taking everything in. Entrancing as it must be to finally see herself in a bridal gown—especially if she was someone who'd fantasized about such a moment since childhood—this seemed undue. Christina's eyes were growing wider and . . . darker. Were her pupils dilating? Or maybe the lighting in the boutique had changed overhead? Just as I was beginning to embrace this explanation, the bride's eyes flashed opaque white in the mirror and my blood went icy.

A second later, Christina's eyes were back to normal. She was blinking and laughing, saying something to Eden about the vexing row of buttons. But I could have sworn I'd seen it—something just like a white contact lens clicking down over her irises.

12

THEN

ON THE NIGHT BEFORE HALLOWEEN, SAM AND I TOOK A BAG of candy into her room to enliven our jewelry-making session. Since our last get-together, I splurged and bought a torch, along with other requisite soldering supplies— a syringe, a fire brick, and a pickling solution in which to dip the jewelry afterward. Sam was working on a wrapped wire ring, but I could feel her attention on me as I directed the blue flame onto a thin wire ring of my own, coaxing the gap closed. Once I mastered this set of simple stacked rings, I'd start branching out to more challenging techniques. Merely thinking about it made me buzzy with excitement: this soldering set was going to be a game changer.

"Can I see that?" Sam's voice pierced my thoughts. When I glanced up, I realized she'd long since let go of her ring, which sat abandoned in the middle of her workspace.

"Let me finish closing up this ring first."

Sam groaned, reaching for a mini Snickers bar and tearing into it noisily.

I focused on the ring. Sam could whine all she wanted— *I'd* been the one to shell out the money on the soldering kit, not her.

"Okay," Sam said, the moment I'd deposited the closed ring in the shallow dish of pickling solution. "Hand it over."

I did, grudgingly. Sam was as entranced with the process as I had been—if not more. I reached for my wire and prepared the next stacking ring as Sam played with the torch, flicking the blue flame on and off. She helped herself to my syringe of solder and, before I knew it, was manipulating her own wrapped wire ring.

"Do you even know what you're doing, Sam?"

"I've watched you long enough."

I toyed with the C of wire in my tweezers, annoyed. Somehow, Sam had commandeered all my soldering materials into her own workspace, halting the creation of my own stacked rings. "Can I have it back now?"

"Hold on. I want to finish this."

I let out a sigh. Ninety percent of the time, Sam was the perfect crafting partner, focused and encouraging. But ten percent of the time, when her bossy side came out, it made me want to scream. A minute later, when Sam made no move to return the torch, I sighed again, got to my feet, and left Sam's room in search of a glass of water.

Sam didn't even look up.

I crept down the hallway outside Sam's room and into the kitchen. It was almost nine by now, the house dark save for the soft glow of fairy lights edging the doors to the deck.

There were little touches like that everywhere in this house, I'd noticed—from the carefully curated basket of seashells in the guest bathroom, to the breakfast bar, perennially set with woven placemats, silverware, and cloth napkins rolled into bejeweled napkin rings. *Stepmom*, Sam had told me with an eye roll, when she'd caught me looking. A few weeks ago, I sat down to dinner here, and Sam's stepmother kicked the meal off with what she called "High/Low": going around the table, each family member recounted the best and worst parts of their day. How foreign it was, to see such effort and domestic harmony. My own family dinners—not that I would ever allow Sam to witness them—were silent, prickly affairs on the nights my parents weren't snarling at each other across the table.

"Happy Mischief Night." The sudden male voice made me jump. Sam's twin—he of the lacrosse-player build and liquid smile—leaned against the doorjamb in the entrance to the living room, regarding me with a sleepy expression. My innards leaped. Since running into Everett at the Guilford Fair, I'd strained to pick him out in the throngs of students during passing time. And even though I was at Sam's house nearly every day after school, Everett always seemed to have plans of his own—including during family dinner—which felt like a crushing disappointment and a relief all at once. Sometimes when drifting off to sleep, I liked to play back the night of the Guilford Fair, the way Everett's gaze had lingered on my body before he'd tossed me a knowing smile. It still made my skin fizz.

Now, my laugh sounded funny in the dimness of the kitchen. "Mischief what?"

Everett uncrossed his arms and sauntered toward me. He was barefoot, his hair mussed in the back. "Please tell me someone's filled you in on Mischief Night."

Another strange laugh bubbled out of me. I felt my heart start to beat harder in my chest, as if I were a cornered animal. "I have no idea what you're talking about."

"My sister has failed you, then. As a friend and as an educator." Everett ran a hand through the cowlick near the base of his neck and looked over his shoulder into the dark hallway. He must have known how infuriatingly attractive nonchalance was on him. I considered Sam's warning about Everett's fuckboy charms, but damn, was it hard to resist.

"Okay," he said, turning back to me. "Here's the deal. Tonight's the night before Halloween, right? Which, in this neck of the woods, means it's time to go around the neighborhood . . . and make some mischief."

I hoped the kitchen was dark enough to hide the heat in my cheeks. "What kind of mischief?"

A dangerous smile flickered across his face. I could tell Everett was pleased with the way I was reacting to him. "Whatever kind you'd like." Everett took another step toward me. His dark eyes looked predatory. "What kind of mischief are you into?"

Sam chose that precise moment to lose interest in the soldering torch and materialize in the hallway. Her eyes narrowed when she saw Everett. "What are you doing here? I thought you were out."

"On my way. Not that it's any of your business." Sam's twin turned on his heel toward the darkness of the hallway and the distance notched back between us. It was probably better off that way—after all, I'd promised Sam I'd resist him.

Suddenly, Everett spun back in our direction. "You should come with," he said, looking straight over Sam's head at me.

Sam wrenched open a cabinet to procure her own glass. "Thanks, but TP'ing trees and egging houses isn't really Liv's style."

I fought down a tidal wave of resentment. There went Bossy Sam again, speaking on my behalf. She hadn't even asked.

"Actually," I said, "I kind of like the sound of Mischief Night. I'll go."

Everett punched the air in victory as Sam fixed me with a venomous look. "Seriously? We're in the middle of working."

"Come on, Sam. We can finish the pieces another time. I just want to . . . I don't know. Take a walk down your street, see what all the fuss is about. I've never done Mischief Night before." I met Everett's eyes over Sam's head again, and the lopsided grin he gifted me submerged my body in heat. In that moment, I was convinced I'd do anything to be the recipient of that smile again.

"The hell," Sam said, but she'd slammed the cabinet shut in defeat. Everett gave me another twisted smile and a shrug—a kind of *What can you do?* expression. I fought to return the smile, even as my stomach squirmed with guilt. Was I betraying Sam by insisting on attending Mischief Night? It kind of felt that way. Regardless, though, I deserved to have my own experiences.

Everett returned to the kitchen and took an egg carton from the fridge. Then he lifted the top and drew out a single brown egg. I stared at his boy-hand in the overhead lights: tanned skin, clipped-short nails with striking crescents of white. Everett's skin touched mine as he set the cool egg in my palm and I flinched. Up close, I could smell his boy-deodorant, and for a dizzying moment, I wondered what it would feel like to be pressed right up against him, our bodies flush.

"Sister of mine?" Everett drew out a second egg and raised it in Sam's direction.

She turned away from him, then—inexplicably—flung a mini Snickers at his chest. "Don't make me kill you."

"Jesus," Everett snapped, kicking the fallen candy bar across the kitchen tiles.

"Come on, Sam," I said. "We'll just go down the street a little and then we'll come right back and pick up with the jewelry."

A prickly silence stretched. Then, wordlessly, Sam snatched the egg from her brother. I couldn't believe she was going along with our plan after all.

Everett marched out of the kitchen, grabbed his sweat-shirt off the coat-tree in the hallway, and opened the front door to the night.

"Ladies," he said, sweeping an arm over the threshold. "Mischief awaits."

After bundling up, Sam and I followed Everett down the porch steps and to the sidewalk. Overhead, sparse tree canopies twitched audibly in the wind. There did seem to be a charge to the air tonight. Snatches of laughter threaded through the darkness. It smelled like leaves and woodsmoke. I took a deep pull of the icy air and it blazed down my windpipe.

"Come on." Someone—it had to be Everett—gripped my elbow for a second. Then, before I could process what was happening, the three of us had broken into a run. Shock registered: we were moving *fast*. Something like ecstasy bloomed inside me. This—this is what had been missing back in Denver: sprinting down darkened streets with a hot guy, sucking down electrifying air as jack-o'-lanterns winked at us from porch steps. Our feet slapped the pavement wildly and I almost had the courage to whoop. Instead, I let out a frantic laugh. "Oh my God, I'm going to drop my egg!"

We skidded to a stop on the sidewalk. Once I caught my breath and looked up, I realized we were no longer alone. A cluster of other high school students had gathered around us. My chest caved with disappointment. Here were Everett's real friends: guys clutching rolls of toilet paper, their voices clamoring to be heard over one another; and even a couple of girls, long hair skimming down the backs of their flannel-and-shearling jackets. I felt a stab of envy just seeing them. This was really it. Before I could dredge up my voice, Everett's friends had swallowed him in their midst. Then they were tearing away from us down the dark street.

Sam must have sensed my muscles sparking as I contemplated breaking into a run after them. "Don't," she said, her hand encircling my wrist.

I let my chin fall to my chest. Who was I kidding? I didn't belong with someone like Everett. That hit of eupho-

ria I'd gotten running with him through the dark was the
best I was going to get.

"I guess we can head back now," I said, resigned.

"Hmmm." Sam assessed the street, hugging herself
against the chill. A gnarled oak thrust from the ground before us, its branches tangled with toilet paper. Evidently, another group of teens had gotten here first. When Sam
turned back to me, her eyes looked so much like her brother's that a spidery sensation crossed my forearms. "Let's not
waste your egg, though," she said.

I shook my head. All the excitement had drained from
my body the moment I'd seen Everett swallowed by his
group of friends. "I'm not really in the mood."

"Hey. You said you wanted to experience Mischief
Night. Come on." Sam gripped me by the arm, pulling me
a few houses down. There we stood, looking at an unassuming gray ranch house with a plastic skeleton seated on the
porch swing. Sam nudged me. "Throw it," she said.

"You throw it." I shoved the egg at her.

"Hey, you were the one going on about needing to experience your first Mischief Night. Come on!"

I huffed out an exasperated breath. In the span of a
minute, the night had gone from intoxicating to infuriating.
Sam was needling me. She was pissed I'd fallen for her
brother's charms, pissed I'd picked debauchery with him
over jewelry making with her. And I knew her: she wasn't
going to drop it. I wound up, aiming for the hedges in front
of the house. The faster I disposed of the egg, the faster this
could all be over.

"No! Don't throw it into the plants. You need to get the

front door. Right smack-dab on the window part. It's the only way."

"God, Sam." I rolled my eyes. I shifted the egg from one hand to the other. It was warm to the touch now. I'd never egged a house before and all at once, adrenaline spiked my blood. Could I really do this? To a random, innocent stranger?

"Knew you wouldn't," Sam said.

How could someone I spent so much time alongside, creating with and encouraging, piss me off so much? Maybe it was because Sam had access to these subterranean parts of me that she was able to jab me where it really hurt. She was making it a habit to speak on my behalf and treat me like a goddamn pet, and it made white-hot rage rear up within me. I had the startling reflex to transfer my egg to my non-dominant hand, the better to slap Sam across the face. I imagined striking my best friend so hard that my rings made her cheeks bleed. The satisfaction this elicited in me was alarming.

Instead, I launched the egg against the ranch's front door.

"Oh my God!" Sam jumped away from me, letting out a whoop. "You did it. You actually did it!"

I stared at the mucousy yolk sliding down the glass. *I* had done that. *I* was a vandal. What's more, there had to be someone living in that house, and if we didn't bolt now—

To my horror, the front door swung open. My muscles screamed at me to run, run, run. But the figure on the doorstep wasn't at all what I expected: a stooped older woman with stick-thin arms. Guilt assaulted me. I never would've thrown that egg if I'd known someone so vulnerable was behind that door.

"What the fuck, Sam." Everett had materialized, his face a mask of rage. To my surprise, Sam was doubled over with almost maniacal laughter.

He shoved her, hard.

"Liv did it, not me!" she sang, and it made me hate her for a brutal second or two.

"You are a fucking psycho, I swear to God," Everett snarled. He reached for his sister again, but she slid out of his grip, tearing off back in the direction of their house.

"Let's go." Everett's voice was grim as he took me by the shoulders and turned me away from the elderly woman on the porch. Even though he was touching me—more than he'd ever before—I didn't feel any of the soaring elation I'd felt earlier in the night. I just felt hollow.

"What was that about?" I hissed, once we were a safe distance away from the gray ranch house.

"That," Everett said through clenched teeth, "was my ex's house. Sam has always had this weird thing about her. Goddammit." He wound up, kicked a jagged pebble down the sidewalk.

Of course. Sam had such a wicked look on her face when she directed me to throw the egg at that particular door. I licked my lips; they instantly went dry in the crackling night. "Who was your ex?" I asked, even though I wasn't sure I wanted to know the answer.

Everett shot a look up at the crisp stars overhead.

"Eden Holloway," he said.

13

NOW

I WENT STRAIGHT FROM EDEN AND CORA'S HOUSE TO THE
police station to drop off the lipstick knife I found in
Sam's makeup bag. Detective Patterson met me in the
same room we'd shared before. He greeted me with a
strained smile.

"I didn't expect to see you back so soon."

"Me neither." I set the decoy lipstick on the table between us. I waited for confusion to flash over Patterson's
face—then I removed the cap to bare the blade beneath.

The detective blinked once, slowly. "Can't say I was expecting that, either."

I nodded, vindicated. "I found this in Sam's makeup
bag. I think she was feeling unsafe. Why else would she have
this?"

Something was unspooling behind Patterson's eyes. I
wished he'd speak his thoughts aloud—I wanted badly to

theorize with him about Sam—but he kept silent. He slipped the lipstick knife into a plastic bag. "Thank you for this. I'll look into it."

It was clearly a dismissal, but I lingered at my seat at the table, unwilling to leave just yet. "I can't help but feel like it reinforces that note Sam sent me," I said. "Like there was someone after her, and she was afraid."

Another strained smile from Patterson. "We're still looking into everything. I can assure you we're in close contact with the family."

"I don't know. It just feels weird."

"It feels weird because it is. Missing person cases—especially when there's a lack of evidence—can drive everyone nuts. Makes you want to grasp at anything and everything to get an explanation."

I bit my cuticle. Maybe, but did that mean this was nothing?

"We're doing everything we can on the investigation front," he assured me again.

"Okay."

The detective gave me another smile. It was unexpectedly tender, and I wondered briefly if Patterson had a daughter of his own. "I appreciate your concern. You're a good friend, Liv."

A GOOD FRIEND. THE WORDS haunted me on my drive to Everett's. Obviously, Patterson couldn't have known how scalding his words would feel; I was sure he'd just been trying to console me. Still, our conversation had left a bitter taste in my mouth.

Sam's stepmom had told me Everett was out the last time I'd been on the property, but I was banking on him being home this time. As I drove, I played back memories of the cake tasting and bridal fitting that afternoon. Why had all the women in the boutique seemed giddy, while the singular man had looked about to squirm out of his skin with discomfort? Was that a natural, gendered reaction to wedding planning? And had I imagined the eerie whitening of Christina's eyes in the mirror? It reminded me uncannily of the moment Eden and I had shared in the girls' bathroom on the first day of school—but that could easily have been my brain, rewriting moments in time to nest within existing memories.

At last, I pulled up into the Mendezes' horseshoe driveway. From there, the guesthouse was almost entirely obscured by foliage—though when I crunched toward it on foot, I realized "guesthouse" was a charitable term. The doorframe of the sagging shed was rotting, paint peeling away in green curls. I bit the insides of my lips, fighting a rising tide of anxiety.

I stood for a moment at the door, working up my nerve to knock. I could do this. In and out—no more than ten minutes. Ask the questions I needed to ask, gather the necessary information, and then get the hell out of there. I rubbed damp palms across my thighs and rapped on the door.

An excruciating minute passed. Finally, Everett answered in a pair of sweats with a frayed drawstring. I tried not to balk at the man in the doorway. His eyes, once dark and alive as flint, had sunken into his face.

"Here she is," he said, and his smile made my belly buckle.

"Here I am. Sorry to show up like this. I was in town and—"

"My stepmom told me." He paused. "Didn't mention how great you looked, though."

I tugged the hem of my dress, mentally berating myself for my choice of outfit. "Thanks." I could see, with crystal-line clarity, what I must look like to him: a polished city girl with her gel manicure and leather riding boots. It seemed almost cruel to show up like this after what Everett had been through.

Everett motioned me inside. I followed him into a dark living room. The coffee table in the center was littered with junk mail, game consoles, and a couple of ceramic plates of cookies and pastries, tinfoil peeled off the top.

"Snickerdoodle?" Everett indicated the sweets on the coffee table. "People keep coming by the house bringing us stuff."

"No, thanks."

"Beer?"

"I'm good."

Everett meandered into the adjoining kitchen and cracked the fridge. It was a kitchen that looked as though it hadn't been updated since the seventies, with overwhelming dark wood cabinets and pea-colored appliances. A pile of water-filled bowls and cups sat in the sink attracting flies.

My stomach sank. Maybe this was just how single guys lived? I wanted to believe the lie, even though I knew my own fiancé wouldn't be caught dead in a hovel like this.

Everett shrugged and settled into a cushion of the couch, one arm thrown over the back. Hesitantly, I joined him, shoving my body into the opposite armrest and crossing my legs twice over at the knee and ankle.

"So." Everett's eyes danced over my face. For a moment, I was jolted back to high school as a self-conscious warmth flickered up my neck. Even all these years later, he still had that same rakish, crooked smile. "How can I help you?"

I cleared my throat. "First of all, I just wanted to say I'm really sorry to hear about Sam. And scared. I came out here to see if there was anything I could do to help find her."

Everett stared at the dead TV screen. "Probably not," he said after a beat and took a swig from his beer.

"What do you mean? Do you feel like the police are doing their job?"

He shrugged, still not looking at me. "They're trying, but there's not much to work with. Who's to say Sam didn't just up and leave Guilford on her own?"

That pit in my stomach again. "I don't know if your stepmom told you about the note Sam sent me."

Everett's eyes swung to me, and they were as blank as the darkened TV screen. "She did."

I frowned. Everett's stepmom had told me Everett was beside himself after Sam's disappearance, but I wasn't see-

ing much distress. Maybe Everett didn't feel comfortable
appearing vulnerable in front of me? Or was he simply
numb by this point?

"Do you have any theories?" I prodded him. "Was there
anyone you can imagine that could have been making Sam
feel . . . uncomfortable?" I didn't want to reveal the lipstick
knife finding just yet—let Everett share his hypotheses un-
clouded by additional evidence.

Everett sighed. "Not that I know of. Sam wasn't dating
anyone, wasn't having any beef with her friends. But then
again, I haven't seen her since Christmas."

I made some hasty calculations. Ten months? Wow—
that was worse than Sam's stepmom had led me to believe.
Hadn't Maddie said that Sam and Everett had been really
close ever since her accident? "Was she that busy? Or did
you guys get into a fight or something?"

"No fight. And who the hell knows? I know she was
working hard on her jewelry because I'd see things online, but
every time I tried texting her, she'd ignore me. Finally I just
gave up. Quite the way to repay your devoted twin, huh?"

I dug my nails into my thigh. "You guys have definitely
been through a lot . . ."

"Ha," Everett said humorlessly, setting his beer down
on the coffee table with a clank.

I wished Everett would crack a window or something—
the air in the living room was thick and smelled of mold. I
felt like leaping off the couch and diving back into the safety
of the car. But I forced myself to stay rooted to the cushion,
to make this visit count. "Sam lives with Eden and Cora
from Guilford High, right?"

"Wow, you've really been doing your research." Everett studied my face and I could see the question in his eyes: *You haven't spoken to Sam since you were a teenager. Why are you even here?*

My throat locked up. *I wrote to her every week for a year,* I wanted to tell him. *Then monthly, after that, just to see if she'd changed her mind. I apologized so many times, the words* I'm sorry *didn't even make sense to me anymore.*

But I wasn't willing to speak those words aloud. Instead, I asked Everett about the dynamic between Sam and her roommates.

He considered. "I dunno. It's kind of weird having your sister move in with your ex, I guess. I know she was kind of judgmental of them in high school, but I honestly think she was just uncomfortable with me dating Eden."

"Why?"

Everett's heavy eyebrows lifted. "Jealousy?"

I laughed. "Sam wasn't into girls."

"I don't mean romantically. I think Sam secretly admired Eden and her friends and hated that I had an in, brief as it was." He crossed his arms and sat back against the couch cushion.

"Interesting theory. It must not have seemed weird to Sam to move in with the girls, though, because she did it."

"Yeah, and really fast, too. Cora met Sam in an art class or something. There was an opening at their house and they were adamant about filling it immediately. Sam had to scramble to get packed up in, like, two days."

"Huh." I worried my lip. "Why the rush?"

"No clue. I think there was another girl living there who

moved out suddenly. Maybe they didn't want to get stuck with her portion of the rent."

"It wasn't Avery?"

"No. Some random girl I'd never heard of."

"You don't remember her name?"

Everett looked at me, his face gutted with exhaustion. I knew, then, that I'd pushed him too far. "I have no idea, Liv."

I squirmed. Why did it feel like I was adding to Everett's suffering just by sitting there on his sagging plaid couch? My voice was nearly a whisper when I spoke next. "Is there anything I can do?"

Everett's eyes trailed to my thighs, peeking out from beneath the hemline of my dress. "Depends. How long are you in town?"

My body blazed in mortification. How did this guy have the guts to hit on me like that, after everything he'd been through—and wearing a pair of ratty sweatpants? It was as foreign as Everett's boy-body had been to me back in high school: that masculine assumption that things would work out in his favor.

"Um . . ." I rubbed at my cheek.

It took a moment for the two carats to register with Everett. When they did, a sneer claimed his face. "That's quite a rock."

"Thanks." Too late, I decided it hadn't been a compliment. Everett was back to staring at the dark TV screen, his Adam's apple bobbing through another swig of beer.

I looked down at the floor. A minute later, I told him I should probably go.

• • •

BACK AT MOM'S A HALF hour later, I was still turning over Everett's words in my mind. Why the urgency to have Sam move into that house? Couldn't she still have made her jewelry living elsewhere? Who had she replaced? And whatever happened to Avery? Eden had dismissed Avery's name quickly when I brought it up. *We fell out of touch.* Had something happened to drive a wedge between them?

There were a lot of unanswered questions—and who knew how Sam was connected to it all. Cross-legged on my bed, I opened my laptop and searched for Avery on social media. Her location was set to Seattle, so clearly we wouldn't be grabbing coffees together anytime soon. Still, a message couldn't hurt.

> Hi Avery! I'm not sure if you remember me from GHS. I'm sure you've heard about Sam's disappearance. Is there any chance you'd be willing to talk with me?

After sending, I checked Avery's profile. A gray cat obscured a cheekbone in her photo. Her profile was set to private, so I couldn't access anything more. Still, I recognized the sharpness of her features. Without the cat, I knew she'd have that signature flush sitting high in her cheeks—back in high school, Avery had always looked as though she'd come straight from a light workout.

For the hell of it, I clicked over to Eden's, and then Cora's profiles. Infuriatingly, they were set to private, as well. I rolled back angrily in my desk chair. But then again, shouldn't I have expected this? The first time I happened upon The Sisterhood, they'd secluded themselves in a gazebo on the fringes of campus. There was always a shroud of mystery around these girls, an impulse to shut out the world, which made it kind of a big deal that they'd included me in their elaborate dinner and invited me to spend the night. Not only that— they'd trusted me enough to help with one of their bridal clients, having never seen my jewelry-making skills in action.

I guess I had to give Sam credit: eight years later, I was starting to understand their pull.

There was a gentle knock.

"Yes?"

Mom cracked the door to my bedroom. "I made a pot of green tea downstairs. Want a cup?"

"That'd be great. I'll be right down." I clapped my laptop shut and swung my legs over the side of the bed.

Mom stood in the hallway. I could only see a sliver of her face through the door. "Were you at a friend's last night?"

I hesitated. No way could I tell Mom I stayed the night at Beloved—I was aware how strange that would sound. Besides, were Eden and Cora even friends of mine?

"Yeah," I said at last. "I'm really sorry about hogging your car."

Mom waved a hand dismissively. "I was working on my pottery all last night and today. It's no problem." She nudged my door open a bit wider. Then she pointed at my bed. "Your phone is lighting up."

I looked down.

Sure enough, the screen was bursting with Google alerts.

14

THEN

*E*VERETT'S EX WAS EDEN HOLLOWAY.

It took a second for the truth to register. When it did, my throat began to burn as twin rivulets of tears streaked down my face. I'd just thrown an egg at Eden's front door. And that poor old woman who'd looked on? She must have been a relative.

So much for choosing a random person.

"Liv," Everett said, reaching for my shoulder.

I squirmed out of his grasp and broke into a run. I was humiliated—to have been manipulated so easily by Sam, to be crying. Humiliated to have done something so vulgar to someone so spellbinding. Sam had undoubtedly wanted me to throw my egg at the home of one of GHS's most high-profile students because she knew how much it would mortify me.

Branches tore at my face as I plunged into the wooded

area behind Sam's street. When I could no longer see the road through the trees, I stopped, bracing myself against a massive trunk. Then I let myself cry. The wind stung on my wet cheeks. Good; I deserved the punishment. I wondered if Eden's relative had seen enough of my face to describe it to Eden. The thought filled me with a sickly feeling.

"Liv! Hold up."

Everett had run into the woods after me. His feet crashed through the fallen leaves as he made his way over. He was breathing hard, his cheeks mottled with exertion. Hurriedly, I turned to hide my swollen face.

"Are you . . . crying?"

"No." I said it through a sniffle.

A leaden silence pressed in around us. I knew I'd made Everett feel awkward with my tears, and it only added another layer of mortification. Why did I have to be like this?

"Um," Everett said presently. I swiped my knuckles across my cheeks and dared to turn toward him. He held a crumpled tissue in one hand, a bashful expression on his face. "I think it may be used, but it's all I've got."

I laughed, in spite of myself. "Gross. No thank you."

He shoved it back into the depths of his pocket. A wind stirred up, rattling the skeletal canopies overhead. I'd run us deep enough into the woods that we could barely make out the tinge of porch lights through the groping branches. The scent of woodsmoke was stronger here. I could feel it seeping into my hair and the fabric of my jacket, along with the dampness of the forest.

"Who was . . . that woman?" I ventured. "At Eden's house."

Everett kicked a foot through the leaves. "Her grandma. She's been the one raising Eden."

Even here, tearstained and humiliated in the middle of the woods, I was ravenous for details about Eden's personal life. I had to know more. "What happened to her mother?"

Everett rolled his shoulders. "It's actually an awful story. She got knocked up super young—practically right out of high school—and was really messed up. Apparently, she almost let Eden drown in the bath because she was so out of it. Eden's grandmother was the one who fished her out at the last minute."

Coldness clawed its way over my spine. "Jesus."

"I know." *Swish, swish* went Everett's foot in the leaves. "Listen, I don't mean to be rude. But can you not, like, spread this info around? It's not common knowledge. The only reason I know is because . . ."

I let his statement hang in the air, taunting us both with its unspoken half.

Because you dated her.

An unwelcome image leaped into my mind: the two of them flushed after sex, limbs intertwined, voices husky as they shared secrets about their lives. Even if their relationship hadn't lasted, Everett clearly still felt protective of her. I remembered fantasizing about pressing close to Everett in his kitchen earlier that night and promptly felt mortified again.

"Sure," I said, too quickly. "Of course I won't." A vein of sadness ran through me. I'd been hoping Everett had chased me into the woods to soothe me after my humiliating egging experience. But now it seemed like he was more intent on shielding Eden. It shouldn't have been a surprise. Of course she took precedence over me.

"Hey." Everett must have picked up on my self-pity, because suddenly he was shuffling toward me through the undergrowth.

"It's nothing," I said, hanging my head as a sob snagged in my throat. This is usually what happened whenever I heard pity in people's voices and was already on the precipice of tears: it pushed me right over the edge.

He paused, and I felt his closeness. I hadn't noticed the heft of Everett's shoulders until now. His chest rose and fell in his hoodie. I fought the urge to press my palm against it, to feel the thudding of his heart.

"It wasn't cool how my sister tricked you," he said quietly. "Obviously, you're still upset about it. For good reason."

Everett's proximity was causing a sparking sensation along my skin. I swallowed, my throat painful and constricted with tears. "What was with her flinging that candy bar at you? 'Don't make me kill you'?"

"Well, I have a pretty bad peanut allergy."

"That's messed up."

"Eh, you know how Sam is. She says these things, but she doesn't really mean them."

The thought ghosted through me: *She doesn't?*

The two of us stood rooted in the fallen leaves, muscles locked. Half of me yearned to turn away from Everett and run headlong into the forest. But the other half of me had a sudden, daring idea. I swung my eyes up to meet his. "Sometimes," I said, very low, "I worry."

It worked; he moved a few centimeters closer to me. "About what?"

Oh God, he was there, *right there*, those vivid lips in line with my forehead. I didn't dare breathe.

"I don't know," I whispered. "That I'm, like, Sam's little pet or something."

Everett looked down at me, and the way his eyelids settled made him look languid. "Please," he said. "You are anything but." Then, to my utter disbelief, he tilted my chin up to him and kissed me.

The contrast between our cold faces and our warm mouths made my head loop. For a few enchanting moments, I lost myself to Everett's lips as his wide boy-hands cupped my face. He touched me like I was so precious. It made me ravenous for more.

A sudden scream pierced the night. Everett and I broke apart, my heart galloping.

"What the hell was that?" Everett's head whipped in the direction of the sound.

Another scream, more like a whimper this time. Everett and I looked at each other. Then we both broke into a run, headed in the direction of the cry.

Running through the woods at night was more perilous than I'd anticipated. Sneaky roots thrust up through the ground, camouflaged by fallen leaves. Several times my toe caught and I managed to correct myself before falling. A sliver of moon peeked out from behind the tree trunks, doing nothing to illuminate our way. The farther we ran, the stronger the smell of woodsmoke grew.

Everett and I stopped short, chests heaving. We'd

reached a clearing. In it was a smoking firepit encircled by rocks, and around that, three female figures dressed in black. I sucked in a breath. I smelled meat. Were they cooking something? The girls wore animal masks: cats or panthers, something feline. But more disturbing still was that the tallest of the girls had rolled her shirt up to expose her abdomen. And another girl with an all-too-familiar slash of hair down her back knelt by one bared hip bone, holding something that looked like a grotesquely large sewing needle about the length of my forearm.

I knew, had it been light enough to see, that hair would've been cornsilk-white.

"Just do it, Eden." Avery—it had to be Avery—spoke through gritted teeth.

Everett and I locked eyes.

"Holy shit," I whispered. "What do we—?"

Eden jumped to her feet and swirled in our direction, her severe hair flipping back. I flattened my back against a tree. How the hell had she heard us? I'd barely breathed the words aloud.

"If anyone's there," Eden called into the night, "I'd advise you leave. Right now."

Everett and I looked at each other again with wild eyes. Then we fled.

15

NOW

I F MY PACKED PHONE SCREEN WAS ANY INDICATION, THERE had been movement in Sam's investigation. I clicked open one of the news articles hungrily.

> Further investigation uncovered partially completed paperwork on Mendez's computer which indicated that Mendez had begun the process of filing a restraining order against boyfriend Brendan Field. Field has since been taken in for questioning.

I stared at my phone in disbelief. Who the hell was Brendan Field? I'd asked everyone I knew if Sam had a boyfriend. Her brother, stepmom, and roommates had all denied it. Had Sam been dating someone in secret? Or was this just some random guy obsessed with Sam and delusional enough to consider her his girlfriend?

I asked to borrow Mom's car again, explaining to her what had happened and that the tea would have to wait. After shooting off a quick text to Maddie, I headed over to the boutique. I needed to talk to Sam's roommates immediately.

The hive of anxiety was back in my chest. Sam had filed a restraining order. I'd been right; she felt threatened, just as she indicated to me in her letter. How long had Brendan been harassing her? Long enough for Sam to procure the lipstick dagger, evidently, to start court paperwork on her laptop . . .

I used the heel of my hand to pound on the front door of Beloved; a polite knock wouldn't suffice today. Thankfully, Eden and Cora rushed to let me in.

"Oh my God, we heard the news," Cora said, pulling her hair away from her face anxiously.

I was already pushing past them into the bridal salon, too distraught for pleasantries. "Have you guys ever heard of Brendan Field before? Who the hell is he?"

"We have no clue." Eden shut the door and followed me into the salon. It felt like a lifetime ago that I'd sat in one of those snowy-white chairs, watching Eden tap at her iPad with her dark nails. "It must have been some random guy that set his sights on Sam . . ."

"Maybe she met him through her brother," Cora mused.

I shook my head. "I talked to Everett. He said Sam didn't have a boyfriend. No one knew about him."

We stared at one another for a couple of dread-soaked moments. Had Sam fled to Europe to get away from Brendan, then? Or was she being held somewhere in this guy's basement . . . or worse? I could tell from Eden and Cora's expressions that their minds were flickering through the same terrible possibilities. But none of us were willing to speak them into existence.

"Well," Eden said at last, through a slight cough, "we should feel good about the fact that he's been taken in for questioning."

Feeling sickened, I excused myself to the powder room down the hall filled with the aggressive fragrance of potpourri. I ran cold water over my hands and dotted the coolness on my flushed cheeks and neck, under the scratchy tag of my T-shirt. My lips looked swollen and bitten red in the mirror. I barely recognized myself.

After exiting the bathroom, I stood for a moment in the hallway, looking out at the slope of lawn and the fringe of the woods just beyond it, the girls' detached studio. From my vantage point, I could see Eden's rolls of fabric looming, the edge of Sam's teal supply box. Before I realized what I was doing, my feet were carrying me, again. Down the corridor, past the living room, and out the back door.

When I twisted the scowling face in the studio doorknob, it gave way without protest. I floated toward Sam's workspace. The calla lilies were beginning to wilt in their vase, as if nodding off to sleep. Next to it was what appeared to be an intricate, half-finished brooch with a thick, spearlike pin. For some reason, I hadn't noticed it the first time I investigated Sam's station. I hesitated reaching toward the drawers of the trunk. I'd felt so guilty sifting through her stuff last time . . . but surely a minute or two wouldn't hurt anyone? Convinced, I snatched open the drawers and ran my fingers through the fine supplies. They put my high school collection, largely cobbled together from Jo-Ann Fabrics, to shame.

In a drawer toward the bottom of the trunk, I found a couple of pearl drops and rolled them around in my palm. Merely touching Sam's materials made me feel a shocking through line to her, remembering the hours after school that had dissolved around us as we'd worked in tandem. Snatches of that damn Google alert pierced the memory, making my heart clench with terror. *Mendez had begun the process of filing a restraining order against boyfriend Brendan Field . . .*

I bit back a gasp. A dark, oblong beetle with that strange blue-and-white marking had clambered out of an open drawer in Sam's trunk and onto the workbench. I swiped at it, sending it skittering onto the studio floor.

"Busted."

Eden stood in the entrance to the studio, smirking.

Hurriedly, I backed away from Sam's workspace. "Sorry. I thought I saw a bug in there—"

"No need to apologize." Eden took a few steps toward me. "Sam was in the middle of designing that brooch for a bride when she disappeared. Gorgeous, isn't it?"

I nodded, my eyes drifting out of focus as I stared at the brooch, the little iridescent pebbles beside it, waiting to be incorporated.

"The wedding is coming up fast. With any luck, she'll be back to finish it with time to spare."

I clenched my fists by my sides. "God, I hope so. How long do you think it takes to get a search warrant?"

"I would imagine they could move pretty quickly once they have reasonable suspicion. Just think about it—that creep is probably sweating bullets under interrogation as we speak."

I allowed myself a small exhale. The scene Eden had painted was a satisfying one.

"Come on." She cocked her head at me. "Let's take a walk."

IT WAS A STARTLINGLY MILD day, fragile October sunlight pressing through the shoulders of our jackets. Cora had filled us both carafes of mulled cider from a steaming pot on the stove, accented with orange rinds, cinnamon sticks, and cloves. I took a pull of it; the spike of alcohol softened the edges of my anxiety. *This is a good thing,* I kept reminding myself, as I followed Eden across the lawn to the beckoning fringe of woodland. *We're getting closer to finding Sam. It's only a matter of time.*

It was quiet here, the only sounds Eden's and my footfalls and the whisk of cartwheeling leaves settling in the dried grass. We passed a massive lichen-spotted oak, its knots resembling a somber downturned face. The smell of earthy decay and woodsmoke brought back flashes from our midnight run in the woods with sparklers. Reflexively, my heart revved.

"I want to know more about how Sam ended up living with you," I told Eden. "And working at Beloved. I know it's been a while since we talked, but I'm just struggling to imagine her fitting in here."

"Hmm." Eden took a thoughtful sip from her carafe. "Valid question. To be honest, Cora and I had our doubts in the beginning, too. But Sam has changed a lot since high school. We all have."

That fiery twist of guilt again in my side. Of course Sam had changed; she just hadn't wanted me around to see it.

Eden held up a finger. "Actually, it's more than that. I think Beloved's origin story resonated with Sam on a deeply personal level. That was the draw for her."

I studied Eden's profile. Sunlight glanced off her bright hair. "Origin story?"

She tilted her head to look directly at me. "Yeah. Want to hear it?"

"Sure."

"Alright, buckle up, chickadee. Here we go." Eden cleared her throat. When she spoke again, her normal gravelly tone had smoothed to honey. "Once upon a time, there was this beautiful girl with long golden hair. She was a cheerleader at Guilford High and two years after graduating, she married her high school sweetheart. The girl was so young, she couldn't even do the champagne toast at her own wedding. But it didn't matter—their marriage was a fairy tale."

I glanced sharply at Eden, suspicious. At first, I assumed she was talking about herself—but Eden had certainly never been a cheerleader. Was she telling me the story of her parents?

She went on. "Her husband used to come home from his construction job with bouquets of sunflowers: her favorite. While he worked, she took nursing classes at UConn. They were so happy."

Okay, definitely Eden's parents. I braced myself, knowing already this story didn't have a happy ending.

"But then," Eden said, "about a year into their marriage, the husband wanted children. The girl was barely twenty-one at the time, still in her nursing program. Her husband vowed that nothing would have to change, that she could go back to school right after the baby was born. He made an ironclad promise to her: they were in this together. Everything would be okay. So the girl, who had only just ordered her first glass of wine in a restaurant, swore off alcohol to get pregnant."

"It was a horrific pregnancy," Eden continued. "The girl was violently ill the entire time, but the doctors told her anti-nausea medication would endanger the fetus, so they refused to help her. She was bedridden for her entire last trimester. Obviously, she had to drop out of school. And even though her husband had sworn up and down that they were in this together, they weren't. He couldn't possibly understand how she was suffering." Her voice dipped to a choked whisper. "She was so alone."

My skin went cold, remembering Penny's words. *Sometimes I feel so overwhelmed, so alone . . .*

"Things only got worse when the baby arrived," Eden said. "It was a traumatic delivery—the girl almost bled to death. She survived, but developed severe postpartum depression. She had no interest in her own child. Worse, her husband didn't seem to understand the severity of her condition, so he left her all day with the baby while he went to work. After all, they couldn't afford childcare. Most days, the girl never even managed to make it out of bed. She could barely keep up with the feedings every two hours. She was in over her head."

I was gripped by that same frantic buzzing I'd felt when my sister had told me about her own experience as a new mother.

"Eventually," Eden said, "she snapped. She couldn't do it anymore. When her husband was at work, she emptied out a fistful of Ambien and climbed into the bath with her baby. With me. And that's where my grandma found us. She had enough time to scoop me out, but my mother's body had already gone bone-white."

My mouth fell open. This tale was even more horrific than the version Everett had shared with me on Mischief Night.

"God, Eden," I said.

Eden shrugged. "Don't feel bad for me—I'm the one who survived. My mom was the victim here. She should've never, ever been pressured to do something she wasn't ready for. Or that she didn't even want in the first place. She lost everything."

I let her words settle.

"What about your dad?"

Eden's shoulders lifted. "Turns out he didn't really want a kid after all. At least not when the responsibility fell on him. He left me with his mother one night, who'd come in to visit from the Midwest. And he never came back."

"Jesus." Both of Eden's parents, gone forever? This story just kept getting worse and worse.

"Yeah," Eden said, and her voice caught.

I felt a flash of protectiveness. "You don't actually blame yourself for what happened, do you? Because you were only a baby. You didn't ask to be born. We're talking about a lot of factors at play here. Mental illness. And, no offense, but your dad sounds like he was . . ."

"A deadbeat. I know."

Eden's story made me profoundly sad. Even though she claimed otherwise, I could see through her words: all these years, Eden had shouldered the blame for her mother's suicide. Something snagged in my chest like a caught zipper.

"The worst part is, it took me a while to realize that I was on the same path as my mother. Replicating her mistakes," said Eden.

I stared at her, aghast.

Eden uttered a little laugh. "Don't look at me like that, Liv. You remember who I made the mistake of dating back in high school."

My stomach churned. "But you and Everett . . ."

"I know. We were only together, like, a grand total of three weeks. But it was enough. He was one of those guys who tore through girls as if they were disposable. Expecting them to make concession after concession for him before leaving them in the dust. After what my mother had gone through, I couldn't—I just *couldn't* . . . "

I swallowed, painfully. "I get it," I said, partially to rescue her from having to say anything more.

"It's not like there's any malice on my end," Eden clarified. "Mostly, I look back and just feel sorry for the guy."

I thought back to the version of Everett I'd seen in the peeling guesthouse. I, too, felt sorry for him.

"Anyway." Now Eden's voice was threaded with cheer. "That's why I launched Beloved. Yes, we make stunning dresses and mouthwatering wedding cakes, but this boutique is so much more than that."

"How so?"

"Well, as you've probably noticed, we take our job extremely seriously. We want to leave a lasting impression on our brides, to ensure they are as happy and confident as possible walking into this next chapter of their lives." Here, Eden's voice dropped to a whisper. "At the end of the day, I guess I just want to give these ladies the happily ever after my mother never had."

"Damn." I shook out my shoulders as Eden laughed gently. "That gave me chills."

"I think it affected Sam similarly. That's why she worked so hard to get moved in here quickly and join our cause. Girls like us . . . we just *get* it."

I drained my cider and peered off into the trees. What a strange statement. *Girls like us.*

Did that include me?

"Oh!" Eden cried, clapping a hand to her mouth. "Excuse me."

I looked over at her, grinning. "Oh my God. Was that your one hiccup of the day?"

"Guilty as charged." The funny thing was, she did look guilty, a lacy flush climbing her throat under the neckline of her jacket.

Standing there under the fiery canopy of trees, I felt a stab of affection for the chilly, harsh-featured girl who'd so intimidated me back in high school. Turns out, Eden was a fallible human just like the rest of us. To see these parts of her—the pain under her ferocious commitment to her business, how she blushed her way through her curse of hiccups—it all made her absurdly likable. Why had it taken me so long to see this side of her?

As if reading my mind, Eden laid a hand on my arm.

"Come on," she said quietly. "Let's go home."

16

NOW

NOAH WAS ONE OF THE FIRST PASSENGERS OFF THE TRAIN Saturday morning. He must have picked me out from the crowd through the window, because he made a beeline for me on the platform, where he kissed and dipped me theatrically.

"Whoa," I said through my laughter, once I'd surfaced. "That was quite the welcome."

"Well, I've missed you. It feels like you've been gone forever."

It'd been less than a week, but I couldn't fault Noah—throughout our eight years together, this was probably the longest we'd ever been apart, barring college breaks. Besides, I was lucky to be with a guy who wasn't shy about showing affection.

On the car ride over to Beloved, I briefed him on what to expect. "Just so you know, Eden can be kind of intense."

Noah shrugged and squeezed my thigh closest to the console. "I'm sure it's nothing I can't handle." He'd dressed up for the occasion—tailored dark jeans and a crisp button-down—which made my heart pinch with endearment. Noah would never be one of those guys who rolled his eyes at the wedding planning process. If anything, I wished he'd take it a little less seriously.

Ten minutes later, the same black-clad shopgirl I met my first time at Beloved came to the door and led us into the bridal salon. For a second time, I sat in that white chair, which was just deep enough to keep my toes from reaching the ground. Even the scent of the studio—a combination of crushed rose petals and lavender—made me feel unsteady.

Cora entered with a silver tray of filigree-like cookies. They looked like miniature lavender doilies; the moment I picked one up, I fumbled it, snapping it in half.

"Bad luck for seven years," Noah joked, bending to pick up the piece I'd dropped.

Cora was smiling, but her voice was severe. "Don't say that."

"Cora's right. Let's not curse the marriage before it's even started." Eden breezed into the studio behind Cora. She wore a couture-looking black dress with a dramatic flared lip just above the knee and a nipped-in waist, her hair an icy sash down her back. Eden was striking—there was no doubt about that—but rather than Cora's soft, doe-like prettiness, she was all severe edges. I caught Noah blinking away his surprise.

"You must be Noah," Eden said. For some reason, her eyes were on me as they shook hands. "So," she said, settling into her own chair directly across from us. "Let's get down to business." It must have been her tagline—it was verbatim what she said when I first sat across from her with Mom and Penny. The memory made my body tense; that visit hadn't exactly gone well for me.

Eden was bringing my fiancé up to speed. "As Liv has probably explained to you, we have a special approach to serving our clients here at Beloved. I design and craft all dresses by hand, and to do so, I like to be inspired by each couple's unique story. That's why I've invited you both here today—to answer some questions intended to bring your relationship to life."

Noah settled into his chair with a smile. "Sounds good. I'm pretty much an open book."

"That's what I like to hear." A smile hooked through Eden's closed lips. "We'll start easy. Why don't you two tell me about how you met."

Noah and I looked at each other. "Go ahead," I told him, eager to shirk Eden's attention for as long as possible.

But Noah was comfortable being the center of attention. I watched the margins of his body expand to fill his chair. "Liv and I met freshman year of college. She was in the common room of our dorm and I remember thinking she was really cute, wearing these ripped-up jean shorts and her polka-dot shower sandals. I challenged her to a game of Ping-Pong and she kicked my ass."

I grinned at the memory. "I can't believe you remember what I was wearing!"

"That is adorable," Eden said, tapping at her iPad again, but her face was blank; she didn't look especially charmed. I guess I couldn't blame her. She'd probably heard hundreds of such stories over the years.

"Tell me, Noah. What's your favorite thing about Liv?"

He made a show of studying me and I laughed self-consciously. "That's an easy one. I love how nurturing Liv is. I've always known I wanted to marry someone like that."

I smiled, taking in the compliment, but my insides were drowning in heat. Nurturing? Of all the adjectives I could have used to describe myself, *nurturing* wasn't one of them, and it was likely one of the reasons I felt a frisson of fear whenever Noah brought up children. Where could this compliment be coming from? Maybe Noah appreciated my fumbling attempts to soothe him after his brother's death? But even that was a stretch—if anyone was a nurturer, Noah was the one for whom care and tenderness came naturally.

"What about you, Liv?" Eden was watching me intently; for a wild, scrabbling second, I was positive she'd read my inner turmoil on my face. "What's your favorite thing about Noah?"

My mind went blank. Eden and Noah stared at me with expectant smiles. What was wrong with me? Here was my beautiful husband-to-be, thick wavy hair lifted off his forehead, luminous gray eyes drinking me in like they always did. But I couldn't point to his physical attractiveness after he just called me *nurturing*. How shallow would that be?

"His kindness," I said finally, because it was true. But the word sounded bland and I cringed internally, wishing I could have scraped together something more eloquent.

Noah reached over and squeezed my thigh again. Thankfully, he didn't seem to be bothered by my response.

"That is so sweet," Eden said, tapping at her iPad. It needled me how she said it with the same intonation she'd used before, that had seemed so insincere.

That is adorable.

I shoved the rest of the lavender filigree cookie in my mouth.

"How about the proposal?" Eden asked. "Noah, were you the one who popped the question?"

"Of course," Noah said. He gave me a sly smile. "I'm not sure Liv was expecting it, to be honest."

"That's an understatement!" I said it through a laugh.

"Really?" Eden cocked her head at me. "But the two of you have been together . . . what, seven, eight years? Hadn't you talked about marriage?"

I withered under Eden's patient smile. "No—of course," I stammered, looking down at my lap. "I knew Noah and I were headed in that direction. I guess we hadn't discussed the specifics, though. And there are a lot of changes going on right now, so I figured maybe—"

"Changes?"

Dammit, why had I said that? I wished I could snatch my words back. "I just got laid off," I explained. "And I'm trying to figure out what comes next."

"Liv is applying to law school," Noah piped up helpfully.

"I mean, that was the plan," I said to Eden. "But now I'm having second thoughts about my career in general and . . . I'm feeling kind of lost these days." The last part slipped out, against my better judgment. I had to bite back the rest of my swirling doubts: *I don't think I'm ever going to be fulfilled as a lawyer. I want something more. I need something more.*

Noah was squinting at me. "I had no idea you were having second thoughts about law school."

A hot, guilty plunge in my stomach. Why hadn't I told him?

"Well, that's part of the reason we're having this conversation!" Eden exclaimed. "Sometimes little nuggets like this come out, and it can be so helpful for couples. I mean, when's the last time someone asked you critical questions about your relationship like this?"

I glanced over at Noah with an apologetic smile. *Sorry,* I mouthed to him.

He took my hand, curled up in my lap, and squeezed it once. *Love you.*

"Let's talk about the future," Eden said gently. "Liv, what are you most looking forward to in your first year of marriage?"

I squeezed Noah's hand back twice. *Love you, too.* "Just making things official, I guess. And continuing to support each other as we both grow as people."

"Great answer. How about you, Noah?"

He didn't even hesitate. "Oh, that's easy. Becoming a dad."

I dropped Noah's hand. "She said the first *year,* Noah."

"I know." A wry smile twisted his lips. To my shock, it was Eden he addressed next. "Liv and I were planning to have kids in a few years, but honestly the more I think about it, I wonder, why not now?"

I blinked at my fiancé in shock. "Because I need to figure out my career."

He shrugged. "There's time for that down the road. Besides, who knows? When we have kids, it might make the most sense for you to stay home anyway. When Ben died—"

"Who's Ben?" Eden cut in.

"Sorry, my younger brother. He died from an aneurysm shortly after our engagement."

"I'm so sorry."

"Thank you. But it really put things in perspective for me. Ben never got around to starting a family and I realized I'd be devastated if I lost the chance myself. To me, that's the most important part of getting married. That's the whole point."

I looked down at my lap, fuming. Why was Noah bringing this up now?

"How many kids do you guys want?" Eden asked.

"One," I said, at the same time that Noah said, "Four." We looked wildly at each other.

"Uh-oh," Eden said, through a laugh.

"Four?" I tried to keep my face neutral, even though my heart was racing. "Whatever happened to 'one, maybe two'?" Never mind that since seeing Penny and the hell her life had become, I'd firmly downgraded to one.

Maybe zero.

Noah gave me a goofy, guilty look. "I guess I've been going through some changes, too."

"Hey," Eden interjected, putting aside her iPad. She readjusted the fan of her black dress over her legs. "Listen. I want you both to know these are things that can be worked out with some healthy dialogue. Trust me on this one—I've seen it a million times before."

I was too ashamed to look her in the eye. There was a special, searing kind of mortification in revealing the cracks in your relationship to a third party. Especially when said third party was Eden Holloway.

Noah chuckled. "I have no doubt about it."

"Let's take a breather, okay? In the meantime, Liv, I don't think I ever asked to see your ring!"

My hand was shaking as I lifted it in her direction. I remembered how round Eden's eyes had gotten taking in my wicked-looking bird's nest ring during my first appointment. But she was right—she'd never actually asked to see my diamond one.

"Oh, this is exquisite," Eden said, taking my left hand in her own. Her fingertips were cool as they slid up to touch the solitaire diamond. For a heart-stopping moment, my vision glitched; instead of a diamond, I could have sworn I saw a white thumbtack buried in the flesh of my ring finger, a ribbon of blood snaking down my wrist.

It was so vivid—so convincing—that I ripped my hand away from Eden with a gasp.

But then, just as suddenly as it had happened, my hand was back to normal. No blood, no thumbtack: just one beautiful diamond glinting maliciously on my finger.

MERCIFULLY, EDEN CUT OUR APPOINTMENT a few minutes short, explaining she and Cora had to head to the Green to start setting up for Sam's candlelight vigil. Noah and I went to browse at a nearby bookstore to kill time. My fiancé was uncharacteristically quiet, and I watched the set of his jaw as he thumbed through a featured hardcover, trying to gauge if he was upset with me. I considered apologizing for dropping the bomb about law school on him, but the thought of scraping together the words exhausted me. Besides, that didn't solve for the bigger problem Eden had identified: the fact that Noah and I seemed to have very different expectations for our marriage.

At last, it was time to leave for the vigil. There was a bite in the air. Twenty to thirty people had already gathered on the Green. Cora, Eden, and Sam's parents were at its center, handing out white taper candles. When it came to be our turn, Eden was the one who lit my wick, cupping her hands around the spark until it took hold.

"Thanks," I said. My hands were shaking, and the tiny disc of cardboard affixed to the bottom of the candle to catch the dripping wax revealed my nerves.

Eden gave me a benevolent smile.

Noah and I joined the crowd. Finally, he closed the distance between us, snaking an arm around my waist. It was the first gesture of warmth since our interview at the boutique, and something unnotched inside me with relief. Soon, we were part of a sea of bobbing white flames under the dark canopies of the Green.

"I'm so glad you're here," I whispered, pressing the side of my face into Noah's shoulder.

"Liv?" The hiss of my name made me jump. Maddie was beside me, her sharp face severe in the low light.

"Maddie, hi!"

But for some reason, she wouldn't match my smile. "Can I talk to you for a minute?"

With a low murmur, I excused myself from Noah, and followed Maddie to a spot on the outskirts of the Green. Above us, the moon pressed up against knotted scarves of clouds.

"I got your text," Maddie said, glancing behind us.

"Oh, yeah. About Brendan."

"Yeah. I was going to respond, but I figured I'd see you in person at the vigil. Here's the thing: I didn't know about him. I don't know him."

"Okay . . ."

"But I have a guess about who he is."

My stomach plunged. "Who?"

Maddie grimaced. "There's this guy that comes into the Marketplace all the time and orders the same latte. He's always wearing a Page Hardware uniform and I'm ninety percent sure his name tag said 'Brendan.' Maybe it's the same guy?"

I frowned. "It's possible. You mentioned Sam was going there all the time to get coffee. They could have met."

"Yeah. That's what I was thinking." Maddie's eyes shone in the dark.

I looked out over the Green, to the darkened windows of Page Hardware. Could our number-one suspect really be so close by? "He hasn't been arrested yet, has he?"

Maddie shook her head. "No. Just interviewed. I've been staying on top of the news."

"Me, too." My hands curled into fists by my sides. "I'll go over there first thing tomorrow."

Maddie opened her mouth as if she were about to say something, but stopped when Noah entered the frame. His brow was furrowed with concern. "Sorry to interrupt. It looks like they're about to start. Everything okay?"

"Yep," I said, slipping my arm through his. I shot Maddie an apologetic look.

"Text me," she whispered, before walking off.

As the vigil began, I nestled against Noah's shoulder, trying to siphon calmness from him. But when Sam's stepmom read Sam's favorite childhood poem—by Shel Silverstein, about searching for a pot of gold at the end of a rainbow—it set my panic aflame. This felt too much like a memorial. I wished I could fast-forward to the following morning, when the hardware store opened again. It was excruciating standing here, holding this candle, doing nothing.

I needed to talk to Brendan.

Later that night, curled up together in my childhood bed, Noah slipped his hands under my shirt. I pulled away, citing my mom on the other side of the wall. We drifted off soon thereafter, but my sleep was riddled with nightmares of thumbtack rings and bloodied wrists and my own quivering white candle overflowing onto my hands.

17

NOW

PAGE HARDWARE SMELLED JUST AS I REMEMBERED IT, OF cedar and oiled keys. Maddie had texted me around four P.M., telling me that Brendan had come in to buy his usual latte, and I'd rushed over to the Green, fabricating some excuse for Noah and my mom about picking up a prescription at the pharmacy. My mother had already voiced her opinion on my following leads about Sam and I was certain if I told Noah I planned to question the number-one suspect in Sam's case, he'd be even less pleased.

Now, I scanned the aisles of the hardware store, looking for an associate who matched the description Maddie gave me. My blood pressure began to climb. Somehow, I'd have to lull this guy into polite conversation before mentioning Sam, otherwise he was sure to disengage. And that was assuming he would even return to the hardware store after getting his coffee.

My heart jumped when I spotted a shaved head bent over the paint counter. It matched Maddie's description, though he was more diminutive than I'd imagined. Taking a deep breath, I approached the counter.

"Can I help you?" Up close, Brendan had disarmingly pretty almond-shaped eyes. I glanced at the name tag on his shirt.

Bingo.

"Yeah, I was hoping for some help finding the right paint color. I'm repainting the trim in my living room. It's like a warm off-white . . ."

Brendan came around the counter and led me to a display of color swatches. He indicated a section of milky hues.

"Like this," I said, stabbing my finger at random.

Brendan took the swatch behind the counter and punched something into the computer. An electronic whine, and a stream of butter-yellow paint shot into a bucket below. Brendan wore a leather wristband on his left hand. I'd been hoping he ran naturally chatty and would start innocuous conversation with me, but he was intently focused on the task at hand. Was he keeping his head down after being interviewed by the police? Or could he sense I'd come here under false pretenses?

The machine began to agitate the bucket of paint and my heart rate climbed another notch. *It's now or never.* "Hey," I said, leaning up against the counter. "You look familiar. Did you go to GHS?"

"Nope," Brendan said. He passed the paint swatch back to me.

"Oh. Then you probably don't know Sam Mendez. The girl that's gone missing?"

A muscle feathered in Brendan's jaw. But he said nothing.

"Have you heard about her? It's all over the news. So scary."

Brendan bent his head lower over the rattling bucket of paint. "Yep. I know her."

"Oh, really?" Perhaps I leaned a little too hard into the question.

Brendan swiped a hand over the top of the paint counter. "She's my girlfriend, actually."

"You're not serious. I'm so sorry."

Brendan made a show of studying the furiously rocking paint mixer. Frustration welled within me; obviously, I was going to have to be the one to press him further.

"When's the last time you saw her?"

"About a week ago. I was the one who reported her missing in the first place."

Liar. I forced the suspicion off my face. "Really? It's just—I've been keeping up with the news, and for a long time, no one knew Sam even had a boyfriend, right?"

"Yeah, well, I reported it anonymously."

God, Brendan. Could you sound any sketchier? It took a great show of restraint to keep a pleasant smile anchored in place. "Oh? Why's that?"

The machine clicked off suddenly, and the silence in the wake of all the furious juddering made our conversation feel vulnerable and exposed. Brendan cast a look around the store before stooping to procure the bucket of mixed paint. "Um, I probably shouldn't be getting into this right now."

Yes, you should, Brendan. That's why I came here. Mom used to tell me I had an "inviting" face, and I tried to use that to my advantage now, tilting my head to one side. "I'm actually really glad I ran into you. I'm an old friend of Sam's, and I'm so worried about her. If there's anything you could tell me . . ."

He seemed to consider my plea as he placed the silver top on my can of paint. Finally, he said, "Sam insisted on keeping our relationship a secret and would never tell me why. My personal theory is that there's someone in her life who is really controlling and didn't want her seeing anyone. Maybe a family member. Maybe her roommates. I don't know."

Sam's fearful letter drifted into my mind's eye. *I need help and don't know who else to turn to.* Who would have objected to her having a boyfriend? Sam's stepmom? Everett? Eden and Cora? Nothing was adding up. Was Brendan merely spinning stories in an attempt to divert attention from himself?

I had to say it. "Didn't she file a restraining order against *you*, though?"

That made his jaw clench more intensely than before. Brendan picked up a hammer from the counter and began to pound around the rim of the container. I drew back a bit, studying the tension in his neck and his practiced battering of the metal lid. It made a chill skitter down my back. What, I wondered, was Brendan like when he was angry? Had Sam gotten to see that side of him?

"I have no idea why she did that," Brendan said, setting down the hammer. Then he appealed to me with his doe-like eyes. "I would never hurt Sam. Honest to God."

Had those puppy-dog eyes worked on the cops? They must have, because here was Brendan, a free man out in the world. He hadn't been taken into custody—at least not yet. I ran a finger down the bridge of my nose, thinking hard. "Is that why you made the anonymous report, then? Because you were afraid of retaliation from this 'controlling' person?"

Brendan said nothing, just handed the can to me with a closed-mouth smile.

"Good luck with your trim," he said.

MY MIND WAS SWIRLING ON the drive back to Mom's house. How had the cops been able to prove that Brendan hadn't done anything to hurt Sam? Why the hell would she have taken out a restraining order against him if he hadn't posed a threat? The more I thought about it, the flimsier Brendan's excuses appeared. For God's sake, he didn't even have a particular individual to point the finger at—just a vague somebody who was *really controlling*.

By the time I pulled into the driveway, I was vibrating with anger. Maybe it was even worth paying another visit to the police station, just to check in to see Patterson's perspective on everything. They had to have plans to keep looking into Brendan, right? I couldn't be the only one to see the massive cracks in his logic.

To my disappointment, Noah was sitting at the kitchen table scrolling on his phone when I walked in.

"There you are! Did you get your prescription?"

I shook my head. "Guess it wasn't ready yet."

"Too bad. I made you an afternoon pick-me-up. Have a seat."

Noah poured me a mug of coffee as I settled across from him at the table. He'd already helped himself to Mom's creamer and sugar, and added the exact proportions he knew I liked before sliding the mug over to me. I warmed my hands on the ceramic, peering into the sand-colored liquid. Thinking about Brendan hammering the lid back onto that damn can of paint . . .

"I think we should talk about a few things, Liv." Noah's voice jolted me out of my reverie.

I blinked at him. "Anything in particular?"

My fiancé stretched out his long legs under the table, brushing up against my ankle. "I've just been thinking a lot after our interview at Beloved, is all."

Dread clotted deep in my belly. *Oh, no. Not this. Not now.* I would've been happy to sweep the thickening tension between us under the rug, but my fiancé—damn him—tended to fly to problems like a moth to light. Try as I might, I couldn't ever comprehend the impulse.

Why start a fight? a little voice sounded in my head every time Noah nudged me into a confrontation. *It'll only end in someone getting hurt.*

I pouted. "Now?"

"Stop using your cuteness to get out of this." Noah kicked me gently under the table. "Come on. Talk to me. Why didn't you tell me you'd changed your mind about law school?"

I shrugged. "Because I hadn't admitted it to myself yet, I guess." Then, teasingly: "Why didn't you tell me you'd changed your mind and suddenly wanted a brood of children?"

But he didn't react with humor, the way that I'd hoped. Instead, Noah pushed his coppery hair back with his hands. "I just hoped you'd be on board. When you think about it, is there really that much of a difference between two and four kids?"

I tried to imagine Penny juggling a second set of twins. I felt ill. "That sounds like a *lot* of work."

Noah shrugged. "I know. But I've been thinking about it a lot since Ben's death. And, well . . . it's important to me to have a big family. I don't think I can budge on this."

Wow. It would've been nice to be included in such a decision. Sudden anger sparked through my fingers; I flexed them at my sides. "Well, the timing worries me, too. Now you want to start a family our first year of marriage?"

"We've had eight years to enjoy each other."

Had we met our quota for enjoyment, then? "But I haven't figured out my life yet, Noah. Besides, have you thought about how we'd even afford childcare for four kids?"

Noah scratched the side of his head. "I mean, you aren't working," he said at last. "The timing couldn't be better."

If I swept my coffee mug off the table, would it yield a shard of ceramic sharp enough to draw blood? The moment the question occurred to me, I pressed a finger to my spined ring to snuff it out.

Stop it.

Our conversation was taking a scarily similar turn to the one Penny had described with Carter, that precipitous slide into assumptions. *It was just assumed that I'd be the one to take the step back professionally. Carter makes so much more.* I'd never seen myself as a stay-at-home mom. With four children, how long would that put me out of the workforce? Eight, ten years? For God's sake, I was only twenty-six. I still didn't know what I wanted to do, who I wanted to be. But Noah's timeline didn't afford me the luxury of figuring any of that out.

Noah set his own mug down. "If you decided to go back to school, you could always do it once the last kid is in kindergarten. Maybe even online."

"So I'd be starting a new career in my late thirties?"

Noah shrugged. "Plenty of people do it. With marriage and kids, sacrifices just have to be made."

"Funny, I haven't heard mention of anything *you're* planning to sacrifice."

Noah looked at me as if I'd struck him. "Are you serious? I'd be the one working my ass off to support everyone!"

So, essentially, his day-to-day life would remain unchanged while mine turned upside down for the foreseeable future. How was that fair? My throat was closing with rage. "No," I said, pushing myself from the table.

Noah looked taken aback. " 'No'? What does that even mean?"

"It means I don't want to be a stay-at-home mom, Noah, and I definitely don't want four kids. If this is your new dream and you're unwilling to budge on it, why are we even getting married?"

The moment I said it, I felt lighter.

Noah's face crumpled. "You're not serious."

To my relief, my phone started vibrating in my pocket. I stood and lifted it out.

Maddie.

"Liv," she said, as soon as I'd answered. "Did you ever talk to Everett?"

I glanced over at Noah, who was gaping up at me from the table. Then I strode out of the kitchen and into my father's old study, shutting the door behind me. "Yes . . ." I said, once I was safely sealed inside.

Silence strung out like a taut clothesline on the other side of the phone. "Sam's stepmom just let me know he's in the hospital. He almost died from an allergic reaction."

My mind filled with static.

"He was checked into the hospital late last night, after the vigil," Maddie continued. "Guess he has a pretty severe peanut allergy and it was triggered somehow."

I flashed to Mischief Night, Sam taunting her twin with a Snickers bar.

"Oh my God. Is he okay?"

"They've stabilized him, yeah. But I was wondering . . . how did he seem to you, when you met with him?"

Shamefully, the memories that surfaced first were of Everett's eyes dragging over my thighs. The scowl that had claimed his face once I'd brandished my engagement ring to ward him off. But then the other details began to slot into place: Everett's hollowed face, the filth of his apartment. "He seemed like he wasn't doing too hot," I admitted. "But he definitely wasn't having any kind of allergic reaction. At least none that I could see."

I heard wind whipping in the background. Maddie must have stepped outside the café on her break to call me, and my heart warmed that she'd thought to make use of my number after all. Half of me hadn't expected to hear from her again.

"His stepmom is really confused," Maddie went on. "She said Everett is usually so careful about eating things that might set off his allergy. He has to be."

I pinched both tear ducts with my thumb and forefinger, my brain working overtime. "Wait a second." Those crumb-strewn plates on Everett's coffee table, tinfoil tops peeled away. "When I went over there, Everett had some baked goods out. He said people had been bringing the family food since Sam's disappearance. Maybe there was something in one of the dishes?"

"That sounds likely." Maddie chewed through the new information. "Yikes," she said at last. "Imagine trying to make a nice gesture like that and landing the other Mendez twin in the hospital."

It was supremely bad timing—not that there was a good time to activate a peanut allergy, of course. Still, what was it about this family? A cold sensation trickled down my back. Why couldn't they catch a break?

While I had her on the phone, I filled in Maddie on my interaction with Brendan.

"Someone controlling?" she echoed, when I'd finished. "Yeah, okay."

The thick skepticism in her voice was vindicating: clearly, I wasn't the only one who found Brendan's explanation a flimsy one.

After hanging up a couple of minutes later, I stared down at my phone, mind spinning. Poor Everett. A hospitalization was the last thing he needed after these harrowing few days. Amidst my sympathy, though, something else was swirling. It was the feeling of all these details refusing to fit together correctly, a sharpening unease. Everett could have died. And for this to happen so soon after Sam's disappearance . . .

"How long have you been standing in here?" Noah's terse voice made me jump. He held the study door open with an elbow, a line of confusion—or maybe anger—etched between his brows.

"I just got off the phone with—"

"We were in the middle of a conversation, Liv. You just walked out."

Anger, then. I picked up my phone, as evidence. "I'm sorry, Noah. I got a phone call from Maddie and given everything going on, I felt like I needed to take it. Everything is okay, but—"

"And we were having an important conversation!" It wasn't Noah's character to cut me off, which clued me in to just how enraged he was. Was he even curious about what Maddie had told me? His voice was severe. "Put your phone away and come back to the kitchen. We need to resolve this."

The itchiness that had plagued me back in the bridal boutique was thorning its way back over my clavicle, spreading to my arms and abdomen. I felt hot, as if my airway were stuffed with cotton. How dare Noah talk to me this way? It made my hackles rise; it made me feel like a cornered animal.

It was the closest Noah had ever come to reminding me of my own father.

"I can't handle this right now." I pushed past him, through the living room, and out the front door.

"Where the hell are you going?"

I didn't know, so I didn't answer him. Instead, I rushed down the gravel drive and onto the sidewalk, praying Noah wouldn't follow. He didn't. As my legs pumped, the neighborhood passed in a brown-green blur: low stone walls slung along the street, saltbox houses in red and smoky blue. Pickup trucks with dusty rear windows and the furrowed rows of crops on Dunk Rock Road stretching to the horizon. An empty gray sky, the smell of decomposing leaves. So much space.

As I walked, I let each of my thoughts loose like a released balloon. Brendan in the hardware store. Everett in the hospital. My fiancé, smoldering across the kitchen table. The more distance I notched between us, the easier I began to breathe. I walked, as if in a trance, until the edge of my slip-on shoes rubbed my heel raw. The split-rail fences along the farmland turned to rocks and vegetation, the same wild flavor of woodland I'd run through with Eden and Cora. Distance, quiet—maybe that's all I needed to untangle the mess my brain had become since arriving in Guilford.

The road snaked right and then left. Soon I was swallowed into a tunnel of trees, sun-shot leaves whispering above me. My feet took me through the dark lace of the tree tunnel, onto the shoulder of noisy Route 1, and back into the sanctuary of River Street, nodding golden stalks lining my way. By now, the sun had sunk behind the tree line, painting the sky lavender. Sam and I would take her car out when we'd gotten restless, but a couple of times, we'd walked like this—aimlessly, meditatively—as we dissected Guilford High relationships and spun stories of our future college years. Sam had helped me outrun the stuff that had been plaguing me back then. My parents' deteriorating relationship, my uncertainty about the future. Stomping down these same roads eight years later, I was markedly alone and—somehow—running from far scarier things.

All too soon, I found myself staring at the back door of 128 Whitfield Street. I craned my neck to look up at the pink scalloped side, those swirled finials, and the warped Pegasus weathervane groaning on the roof. My neck prickled. How had I ended up here?

Before I could unearth any hope or intention, my hand raised into a fist and knocked.

18

THEN

I T WAS ONE WEEK AFTER EVERETT AND I HAD STUMBLED UPON
The Sisterhood in the woods around the fire, and I still
couldn't banish the incident from my head. It drove me
wild that I had no one to talk to about this. Sam and I
were on speaking terms again—we'd been chilly toward
each other for a grand total of forty-eight hours, after
which she thawed me by dragging me to get milkshakes at
Friendly's one day after school. But I still didn't feel comfortable broaching the topic. I knew how she'd react the
moment she heard Eden's name come out of my mouth:
not well.

I agonized for the full school week. Finally, on Friday, I
lingered by Everett's locker on my way to physics. My heart
lifted in that predictable way the moment I spotted him.
Gray waffle shirt tight across his forearms, scuffed All-Stars.
He looked startled to see me there.

"Hey," I said.

He cast a look over my head at the hallway, a surging artery during passing time. "Hey."

"Can . . . can I talk to you for a minute?"

Everett began spinning his locker combination. But he didn't tell me to leave.

I lowered my voice. "I want to talk to you about Mischief Night. About what we saw," I added, lest he think I was referencing our kiss.

"Liv," Everett said, hefting open his locker, "just leave it."

Just leave it? How was I supposed to forget what I'd seen, to carry that burden alone? "Please, Everett. I've been trying to make sense of things all week, and I could really use someone to talk to . . ."

Everett groaned, dumping a couple of textbooks into his backpack. Then he slammed his locker door and looked at me. "Fine. But not here. I'll give you my number."

"Right. Okay." I fumbled with my phone, opening up a new contact form. There was hope after all; I'd finally be able to release all the memories I'd been holding. That it happened to include getting Everett Mendez's phone number? All the better.

Everett entered his number into my phone and handed it back to me. "Don't tell Sam about this," he said.

I nodded. "Obviously."

Everett hefted his backpack over one shoulder. "Text me later," he said, before being carried away in the tide of students.

• • •

AVERY SAT A ROW AHEAD of me in class. She wore a high ponytail in a brass-adorned elastic, the ends of her hair meticulously curled. I inched forward in my seat to observe her. She was sitting normally in her chair, back straight, legs crossed. She didn't appear injured at all. But then again—I scooted farther forward in my chair—she was wearing a loose, gauzy top over her jeans. Had she intentionally picked a forgiving shirt to avoid aggravating whatever injury Eden had inflicted upon her? What had Eden done with that creepy-looking needle, anyway?

I settled back against my chair as a shiver claimed my body. I needed to talk to Everett about this face-to-face—but how would that even work? Sam didn't participate in any extracurriculars, so she was sure to be at home outside of school hours. Expecting to hang out with me. Somehow, Everett and I would have to circumvent her, and my stomach clenched at the thought. I'd explicitly promised Sam I wouldn't be tempted by her brother. What kind of friend did that make me? I remembered pinky-swearing with her in the fair fun house and the memory made me want to vomit. But then again, I wasn't going behind Sam's back to hook up with her brother; I was doing it because I needed answers.

That night in bed, I was assaulted with images from Mischief Night. I turned over again and again, dragging my face across a humid pillow. They were getting confusing, too, all the sounds and smells of the night muddling together. Feet slapping the pavement on a run through the neighborhood. The mucous-like creep of the yolk against the door of Eden's house. Eden calling into the night, *If anyone's there, I'd advise you leave.* Leaves and woodsmoke and Everett cupping my face and kissing me.

Under the sheets, I forced my legs together, ashamed of the way my body was reacting to the memories. Yes, my kiss with Everett was tangled up with all kinds of disturbing imagery. But, still, my mind should have been capable of parsing the difference. There was no reason I should reflect upon that night as a whole and feel aroused.

It bothered me deeply that I did.

THE FOLLOWING MONDAY, I LIED to Sam about having a doctor's appointment after school. It was the first time I'd ever lied to Sam and that nauseous feeling rose inside me again. This wasn't a good precedent to be setting.

I walked to meet Everett in the lower lot where the seniors parked. I recognized his car from Sam's driveway—an army-green Jeep with a battered back bumper. Sam had told me, with an eye roll, that her brother had patched it up with zip ties because he didn't want to pony up the cash to get it fixed properly.

I held my breath. How was this supposed to work?

A moment later, the driver's side window rolled down. Everett stuck his head out. He had something in his mouth— a mint or gum—that made him look even more nonchalant than usual. "You gonna get in?" he called to me.

My heart began to pound. Suddenly, I couldn't stop thinking of the way Everett's mouth had felt on mine. I'd played back our kiss in the woods so many times I'd started worrying that maybe it wasn't the memory itself anymore, but rather a cheap facsimile of events, dog-eared from overuse. How was I supposed to just sit there beside him, in that big masculine car, and pretend that kiss had never happened?

Everett was blasting some band I'd never heard; he turned down the volume as I scrambled into the front seat. Then, without saying anything to me, he tore out of the senior lot.

"Where are we going?" I asked.

His eyes cut to me. "Somewhere no one will see us."

The comment could easily have been construed as creepy, but in that moment, I felt only a dark thrill. Shyly, I watched the muscles flicker in Everett's forearm as he maneuvered the steering wheel.

We pulled into a part of Guilford I'd only seen before in passing—the marshland full of tall, nodding grasses. Everett threw his gearshift into Park and my heart bumped right along with it. The rustle of those nodding stalks and the smell of peat and salt curled in through the open windows, making me heady. Down a set of shallow stone steps, an X-shaped gate with black iron hardware led to ribbons of water wending back and forth, silver as the sky.

Everett was silent.

I screwed up my courage. "So," I said.

He unbuckled his seatbelt, pushed his seat back, and sighed. Then he turned toward me, expectant.

Great. He was really going to make me do all the heavy lifting here. "Thank you for meeting me," I said, and my voice came out so stiff and formal that I winced internally.

Everett guffawed. "You are most welcome, madame." But even though we'd broken the tension in the Jeep, he wouldn't move the conversation forward.

I ran damp palms over my jeans. "So, what do you think about what we saw in the woods? Those cat masks? That . . . needle?"

Everett flinched at the word *needle*. "We're not sure that's what it was."

"Okay, even if it wasn't a legit needle, it looked like it could cause some damage. And that was Avery, wasn't it, getting . . . ?" I wasn't sure what word to use here, as Everett seemed set on downplaying the incident. Surely, *stabbed* was a bit melodramatic. But *poked* didn't seem to convey the gravity of the situation.

"I think so." Everett ran a hand through his hair and looked out the window at the curtain of long grass.

"And . . ." I didn't want to say it, but I had to. "That was definitely Eden, wasn't it? With the bright blond hair?"

Everett clamped his lips together, said nothing.

"What do you think they were doing?" I whispered.

"Who knows," Everett said. "Eden and her friends were always into . . . that occult shit. Tarot cards, tea leaves, that kind of thing."

"Did you ever know of them hanging out in the woods like that? Around a fire?"

"Not specifically. Eden was always hush-hush about things she did with Avery and Cora."

A wild intrigue stirred within me. "So you've never seen anything like this before?"

Everett's brow furrowed. "There was this one time . . ."

"What?"

He passed a hand over his eyes. "It was probably nothing, but there was this one time I showed up early at Eden's house. Her friends were still there, and they were pissed I'd come over. They were all huddled around something in Eden's bedroom, trying to keep me from seeing it."

"What was it?"

Everett looked vaguely sick. "I don't know. But it looked like a piece of bone or something."

A piece of bone? Could it have been one of Avery's animal skulls? "What do you mean? Like, a human bone? Or an animal one?"

"I don't know!" There was a snap to his voice now— I knew from the way he turned away from me to look out his window that he was done entertaining questions on the matter.

I tried a different angle. "How long did you say the two of you were dating, again?"

"I didn't." Everett's lips were pressed together again, practically invisible.

"Well?"

He sighed. "I guess 'dating' is a loose term. We were never official or anything. Eden didn't seem to want anything . . . serious. You know. Anyway, things got awkward after that day I walked in on her and her friends. Everything kind of went downhill after that."

I detected an undercurrent of hurt in Everett's voice. So Everett had wanted Eden but Eden had rejected him.

How many other girls could claim the same of Everett Mendez?

Suddenly, I was gripped by the same desperate need to know more about Eden that had struck me on Mischief Night. Not merely because she was so mysterious—what the hell could she and her friends possibly have been doing with a piece of *bone*?—but because I was fascinated by this girl who didn't seem to give a shit about guys. Guys like Everett, no less. How did she do it? How had Eden managed to surround herself with a group of girlfriends who seemed to satisfy everything for her?

I tried, unsuccessfully, to put my confusion into words. "How is Eden so . . ."

". . . untouchable?" Everett finished. He shrugged. "I have no idea. Clearly, I didn't make the same impression on her, though."

"Ouch."

"Ha." Everett shifted in his seat. "No need to feel sorry for me."

"I mean, you've already seen me cry, so."

Everett turned to look at me. I colored furiously—had that tread too close to our kiss in the woods? It's what immediately preceded it. Now, all I could think of was the feel of Everett's plum-soft mouth, his hands in my hair . . .

"Sorry about my sister. Again," Everett added. His energy had shifted; something hungry stirred behind his eyes.

I laughed, awkwardly. "It's okay. Sam will be Sam."

"Hmm." Everett draped his arm over the center console. His fingertips brushed my knee and my entire thigh electrified at the sudden contact. A strange coiling sensation built deep in my core. I wanted to leap on Everett like something feral, to straddle him in the driver's seat. But my body betrayed me, muscles locked like a prey animal's.

To my shock, Everett reached over and toyed with the end of my ponytail.

I held my breath. I thought about asking Everett, *What are we doing?* but I was terrified of fracturing the moment.

Besides, I knew exactly what we were doing.

From my ponytail, Everett's thumb shifted to my jaw. Soon I'd tumbled back into the soft mouth and calloused hands from Mischief Night. The feral part of me took hold and I climbed into Everett's lap in the driver's seat, the more to take him in. Everett's fingertips crept under my shirt, skating over my ribs, making me shiver.

A harsh vibration against my stomach made me rear back. Everett frowned, reaching for his phone. Even though he stowed it quickly, I saw the contact displayed prominently on the screen.

Sam.

"Shit." I slumped back into the passenger seat, running my hand over my now-lopsided ponytail.

"I don't—I'm not taking it," Everett said, pointing to his pocket where he'd stuffed his phone.

"I know." But Sam had butted into the moment and ruined the mood. Reminding me that I was being a shitty friend. I'd lied to her to go sneaking around with her twin, when I should have been making jewelry with her. I'd never forget Sam's face the night of the Guilford Fair. She'd looked murderous, when all she'd seen was Everett looking at me. How would she react if she'd seen the way we'd been entangled a minute earlier?

"She probably locked herself out of the house," Everett said gruffly, turning the key in the ignition. "Again."

I pulled out my hair elastic and fluffed out my hair, partially to hide my face from Everett.

We drove in relative silence to drop me off at my house.

19

NOW

AT FIRST, NO ONE ANSWERED THE DOOR TO BELOVED. Something brushed my hand and I snatched it away. On the green door: movement. A shock of white against black—that beetle again with an eye painted on its back, wedging its plump body into the keyhole. A shiver ran through me. What were these things? And why were they infesting this pocket of Guilford . . . not to mention my dreams?

The door swung open. It was Eden, mouth witchy with dark lipstick.

She smiled at me, those vivid lips splitting over white teeth. Then, without a word, she led me inside.

I followed Eden through the mazelike interior of dark wood and candlelight. I caught a glimpse of myself in an antique oval mirror in the hallway, its silvery skin pocked with shadows. Maybe it was because of all the miles I'd just walked, but my neck was mottled pink, my mouth nearly as dark as Eden's. Or maybe it wasn't the walk at all; maybe it was this damn house again, playing games with me.

Those candles were out in full-force tonight—thick white columns pooling wax, candelabras boasting tapers with dots of flame perched on the wicks. Cora materialized clutching a couple of Band-Aids.

"Here," she said, handing them to me. When I gave her a look of confusion, she pointed to my feet. Unbeknownst to me, the raw skin on my ankles had opened to bleed, tingeing the backs of my slip-ons with rust-colored stains.

"Thank you." I dragged out one of the heavy rail-backed chairs from the kitchen table to sit down and apply the bandages. Cora and Eden stood watching me, their heads tilted close to each other.

"To what do we owe the pleasure?" Eden said softly, once I finished.

I anchored my elbows to the table. I tried to figure out where to start, but the past couple of hours had kicked up such a storm inside me that my body slumped from the effort.

Cora and Eden watched me patiently. Cora went to the refrigerator and poured me a glass of something pinkish from an elegant pitcher. I took a sip. It tasted like a mashup of pink lemonade and lavender. I felt the granules of sugar on my tongue—more refined than the sugary drinks of my childhood, but still, somehow, nostalgic.

After draining half the glass, I felt fortified enough to begin talking. The story tumbled out: questioning Brendan in the hardware store. My argument with Noah; his assumption that I'd have no problem stalling my life to raise the family he wanted. The call from Maddie, the news about Everett in the hospital, and the way my overwhelm had me wandering for miles along the back roads of Guilford. Presently, Eden and Cora joined me at the table, leaning ever closer to me as my tale unspooled.

"We heard about what happened to Everett." Cora's hand crept to mine on the tabletop. She covered it with her soft palm. "It's really scary. Those peanut allergies are no joke."

"I don't know how that could even happen," I said.

"Do you think . . ." Eden started.

"Hmm?"

"I mean," she said, "is it possible someone did that to him? Intentionally?"

The three of us sat staring at one another, our faces mirroring our fear.

"I just want Sam to be okay," Cora whispered. Her eyes were wet, like when she'd called Sam her sister.

Eden laid her head on Cora's shoulder. The intimacy of the gesture ignited something inside me. I couldn't remember the last time one of my girlfriends had touched me with tenderness. College? When we'd been wasted? Sure, my friends nowadays and I gave one another perfunctory hugs when we met up, but even synchronizing calendars these days was becoming a Herculean task.

"What did your fiancé make of Everett's hospitalization?" Eden asked. "Did he seem concerned?"

I frowned. "Maddie called in the middle of our argument, actually. And Noah was so hung up on reaching some kind of resolution that I couldn't even get the story out to him."

Eden's dark eyes flared. "Really?"

"Really." I put my head in my hands. "Ugh. That probably makes him sound like a monster. But you met him! You know he's not. He's been so supportive through this entire thing." Maybe it was my fault Noah had acted the way he had; maybe my tendency to avoid and his to confront was a pairing destined for disaster.

"Of course," Eden murmured. She gave me a reassuring smile, held my eyes with hers. "I know Noah isn't a monster, Liv. Sometimes these things happen in relationships—people change their minds about what's important to them. Unfortunately, it can mean the other partner is totally blindsided."

"Exactly." I tilted my glass to one side with shaking fingers.

"It takes courage to commit to someone for life," Eden went on. "You have to do so based on a handful of assumptions. And when one of those assumptions proves untrue . . . well, it's like the bottom falls right out of everything."

Maybe it was Eden's expertise in her field, but it felt as if she'd climbed into the recesses of my mind and plucked the thoughts straight from it.

"Yes," I breathed.

Eden and Cora exchanged a look.

"We want to show you something," Eden said.

"More sparklers?"

"Not this time."

I followed the girls out of the kitchen and down the narrow hallway with the mirror. Up the creaking, narrow staircase, past the reading nook with its rose sealed in a stained-glass circle. As we walked through the dark upstairs, I felt the house breathing around us: the doorframes sighing, expanding and contracting, the floorboards straining to anticipate our footfalls.

Eden walked to the end of the hallway and reached up to pull a chain from the ceiling. A splintering set of stairs folded down. "Up we go," she said, starting to climb.

I couldn't think of a good reason Eden would be taking us up into the attic. But her back was to me and I had no choice but to follow. The staircase was steep. Mustiness filled my nostrils almost immediately—the smell of damp and rot. A cobweb brushed my cheek and I swatted it away, repulsed.

We reached the top of the stairs. I don't know what I had been expecting, but it wasn't what I found: an old-fashioned fainting couch piled high with pillows. The entire space blushed with soft candlelight.

How had the candles up here already been lit? Wasn't that dangerous?

"This is cute," I said.

Eden waved a dismissive hand at the room. "That's not what we brought you up here to see. C'mere." She crossed the room to a darkened window, which she hefted open with the heels of her hands, bringing in a blast of night air. Then she lifted her dress up around her hips and began to climb outside to the roof beyond. Cora followed behind her, as if it were the most natural request in the world.

"Eden!" Was she really expecting me to follow her out onto the roof?

She didn't respond.

Feeling awkward, I maneuvered my body through the open window, scrabbling to gain purchase on the roof outside. I expected to set my feet down on tiles, but I stepped out onto wooden planks instead.

"This is a widow's walk," Eden said. She had her elbows propped up on a banister, gazing out to the dark quilt of Guilford spreading beneath us. I gasped. I'd never seen the town from this perspective before. The scenery before us—the postcard of the Green, its spired churches, and the clapboard colonial homes clustered around it—looked like kids' toys. The grid of downtown Guilford gave way to the winding roads that led to my own neighborhood, smothered by forest.

"In the daytime, you can just make out the ocean," Cora said, the wind stirring her hair.

"Uh-huh," Eden said. "Way back when, the woman of the house would come up here to look for her husband's ship at the port. I can almost taste her desperation, can't you? Hoping against hope that she wouldn't become the namesake of this structure."

A widow.

"Liv," Eden said, turning to me at last. "Tell me again why you stopped making jewelry."

I looked down at the ground. I would never be able to give her the real answer to this question. "I didn't have time at the law firm," I mumbled.

"Yeah, okay." Eden waved a hand, dismissing my flimsy excuse. "Here's the deal, Liv. There are all different kinds of paths in life. And we want you to make sure you don't forsake a path that we truly believe will be so rewarding. So fulfilling. You have the ability to be so . . . powerful."

"Truly," Cora said, nodding. Her eyes were moons. "Your talent amazes us."

I opened my mouth to laugh, but Eden silenced me with a hand. "No, stop that. I saw you admiring Sam's things. The way they called to you. And I've seen how you infuse your jewelry with intention."

Eden must have seen the confusion on my face, because she frowned. "Don't play dumb, Liv. That bracelet you wore back in high school that calmed your nerves when you needed it. The ring you're wearing right now that pulls you from your own . . . darkness. Both of those pieces: functional and beautiful."

I stared at Eden as if she were speaking another language. I hadn't made those pieces with any kind of plan or intention. They'd just happened. And what did Eden mean by my "darkness"? I didn't like the phrase, didn't like what it implied.

Eden's bare arm rubbed up against mine and I felt a frisson run through me, ink unfurling through water. "Do me a favor and tuck this moment away in your memory, okay? You have the opportunity to invest in yourself and your creativity. You really do."

I stared at the ground, mute. Where was this coming from? Had Eden intuited the pang of jealousy I'd felt sifting through Sam's jewelry supplies? Or had she been as both-ered by Noah's bait and switch as I had?

"As women, we're trained to deny what feels right, aren't we?" Eden went on. "If something feels good, it's an indulgence. There's always that nasty little voice in the back of our heads, telling us we don't deserve it. That we should be *sacrificing*, not creating. We should be tending to others, not enriching ourselves. And we certainly shouldn't be structuring a life solely around cultivating all that makes us powerful and vital."

I dared to glance over at Eden. Her teeth were shad-owed in the dark and for a moment, the sight scared me. So many questions jumbled in my mind. What was Eden really talking about? What kind of power did she see in me?

"I mean," Cora said, "you must recognize what Eden is talking about, right? Think about the feeling you get when you're working on your jewelry. When you're surrounded by your closest girlfriends."

Eden's words called to mind the electric feeling I'd had making jewelry with Sam back in high school. But I hadn't felt that for years now. I grimaced, feeling suddenly exposed, just as I had during my interview with Noah.

"Actually," I said in a tiny voice, "I don't see a lot of my girlfriends anymore. We've . . . kind of drifted apart over the years."

"Why?" Eden said sharply.

"Well, we're all in long-term relationships now. Couple's stuff can really monopolize the weekends. A lot of my friends are moving outside the city, I'm busy planning the wedding . . . I guess it just got too logistically difficult trying to see each other."

Eden didn't even attempt to curtail the disgust crossing her face. "That's the most fucking depressing thing I've ever heard in my life."

Defensiveness closed over me like a claw. Was it depressing, or was it just the natural progression of growing up? We were turning inward to our partners; in a few years, these cozy little lives would include our children. Girlfriends would just have to take a back seat to family; it was inevitable. I opened my mouth to address Eden's remark, but to my shock, she threaded her cold fingers through mine.

"Look," she said, lifting her chin at the night sky.

A single star streaked through the blue-blackness.

"Whoa!"

Beside her, Cora looped an arm through Eden's. The three of us stood like sentinels at the edge of the widow's walk, heads tipped to the sky as the cooling wind toyed with our hair. Moments later, a second pinprick cut a searing path through the night. Three others followed close behind, little gemstones pulling stark necklace chains behind them in the sky.

I gasped, attempted to pull away from Eden to address her. "How did you know—? Does this happen often up here?"

Eden just clutched my hand tighter. "Don't ruin it by questioning, Liv. Just take it in."

It was so counter to how I usually moved through the world—always asking questions, always worrying. But tonight of all nights, Eden's approach was worth a try. I forced myself to relax my hand in Eden's grip. Two more bits of silver scarred the sky. They made me think again of delicate jewelry. I could make a pair of earrings just like shooting stars, I thought; an instant later the design was sketching itself in my mind. Tiny pearl drops, the slightest of chains, one and a half to two inches in length. Something sparked within me like a long-dormant pilot light switching on.

But I reined myself in before I went too far. The meteor shower—right now, in this moment—was just a bit too perfect. How had Eden known this was going to happen? I hadn't seen anything on the news predicting this . . . but then again, I'd been preoccupied with following Sam's investigation. The more I thought about it, the more uneasy I felt. There were too many other odd occurrences in the house. The feverish feeling I got each time I entered, the beetles with the patterns on their backs . . .

I had to say something. "Don't take this the wrong way, Eden, but I feel really strange each time I come over here. Weird things keep happening."

Eden and Cora exchanged a look.

"Weird things?" Cora echoed innocently.

"Yeah. Remember when we were running through the woods and our sparklers snuffed out? They just suddenly . . . reignited. How? And then the next morning, when I saw that bride trying on that dress you made her, I could have sworn her eyes . . . well, I thought they turned white in the mirror . . ."

Another look passed between the two girls. Cora opened her mouth.

"It's okay," Eden said, cutting her off. She turned to me

and said, more gently, "Liv, I feel like I've really connected with you over the past few days, given everything that we've gone through together."

"Me, too," I said, surprising myself.

A small smile graced her lips. "Good. I think it's time we pulled back the curtain for you, then."

My heart thudded in my chest. Where was she going with this?

"Remember when I told you the backstory to Beloved?" Eden said.

I nodded.

"Well, there's a bit more to it, and I think you're ready to hear it now. You see, there's a reason we have such a rigorous application and interview process. It helps us identify those brides that . . . need a little help seeing more clearly."

I waited a moment for her to elaborate, but she didn't. "Seeing clearly?" I prompted her.

"Okay, chickadee, it's time for another story. Let's rewind to the summer after college graduation. A disgusting, sticky day in June. Cora and I were sitting at the wedding of a girl who'd gone to UConn with us. We didn't want to be there. We knew the relationship was doomed from the terrible way her fiancé treated her, but there was nothing we could do. Over drinks at the reception, we got to talking. What if we *could* have done something to intervene?"

The tiny hairs lifted on the back of my neck. "Like what?"

"Let me connect the dots for you. At Beloved, when we've identified a bride in need of our assistance, I help her see the cracks in her relationship. She'll start noticing the ways in which her partner mistreats her, takes advantage of her. She might even see a vision of herself in her not-so-rosy married future. Just as you have a gift for infusing intention into your jewelry, I'm able to help people see what they need to."

I flashed back to the memory in the girls' bathroom that had haunted me for years: Eden with her cold fingertips against my skull, the whisk of that mysterious fluffy brush over my cheeks. I would've done anything to gain clarity on what had happened. But standing before Eden now, my tongue felt Velcroed to the roof of my mouth.

"Right," Eden said. "You know exactly what I'm talking about."

"The bride's eyes," I choked out. "The other day in the boutique."

"You're catching on."

"But none of it is real, is it? They're just illusions."

Eden sniffed. "They're based in reality, and that's what matters."

"Me next," Cora whined, tugging at Eden's arm.

Eden rolled her eyes. "Cora wants you to know how she fits into Beloved's mission. Do you have any guesses?"

I shook my head, utterly bewildered.

"Cora has the very special ability to embed dreams in her food," Eden said. She ran a hand over Cora's hair, the crown of her head. "Happy dreams, nightmares, you name it—Cora can cook it up. Ultimately, these dreams reinforce the message we're imparting to brides."

Eden and Cora stared at me, waiting for my reaction. My hand tremored by my side. I wanted to snap at them that this was ludicrous. Dreams, baked into cupcakes? But then I remembered the nightmares that had gripped me after my couple's interview at the boutique: the thumbtack ring buried in my finger, fresh blood snaking down my wrist.

"Are you trying to get Noah and me to break up?" I whispered.

The girls continued to stare at me for a moment before tipping their heads back and laughing.

"Oh, no," Eden gasped, once she'd recovered. "You've got this all wrong, Liv."

"But after our meeting, I dreamed—"

"That must have been your own intuition," Eden cut me off. "We took you on as a client because you're a friend of Sam's—that's all."

My body chilled. "And where does Sam fit into all this?"

"Think of it this way," Eden said. "I help the brides see the cracks in their relationship. Cora reinforces this through dreams. And Sam's jewelry gives the brides the courage to do something about it."

"You're like her," Cora said quietly. "Able to craft jewelry with intention. Such a gift!"

My hand was shaking at my side again, more erratically now. I closed it into a fist and forced myself to breathe deeply. So this was the real reason Sam had been invited to room with Eden and Cora. Cora must have become aware of Sam's abilities after taking that art class together.

"If it makes you feel better," Eden went on, "we leave most relationships be. But a small minority are so egregious it would be unethical not to intervene. These are the relationships where there is emotional abuse. Where a woman is taken for granted and falls into that all-too-familiar trap of sacrificing herself entirely . . . not unlike your sister, to be frank."

I bristled at the unexpected mention of Penny. Why was she getting pulled into all of this?

Cora must have misinterpreted my stiffening, because she approached me in the dark then, rubbing a gentle circle on my back. "I'm so sorry. If she had come to us sooner, maybe we would have been able to help."

I shook off her hand. Under different circumstances, the gesture might have pleased me—a sign she was drawing me into that fold of female friendship I'd been missing in my own life. Instead, I felt frantic. Eden and Cora were introducing too much, too fast. I didn't want them near me.

"I feel sick. I need to go home."

"Of course." Eden was staring out at the dark patchwork of Guilford below us. She didn't even turn to look at me.

Cora stepped away from me a bit, likely sensing I needed space. "Yes, please go home and rest, Liv. Take all the time you need."

"And when you've processed everything," Eden said, still looking out at the streaking stars, "you know where to find us."

20

NOW

I FOUND NOAH'S LETTER THAT NIGHT, FOLDED ON A RAGGED-edged piece of notebook paper and placed on my pillow:

> *Liv,*
>
> *I took the train back to Boston to give you some space. I get that you're feeling overwhelmed with everything going on & that's understandable, but please try to see the situation from my POV. Let's talk soon & figure this out.*
>
> *Love you.*
>
> *N*

I ran a fingertip over the spiky stems of Noah's T's and I's and something fractured inside of me. There was something so vulnerable about a man's handwriting, and I'd been gifted Noah's over the past eight years: usually in the form of anniversary cards with funny-looking animals on the front and a single, shockingly sincere line inside. The last one had said, *I don't even want to think about what my life would be like without you.*

The grief that rushed in then left no room for me to even consider the absurdity that Eden and Cora had just dumped on me. My relationship with Noah was the central relationship of my life; over the past eight years, our lives had grown so entwined I wasn't sure where mine left off and his began. We'd weathered college together. We'd built a home together, Noah commandeering the hanging of the pictures when I worked myself into a rage setting each one askew. We'd picked out furniture together. Kitschy saltshakers (only to discover once we got home that the pig figurines were—horrifyingly—anatomically correct, and laughing until we cried). We had our own language: that one-two squeezing of each other's hands, the way we called sleeping dogs "loaves."

The idea of scrubbing this man from my life was almost unthinkable. And all because of—what? The fact that we wanted a different number of children?

Because I was starting to think I might not want any children at all?

I crawled into bed clutching Noah's letter as my tears seeped into the fabric of my pillowcase. I didn't want to think about life without Noah, either. It made me feel panicky and out of control, as if my body was vibrating at a dangerously high frequency and might spontaneously shatter. Soon, the quiet tears turned to barks of grief, which I muffled into my pillow so Mom wouldn't hear through the wall.

I don't even want to think about what my life would be like without you.

Before this horrible week—before tonight, really—I simply hadn't dared.

THE ENTRANCE TO STRAWBERRY HOLLOW Farm was a riot of color. In front of the rustic cottage, a large wooden wheelbarrow was piled with pumpkins, its sides studded with husks of blood-red ornamental corn and bunches of bittersweet berries tied with twine. Terra-cotta flowerpots crowded the ground, bursting with farm-grown blooms in shades of gold and rust. Here were the oddly flattened white pumpkins, those wart-covered gourds lolling on bales of hay; a flag depicting a cheery jack-o'-lantern hung from the peaked roof of the cottage. Beyond its roofline, a fiery wash of foliage: the leaves in Guilford had finally changed.

Inside the cottage, garlands of colored leaves snaked around the rafters; a stout wood-burning stove sat working in the corner. Mom lifted Halloween decorations—a green-faced witch with a crow perched on the end of her broom, a skull with frantic eyes lodged in its sockets—to peer at the handwritten price tags. My hand tightened around the MISSING flier I'd brought in for the shopkeeper. Eden and Cora had printed off a stack and I'd taken a bunch of them after spending the night at their house. I'd thrown myself into canvassing the town over the past couple of days because it was one of the only things that made me feel purposeful. It was also a useful distraction for whenever my thoughts drifted to Noah or 128 Whitfield Street.

The photo on the flyer was the same picture I'd first seen on social media with the announcement of Sam's disappearance, and the more I saw it, the more it unnerved me. Sam looked like she'd been preparing for a night out— lots of eyeliner, blush painted on the apples of her cheeks. But despite the mask of makeup and her signature gummy smile, her eyes were vacant as a ventriloquist dummy's.

Who had taken this photo of Sam? I tried to imagine Eden, Cora, and Sam tromping through the pink Victorian in blocky heels, preparing for a night out. Touching up their dark pouts in the antique hallway mirror, drinking from little goblets of violet alcohol. Imagining it all gave me an inexplicable pang.

Eden's words still bounced around my head like a loose penny rattling in a washing machine. She and Cora had scared me up on the widow's walk. Plus, I was still coming to terms with the fact that Sam was a part of their operation. While in theory it sounded profound—who wouldn't want to free women from problematic relationships?—it still freaked me out. At the end of the day, these girls were still intervening in strange ways to ruin potential marriages. Weren't they? Manipulating their brides. Manufacturing nightmares and visions. It was so absurd I was tempted not to believe it—except, of course, that I'd experienced it myself. Since our talk on the widow's walk, I'd wondered about the bride I'd seen trying on her gown at Beloved, the one whose eyes had flashed white in the mirror as Eden had tenderly fastened that row of tiny buttons. What exactly had she seen, in that moment? Had it scared her?

After giving the flyer to the shopkeeper, I slipped into

the pumpkin patch out back. There, I tipped my head up to the trees and let the crisp wind lift the hair off my shoulders. Decorations filled the field: an assemblage of fake tombstones, skeletons, and a hunchbacked zombie wearing a top hat and red-lined cape. A few yards to my left, a little girl in a stocking cap and ribboned knee-socks shrieked, chasing her younger brother around a wishing well. I thought of Noah and how he'd grin at the sight. He hadn't texted or called since leaving for Boston and I appreciated the space—I was already overwhelmed enough as it was.

A bit of red flashed in my peripheral vision. A petite woman with coarse coppery hair and a blue flannel knotted at the waist was crouching to study a pumpkin on the ground. Something about the combination of her shiny forehead and snub nose tugged at me until realization dawned.

What were the chances? It was the bride I'd seen at Beloved.

"Christina."

I hadn't meant to say the name aloud, but she spun when she heard it.

"Do I know you?"

"Sorry, no, not really." I felt my face flushing. "I think I might have run into you at Beloved, the bridal boutique on Whitfield Street? I was helping Eden with something, and I saw you trying on your wedding dress . . ."

"Oh." Now Christina's cheeks were flaming. "That feels like forever ago," she mumbled.

"Your wedding must be coming up, then." It was the only thing I could think to say.

Christina swayed a little, from one foot to the other. "Well. We called it off, actually."

For a moment, I forgot entirely about what Eden and Cora had told me the other night. The woman I'd seen in a bridal gown mere days ago was now single. All those hours spent picking out invitations and place settings and flowers—it had all been for nothing. In the apples of my cheeks, I felt Christina's shame as if it were my own.

"Oh God. I'm so sorry."

"Please." Christina gave a delicate flick of her wrist. "Don't be!"

My eyes widened. Christina sounded as if she were brushing off a compliment, rather than refusing condolences for a ruined engagement.

She offered a small grimace. "Maybe I should be more upset? I know how terrible it sounds."

"N-no," I stammered, trying to right myself. My disgust must have been written across my features. "It's not—"

Christina cast a quick look behind her. The shrieking siblings were throwing leaves at each other now. "Can I be candid, just for a moment?"

"Okay . . ."

"Things with my ex . . . they weren't exactly the best."

My heart was beating fast. "No?"

Christina winced. "Sorry if this is TMI. I'll just say this: I wasn't feeling super confident as the wedding day approached. But we'd already put down our deposit on the venue, everything was ready to go . . . I brushed it off. I told myself it would be okay."

The urgent thumping of my heart returned, but now for an entirely different reason. Didn't all brides walk down the aisle clutching *some* sliver of doubt? Realistically, how could you commit to spending the rest of your time on earth with someone, knowing with one hundred percent certainty you were choosing the best configuration of your life possible?

It took the bite of metal in my finger to realize I was pressing the face of my spined ring.

"So there was this incriminating text I found on his phone," Christina said, ticking off items on her fingers, "and honestly, my best friend had overheard a conversation—an argument—we'd had about the seating arrangement and she was shocked to hear how my ex spoke to me. Is it sad I hadn't even noticed, because it'd become so routine?"

I blinked at her, flabbergasted, until I realized she was waiting for a response from me. "I'm so sorry," I said again.

"But that's why you don't have to be!" Christina's face blossomed. "It all ended up being for the best. I'm telling you, I have never felt so free in all my life."

My mind scrambled to keep up with Christina's tale. I surprised myself by feeling something dangerously akin to envy.

"Wow," I said.

"I know. No more dirty boxers to pick up. No more rushing to get dinner on the table by seven—that had just become the expectation. I just rented the cutest place right off the Green. I got falafel delivered last night at eleven-thirty and ate it standing over the kitchen sink. And honestly?" Christina flashed a reckless grin before covering it with a hand, as though she'd had a scandalous revelation. "I've never been happier."

AFTER MY RUN-IN WITH CHRISTINA, I made a slow circuit around the farm. I knew Mom was waiting for me back in the gift shop, but I needed a moment to think through what I'd just learned. Insects clicked and whirred in the grass; the tattoo of a woodpecker started up along the fringe of woodland.

There was no doubt about it: Christina was happy as a newly single woman. But to what degree had she been manipulated by Eden and Cora? Would she have eventually reached this very same conclusion five years into her failing marriage? *We leave most relationships be,* Eden had told me. *But a small minority are so egregious it would be unethical not to intervene.* Judging from the tidbits of information she'd just shared with me, Christina's sounded pretty miserable.

I imagined Sam crafting jewelry for brides like Christina. A sparkly pin, like the one I'd glimpsed on her worktable. *Beloved's origin story resonated with Sam on a deeply personal level,* Eden had said. *That was the draw for her.* Framed this way, things were—finally—starting to make sense. Sam had never been one to stand by and watch injustices happen. She hadn't let me drift, lonely and lost, on my first day of school; she sure as hell wasn't going to let problematic relationships continue if she had the power to do something about it.

Apparently, Eden and Cora had granted her this power. And I couldn't deny it: that was pretty amazing.

I marched back to the cottage gift shop and asked Mom to drop me off at 128 Whitfield. As her battered car drove away, I stared up at the pink house, feeling that familiar prickle on my neck. Two days: that's how long I'd managed to stay away. Had Eden known about the tether that was beginning to grow between me and this place? She must have, because she'd spoken with such confidence the other night. *When you've processed everything, you know where to find us.*

Eden was eating an apple when she answered the door, the white flesh of the fruit vulnerable under her eyeteeth. She closed her mouth and smiled at me.

"I ran into Christina," I blurted out. "She called off the wedding."

Eden's face blossomed. "That's the best news I've heard all week." Then she turned to call into the hallway behind her. "Cora! Get over here!"

Eden grabbed my wrists and began to swing them gleefully back and forth. "Tell me everything."

"Well, she just seemed so . . . happy. She couldn't stop grinning. She was practically glowing."

"Oh my God." Eden covered her eyes like a delighted child. Then she turned back to the hallway. *"Cora!"*

In the distance, the patter of Cora's footsteps. What followed was a blur—Eden grabbing our hands and pulling us beyond the bridal salon. Soon the three of us were thundering up the rickety stairs to the attic, hand in hand, Cora's whining questions going unanswered. I wasn't sure why Eden wanted to take us up there, but I was too excited to care. I was already rehearsing how I'd fill in the details of running into Christina. The incriminating text on her ex's phone. Christina relishing that falafel over her sink.

The attic air felt warm against my face. And it smelled curious—not of the mustiness from before, but sharp, like tin. When I reached the top of the attic stairs, I blinked. The fainting couch with its pile of pillows warped and flickered in my vision. But when I blinked again, it had disappeared.

I stood in a decrepit chapel. Missing panes of stained glass gave way to evening sky just starting to bleed of color. Scattered across the marble ground was a myriad of fairy-picnic props: tasseled cushions in jewel tones, throw blankets, bottles of wine, and tiered plates piled high with fruit and latticework pastries. A fast-moving stream cut through the stone floor, its sides slick with moss. I looked up, past the soaring ceiling to the stars just beginning to pierce the darkening sky, and warm, tin-scented air caressed my cheeks. Magenta flower petals with white bellies sifted down through the church's bared skeleton.

I gasped. "What is this?"

Cora was already snatching pastries off the tiered plates. Eden looked over at me and smiled. "Our playground for the day," Cora said. "Isn't it amazing what Eden can pull off?"

They let me explore the space on gelatinous legs. I knelt to touch the velvet of the pillows. Scooped a handful of snow-colored petals from the ground and cradled them in my palm.

Cora reached into my cupped hand, plucked a couple of petals, and put them in her mouth. "Taste them!"

I dared to place a single, silky petal on my tongue. It dissolved in an instant, tasting of cotton candy.

Eden looked on, an abashed-looking flush creeping up her neck. I found that endearing about her, the fact that she seemed to be slightly discomfited by Cora's praise. She snatched up a bottle of wine—conveniently already opened—and poured glasses for us all. Then, slowly, she raised hers. "Liv and I have news."

"Liv and you?" Cora's eyes jumped between the two of us as emotions scrambled across her face.

Eden gifted me a secret smile. Then: "Liv ran into Christina today. And her eyes have been opened."

Cora erupted into whoops. I laughed, watching as she streaked away from us to riot in the gorgeous ruins—tossing handfuls of flower petals, leaping into the river and sloshing through it, up to her thighs.

Maybe it was the enchanted attic, or the wine, or the feeling of being in on a secret before even Cora. Whatever the reason, a groundswell of emotion opened within me. Eden and Cora had really done it. I thought back to the night I'd run from this house feeling sick to my stomach. Any remaining doubts dropped away remembering Christina's radiant face at the pumpkin patch. Eden and Cora had known they were needed, and they delivered. They'd saved Christina from a terrible marriage.

Eden looked over at me. "Not going to run around like a banshee?"

I shook my head, grinning. "No, thanks."

"Have a seat, then." Eden indicated a copper-colored cushion below us. "Enjoy."

Obediently, I sat cross-legged on the cushion. Then I raised the velvety wine to my lips, the blossom-strewn chapel thrumming around me.

Eden settled beside me. "Having fun?"

"Seriously? This is unreal. I can't get over this. Any of this."

"Good." Eden smiled, this time with teeth. "Don't. Don't ever."

21

NOW

IT WAS IMPOSSIBLE TO PIN DOWN TIME UP IN THE ATTIC. THE bled-out evening sky behind the missing stained-glass panels was unchanging. By the time the three of us stumbled back downstairs, morning light was streaming onto the dark wood underfoot. I thought I'd be retiring to Sam's room alone, but Cora and Eden followed, flopping onto the mattress on either side of me. Nearly delirious, I fell asleep as Eden ran her fingers through my hair.

Hours later, I woke to an empty bed and the sound of shattering glass. I peered groggily around the room.

"Eden? Cora?"

Silence.

Had I dreamed the breaking glass? Unnerved, I slid out of bed and crept barefoot down the stairs. My head pounded from alcohol and sleep deprivation. A peek into the kitchen and living room yielded nothing. That left the bridal salon—

but would the girls really be back to work so soon after our festivities? I'd slept longer than them, and still felt like I needed a couple of painkillers and a massive cup of coffee.

Inside the boutique, I finally located the source of the sound: shards of glass sat in a puddle of water on the ground. The frilled neck of a vase was still intact, the rest of its body cracked into several triangular fragments. It looked as though someone had knocked the floral display off the table in the seating area.

"Shit, shit, shit!" Cora came rushing into the room.

"What happened?"

Cora pulled her hair back from her face, a gesture I was coming to recognize as her signature nervous tic. "It's Eden. The delivery person came to drop off a fresh floral arrangement for the week but no one had warned them . . . they gave us a bunch of sunflowers!"

I studied Cora's face, searching for clues. Finding none, I said haltingly, "Dare I ask what's wrong with sunflowers?"

"It's—a personal thing." Cora stooped to pick up the blooms. In her fists, their cheery faces mashed against one another, as if she were handling garbage. After she picked up the final sunflower, she began plucking the shards of glass from the puddle, depositing them on the circular table with little *clink*s.

I frowned, reached for a shard of glass by my foot.

"Careful." Cora eased the cold fragment from my hands. The intimacy of the gesture reminded me of the night prior, when the three of us had held hands in the attic amidst Eden's riches.

"I won't tell Eden you told me," I coaxed.

Cora sighed, casting a look over her shoulder. When she spoke next, her voice was pitched low. "Okay, I'll be quick. Eden had a pretty screwed-up home life as a kid. Before her parents' relationship imploded, I guess her dad always used to bring her mom sunflowers—"

"Oh. Right." Eden's story snapped back into place in my mind: *Her husband used to come home from his construction job with bouquets of sunflowers: her favorite.* "Eden told me about that."

Cora's face was pale. "She did?"

"You're up." Cora and I both jumped to see Eden had materialized in the bridal salon. She handed me a cobalt mug topped with cappuccino foam. "I figured you could use some caffeine."

"I could, too," Cora muttered at the ground, but Eden didn't seem to hear.

"What are your plans for today?" Eden asked me.

I took a sip from the mug, eyeing her warily. Eden didn't seem to even register the broken glass or the puddle on the floor. Was she simply pretending it didn't exist? The cappuccino burned the roof of my mouth. "I hadn't thought past coffee," I admitted.

"Well, why don't you enjoy your cappuccino, freshen up back upstairs, and come join me in the workshop," Eden suggested. "I have something I want to show you."

I glanced over at Cora.

"I'll be in the kitchen making up some vanilla-rose batter," she said, in a clipped voice. Then she headed to the door, chucking the glass shards into a nearby wastebasket as she exited.

. . .

AFTER WASHING UP, I SLIPPED outside and shyly approached
the detached studio. The bronze face on the doorknob
smirked up at me today, as if in recognition. It took only the
tiniest of twists, and the Dutch door swung open. The familiar smells rushed back to me: hearth and hot cocoa and
sun-soaked floorboards. Almost a shorthand in my brain by
now for coziness and creativity.

Eden sat bent over her worktable, the upper knobs of
her spine visible where she'd swept up her hair. It took her a
long moment to disengage from the scraps of fabric she was
moving around the table to register my entrance. "Come
in," she said.

I approached her worktable, my eyes sliding over Sam's
workspace. It was impossible to overlook. The edges of the
calla lilies had turned brittle and brown by now, and the
sight made my heart clench.

Girl, you need to get back here and water your plants.

"What did you want to show me?" I asked Eden.

She gave me a chagrined look. "Okay, okay. I might
have had some ulterior motives luring you out here to the
studio. The truth is . . . I'm really starting to worry about
this bridal pin that Sam was working on. The wedding is
coming up fast and—maybe this is my fault, but I haven't
had the heart to tell the bride."

I peered down at the beautiful canoe-shaped piece on
the tabletop. My fingers itched.

"I wonder," Eden said quietly, "if you'd consider stepping in during Sam's absence. To finish the brooch, and

avoid disappointing our bride. We would pay you for your time, of course . . ."

I shook my head. "No. I don't think so."

"Why not?"

"Because. It just . . . wouldn't feel right."

"I understand." Eden touched her chignon, looked down at the ground. "Though, if I'm being honest? It's what Sam would want. I know her and she would hate the idea of one of her brides being caught in a bind."

Against my will, my feet carried me directly to Sam's workbench. There, I closed my fingers over the loose pearl drops. Eden was probably right—Sam was the kind of person to throw herself into projects with abandon. Back in high school, when we were working together on jewelry for long stretches over the weekend, she'd often forget to eat, forget she had a phone. It made sense that she was so fiercely dedicated to her bridal clients here at Beloved.

"I can try," I said quietly. "But I'm not taking any money." Maybe a superstitious part of me hoped that if I started fooling with Sam's jewelry, she'd feel it, like she was still tethered to it all by an invisible thread. If there was any chance of yanking her back home, I'd take it.

"Deal."

I released the pearl drops onto the workstation; they rolled to a halt inches from the ceramic vase, sitting there like rounded molars. My palms prickled, grabby and eager to finish this brooch, then create the earrings I'd envisioned on the widow's walk. But my impulses were all tangled up in guilt. Was this even appropriate to be doing when Sam was missing? Shouldn't I be out doing something more active—

putting up more posters, checking back in with the Mendezes—rather than making jewelry?

"It would be such a help to Sam," Eden said, as if reading my mind. "To us all. Maybe just play around for a few minutes and see if you get any ideas?"

I swallowed. "I don't know. I haven't done this in a really long time."

"Courage, Liv. Have some courage. Besides, it's just like riding a bike. I think Sam had a sketch somewhere around here . . ." Eden came over to Sam's station, crouched down, and pulled a lavender notebook from a wire shelf near the ground. She flipped through it for a minute before setting it in front me. "Bingo."

With a jolt, I recognized Sam's meticulous pencilwork from high school. The same fine lines and crosshatching that built shadow and depth and lifted her figures off the page. I dared to touch my fingertip to the textured graphite.

"I'll be right over here." Eden was already back at her own sewing station. She tapped her phone and languid electronic music swelled through the studio. Then Eden smoothed her pale hair, dropped into her battered rolling chair, and resumed fiddling with her swatches of fabric.

I studied Sam's drawing closely. She clearly had grown as an artist since high school—likely through those art classes she took and her subsequent work at the boutique. Working alongside other artists had probably pushed her, too.

I sifted through the supply trunk and found some additional beads that looked as though they might match her drawing. Then, I began to arrange them on the tabletop, using the sketch as reference. *Courage,* I reminded myself. I knew how to do this. Eden's ambient music filtered through me, melding with my heartbeat. My breath slowed and deepened. This felt . . . good. Eden was right. Just like riding a bike.

Next came measuring and cutting the wire. Sam's pliers bit through the wire as if it were made of butter. There was something so delightful about using such high-quality tools. It made me almost giddy.

Soon, I lost myself. I'd once read an article online citing research from some psychologist who'd described "flow": a state of complete immersion. I'd felt it before while making jewelry with Sam, but never to this extent. Working on this brooch felt like ceding myself to the ocean. I'd been swept away—and yet somehow, I was acutely aware of Eden beside me at her own workstation. So aware, in fact, that for a moment, I looked down at my workstation and saw Eden's dark nails manipulating the gauges of wire I'd so carefully cut.

A blink, and Eden's hands snapped back into my own skin. But now I felt a second presence, like a phantom appendage. Was it possible I was feeling Cora, at work in the kitchen? Whatever it was, it felt a part of me, just like Eden had. Nested in my very cells and tacky as Saran Wrap.

Minutes passed, or maybe days.

Then—Eden wrenched me from my trance by jostling my shoulder. "Liv, hey. You okay there?"

I dropped my tools with a clatter on the workbench, pressed a hand to my collarbone. It was fiery to the touch. "I . . ."

"You've been at it for three hours. I didn't want to disturb you, but Cora and I—"

"Three hours?"

Eden nodded.

I shook my head in disbelief, running a hand through my tangled hair. It was the same sensation of losing time with Sam back in high school. Sam's stepmom had always barged in with plates of snacks or drinks, concerned we didn't feel the need to eat or hydrate. But what I'd experienced here in Eden's workshop was ten times more powerful, as though some invisible force had snaked around me and buried its talons in my brain, refusing to let go.

Now, I glanced up at Eden. "Is it always like that when you guys are working here? So . . . electrifying?"

A small smile crossed Eden's face. "I guess you could say that."

"Why?"

A shrug. "Must be something in the water."

"Bullshit, Eden." I wasn't going to let her get away with brushing off my questions again.

She sighed. "Fine, okay. How do I explain this?" She thought for a moment, eyes rolled up to the ceiling, then snapped her fingers in revelation. "You know that feeling when you look up at the stars, and it really hits you: those pinpricks of light are suns? With other solar systems rotating around them? And then you feel connected to something so much bigger than yourself, but you don't stop too long to think about it because you know it would just freak you out?"

I nodded.

"It's the same thing. Whenever we're at work—together, in this house—I truly believe we become a part of something greater than ourselves. Because let's be real: Cora and I aren't the first women to band together in the name of mutual creation. Think of all the artist colonies before us. When we work on our craft, together, it's like being pulled into this slipstream. We're somehow able to tap into the very same energy produced by generations of creative sisterhoods before us. And if you're anything like me?" Eden lowered her voice to a whisper. "Once you get a taste of it, there's no walking away."

I fought down sudden goosebumps marching across my neck. Without a doubt, it was the same feeling that had seized me making jewelry with Sam, and up until now, I hadn't allowed myself to relive it.

I could see how Eden might be right about being unable to walk away.

"Now I'm really sorry, but Cora and I have plans tonight. I don't mean to be rude, but . . ."

I stared at Eden. It took me an embarrassingly long moment to realize she was asking me to leave.

"Oh! Okay. No problem. I should be heading home, anyway." I began gathering the tools on the workbench and packing them carefully back into the teal supply trunk.

"You can just leave that," Eden said curtly. When I looked at her in question, she gave me a tense smile. "Cora and I will take care of it."

Eden left me in the driveway outside the studio, trying to gather my wits. I was still in a trance from working on the pin; Eden's abrupt dismissal had given me whiplash.

Was it something I said?

Reluctantly, I headed to the front of the property to call an Uber. The temperature had dipped overnight, leaving frost crystals on the fallen leaves and browned shrubbery. But the further I got, the more resistance I felt, as if my very joints were being yanked by rubber bands. What could Eden and Cora be doing that was so important right now? And why couldn't they have done whatever it was in front of me? Eden had seemed so eager to kick me out of the studio. Had she gotten annoyed at how absorbed I'd been in my jewelry making? Unlikely—she seemed to relate to that tidal feeling of immersion I'd experienced. But it seemed almost cruel to offer me a taste of it . . . only to rip it away.

In fact, the more I thought about it, the more it pissed me off.

Impulsively, I circled back to the bank of windows to the bridal salon and knelt on the grass. The cold seeped through my jeans, chilling me instantly. Then I dared to lift my head, fingers gripping the outer sill, just high enough to peek within the salon.

While I'd been absorbed in my work in the studio, Cora must have set up an easel at the front of the room. Eden stood beside it now. I shifted to get a better view. There was a large photograph poised on the easel, but from where I crouched, I couldn't make it out.

Eden said something, and it sounded like a growl through the windowpane. From my vantage point outside, the soft lighting glowed warm through the window. Inviting. If I thought hard, I could even summon the floral smell of the bridal salon. It had made me lightheaded during my initial consultation—why hadn't I appreciated it then? I clutched my jacket tighter around my body and shifted in the wet grass to keep my legs from falling asleep beneath me.

Cora was lighting candles throughout the salon with a long match. Why the fanfare? There were only two of them standing there. It made me think of what Everett had told me back in high school. *Eden was always hush-hush about things she did with Avery and Cora.*

That same wild intrigue stirred within me again. What the hell were they doing?

A loud snap in the trees by the driveway had Eden and Cora whirling to look in my direction. I flattened myself to the ground, heart hammering. Had I acted in time? It was too risky to look back in the window just yet.

I held my breath, waiting for Eden to resume speaking. *Go back to your candles,* I thought, desperately. *Please.*

Silence yawned back at me.

Suddenly—the groan of the front door.

Shit, shit, shit.

Eden's tall leather boots appeared in front of me.

"Oh," she said. "It seems we've got ourselves a little Peeping Liv."

Make up an excuse. Think fast.

But I didn't even have the time. A second later, Cora had appeared beside Eden and forced a blindfold over my eyes.

22

THEN

EFORE LONG, EVERETT AND I WERE MEETING UP AS OFTEN as once a week. I lied to Sam and told her I had started working with a math tutor to cover for my absences. The days I planned to meet up with Everett, I'd wake a half hour early to shower and go through the painstaking process of removing every errant hair on my body. Exfoliate and moisturize. The school day would crawl by until I finally got to meet Everett in the senior lot. Then he'd drive us somewhere scenic and appropriately remote—Jacob's Beach, Stony Creek. During the drive up, waiting for Everett's touch, my body would coil around itself, so sore and hungry. It scared me how much I craved him. Maybe it was this feral quality of mine that attracted Everett and kept him coming back for more.

For months I suffered whiplash, feinting back and forth between the Mendez twins. Both Sam and Everett elicited fierce reactions in me. With Sam, it was all about being swept up in that tidal thrum of mutual creation; with Everett, it was carnal, but no less consuming. Not surprisingly, my grades began to falter. It took Herculean mental energy navigating this dance, but giving it up—either side of it— was unthinkable.

Everett never asked me to be his girlfriend. I told myself I didn't mind, that there were obvious obstacles in place. Sam. Our very different social strata. But sometimes, lying spent in the back of Everett's Jeep as he trailed his fingers over my flushed skin, I thought of what he'd said about Eden. *Eden didn't seem to want anything . . . serious.* Clearly, Everett had. Eden must have had some edge over me. Rather than feeling jealous, I grew fixated on her. I stared at her when we passed in the hallways, trying to peel back the layers of her enigma. Was it the tattoo? The striking brows and distinctive nose? Or maybe it was the rusted edge of something secret and dangerous that Everett and I both glimpsed on Mischief Night.

Because Everett never made any attempt to define our relationship, it surprised me when one afternoon in the back of his Jeep, Everett grazed my collarbone with the tip of his finger and said, "I'm thinking of taking a gap year before college to explore Europe. You should come."

I sat up, with a harsh laugh. "Yeah, right."

"I'm serious." And his face was. "Imagine what it would be like not having to hide like this. Just to be together out in the open."

My heart jumped into my throat. I'd never heard Everett so earnest before. I'd also never dared consider the fact that he wanted to be with me, where everyone could see.

"You know I applied to RISD," I said, in a low voice. "With Sam." We planned on requesting each other as roommates—which frightened me just a little, if I was being honest. Sam had already picked out our future mini fridge and curtains.

"I know. Just think about it, though."

I did, toying with Everett's words over the next few days like ocean-smoothed stones.

Soon it was Valentine's Day. Our school had set up a flower-delivery service. For a dollar, you could buy a friend a carnation and send a personalized note on a heart-shaped card. I should have anticipated that the students would, of course, twist the event into a glorified popularity contest. Accordingly, girls paraded down the hallways with clouds of carnations and stacks of cards they riffled through like dollar bills. But the true envy of the school? Those handful of girls who had managed to snag boyfriends and received full bouquets of carnations, all deep red.

I got one carnation for Sam and received two. One pink with the note *Can't wait to be RISD roomies xoxo S.* The other one was yellow, and said, simply, FROM: YOUR PARAMOUR.

"What is *that*?" Sam howled, snatching at the card to read it closer.

"Must've been a joke," I said, pulling it away from her. But just then, I caught Everett's eye two tables over in the cafeteria. The small smile on his lips told me everything I needed to know, and my heart began to thump with emotion.

This was way better than a bouquet of red carnations.

The Sisterhood, it seemed, had taken a different ap-proach to Valentine's Day. They entered the cafeteria toting identical bouquets of strange gray flowers tied with bits of ribbon.

"What are those?" I asked Sam, nodding in their direction.

"Dried snapdragons," she said, rolling her eyes. "They bring them in every year."

"You mean, The Sisterhood got each other dead flowers for Valentine's Day?"

"I shit you not."

I couldn't stop glancing in their direction, trying to see more of these odd, desiccated bouquets. Where had the girls gotten those strange blooms? Had they tied them up with ribbons themselves? It wasn't until I sat down in my sixth-period English class that I got a close-up view. One of the girls must have been sitting in my seat the period before, because there was a single dried flower lying in the pencil groove of my desk. I picked it up, rotating it between my fingers. I held a gray, oblong seedpod with three scalloped-edged holes, coincidentally in the configuration of a human face.

It was the most exquisite little skull I'd ever seen.

23

NOW

HANDS GRABBED MY SHOULDERS, HELD ME DOWN.

Reflexively, I struggled away.

"Hey, it's okay, Liv. This was all part of the plan, right? You want to be a part of our group, don't you?"

To my humiliation, a whimper caught in my throat.

Cora clicked her tongue. "Oh, hush. It's going to be okay. Take my hand." Cold fingers against mine. I gripped out of fear, because it was the only thing tethering me to the world.

I let her pull me away.

When the blindfold was removed, I found myself sitting in a wicker chair in Sam's room. With the shades drawn, the room was dark, save for a single candle guttering on the bureau.

Eden materialized from the shadows.

"W-what's going on?" I demanded.

"Liv, relax. There's nothing to be afraid of. In fact, you should be excited." Eden's black brows leaped into peaks. "Tonight, you get to become one of us!"

"That's right," said Cora, beside me. "Eden and I talked, and we think you're ready to join. Officially."

I was breathing hard, my chest rising and falling in the mirror across the room. The tender spot in the back of my head where the blindfold had been knotted pulsed with pain. I had the sensation of stepping back into the Guilford Fair fun house, the entrance shifting underfoot. This was absurd. I'd volunteered to help the girls with a brooch. I never asked to join . . . whatever Eden and Cora had going on in their bridal boutique. Some bizarre reincarnation of The Sisterhood from high school, maybe? I remembered Cora's words on the widow's walk. *Your talent amazes us.* Running through the woods with sparklers, gallivanting through that enchanted attic raining with flower petals.

Of course this was about more than just a brooch.

"What . . ." I wet my lips. "What about Sam?"

"I'm glad you asked," Eden said. "It's time we came clean about that. Sam is safe, Liv. She's in Cora's aunt's cabin in upstate New York, hiding out from her abusive ex."

My mind scrambled with the new information. Hot anger was the first emotion to register.

I spun around in the wicker chair. "Why the hell didn't you tell me this earlier?"

"We can't tell anyone because Brendan hasn't been detained yet," Cora supplied. "The second the information leaks, he'll go straight to her."

My chest was heaving. "You can't just keep this information to yourselves. There's an active investigation going on. And Sam's poor family—"

"Stop it, Liv." Eden gripped my wrist with startling force. "We know what we're doing, okay? We have to protect Sam. Brendan nearly broke her arm the night she fled town."

I sat back in the chair, shivering. I thought of Brendan hammering the lid of my paint container back in the hardware store.

I knew there was something I didn't like about him.

"Once the police take Brendan into custody, it'll be safe for Sam to come back," Eden said, releasing her grip of my arm at last. "We couldn't tell you because we didn't know how you'd react if you knew the truth. After all, you'd been out of Sam's life for so long."

I scrambled to make sense of everything. Had Eden and Cora really orchestrated this whole production to shuttle Sam to safety? It was a risky move, sure to get them in deep trouble with law enforcement if the truth ever came to light. But if they were as dedicated to Sam as they seemed . . .

"It's a lot to take in," Eden acknowledged.

I gripped the arms of the chair, gnawing the inside of my lip. The girls' explanation, at least, connected all the dots from the investigation thus far. Sam's hasty departure. The restraining order and the lipstick knife and even the alarming letter Sam had sent to my Boston apartment. But something still wasn't sitting well with me.

"When it's safe for Sam to come home, she'll be overjoyed to find you here," Cora said quietly.

"She wants you to be a part of this so desperately," Eden agreed. "One could say it's all she ever wanted for you."

That let loose an avalanche of emotion, so intense I felt woozy.

"Take a moment," Eden murmured.

I steeled myself, drawing in a giant breath. Then I opened my eyes and looked directly at her. "What exactly would this entail?"

"We-ell." Eden slunk a bit closer. "To be a part of The Sisterhood, you must exhibit commitment of the highest caliber. You must be *focused*—on your Sisters, on your craft, and on The Sisterhood as a whole."

So The Sisterhood had never fizzled out after graduation. The invocation of their high school group name chilled me. But the truth of the matter? Something about these girls—their siren song of a house, their gorgeous dinners and sun-warmed studio—yanked at me on a cellular level.

"That means," Eden went on, "eliminating distractions. Like any work outside of The Sisterhood."

Fortunately, I didn't have any other work to speak of.

"And romantic partners," Cora said. "Boyfriends, fiancés, et cetera."

And just like that, a harpoon of panic shattered the spell.

"I know," Eden said, towering over me now. She smoothed a hand over the top of my hair, just as she'd done to Cora the other night. "I figured that would be a bitter pill for you to swallow. But I want you to slow down and think very carefully about what you say next, okay?"

My heartbeat was thunderous now. I thought of Noah. Sweet, patient Noah.

This was such a ridiculous ask, I was rendered speechless.

Wait a second. A sickening realization dawned. No romantic partners, Cora had said. *Boyfriends, fiancés, et cetera.*

Yet the girls had claimed not to know about Brendan.

We have no clue, Eden had said, when the news broke about the restraining order. *It must have been some random guy that set his sights on Sam . . .*

Slowly, Eden pulled her hand away from my hair, leaving me cold. "Take a minute to process everything. You're standing at a crossroads."

She was damn right I was at a crossroads. How could Eden have forgotten her slipup? Sitting there in Sam's darkened room, the knowledge spread through me like a poison: Eden and Cora had known Sam had a boyfriend—and Sam had ostensibly joined The Sisterhood pledging never to have a romantic partner. Had Eden and Cora found out about Brendan and gotten upset? Could this have been motive to threaten Sam?

Hurt her?

My heart plummeted in terror.

Cora made a cluck of sympathy. "She'll make the right choice," she said, as if I weren't sitting right there before them, vibrating with anxiety. Then she tilted her head to one side. "Or maybe she won't."

"It's just—"

Eden silenced me with a finger to my lips. "I saw you

working in the studio today, Liv. It's intoxicating, isn't it? I'll admit, I felt a pang of envy just watching."

Despite my churning panic, a flicker of curiosity registered. Eden Holloway, jealous of *me*?

"But," Eden added, "I worry about you. I see you with all this potential. And yet you're so afraid of your own power." She reached out to turn over the pad of my index finger. Even in the dimness of the room, that angry welt was visible: the site of my self-inflicted punishment to halt unwelcome thoughts.

"This?" Eden said, gripping my finger. "This drives me absolutely batty." Then she let it drop to my lap. In a quieter voice, she added, "Why turn this against yourself? You shouldn't be afraid of your own power, Liv. What you should be afraid of? The world trying to strip you of it."

I looked down at the wicker armrest, the straws swimming huge in my vision. I'd tamped down unwelcome, violent thoughts because I'd been terrified of losing control. Of summoning the monster that stewed beneath the polished Liv-veneer, that I'd watched rage in my own father's body. Could it be that this same impulse was wrapped up in the "power" that Eden was citing? That part of what made me so valuable in Eden's eyes was something I'd actively resisted my entire life?

But more importantly: Was I looking into the faces of the people responsible for Sam's disappearance? The longer I sat with the possibility, the heavier it grew. What had Brendan told me? *My personal theory is that there's someone in her life who is really controlling and didn't want her seeing anyone. Maybe a family member.*

Maybe her roommates.

"Thus tonight's crossroads," Eden was saying. "Of course, it's up to you. There will be no judgment at all if you decide this isn't what you want. But my wish for you, Liv?" She took my chin in her hands, tilted my face up to her. "I want you to thrive. I want you to be buoyed by the support of your Sisters. I want you to be creatively fulfilled all the days of your life." She paused. "That being said, I'm afraid if you decline our offer, we really can't be spending any more time together."

My heart sped. *No.* I couldn't lose this lead on Sam, moments after discovering it. If Eden and Cora had anything to do with Sam's disappearance, I needed to stay close to them. I needed to find incontestable evidence to bring to Detective Patterson—

Keep them talking, I commanded myself. *Don't let on that you've spotted their lie.*

"Are you sure . . ." I called up more saliva. "Are you sure I can't have all of that *and* a fiancé?"

The girls were nodding, solemn-faced.

"If you can't handle it, best let us know now," Cora said.

Eden crossed her arms over her chest. "Remember I told you about how important it is for us to eliminate distractions? Well, you could choose to embrace them, as so many women do. Get married to that boyfriend of yours. Start a family. And that's just great, if that's what you want. But I warn you: that choice comes with a price."

Cora's tongue flicked out to touch the edge of her mouth.

"What price?" I whispered, even though in the attic-like recesses of my mind, I knew I'd already stuffed the answer.

"A life of self-sacrifice," Eden said, "and an excruciating creative death."

"Ha!" I blurted, thinking she must be kidding. When no one laughed, I added, in a small voice, "That sounds a tad extreme, doesn't it?"

Eden and Cora remained silent.

I cleared my throat. "I mean, is it really that black-and-white? Come on, guys, it's not the 1920s anymore. Plenty of women have families and careers and fulfilling personal lives at the same time. They can . . . what do they say? They can have it all."

The girls stared at me. Then they burst out laughing.

It was such an ugly laugh.

Once they sobered, Cora and Eden watched me as I trembled against the biting wicker chair. They were really serious about this. But how? How had they made such a gutting decision themselves? Rationally, I understood why they had built their mission around the wedding industry: because, as Eden explained, it represented a unique touch-point for them to reach brides. But how did they move through all the fixings of the wedding world—all the bridal gowns and jewelry and cakes—knowing they'd never have any of it for themselves?

"I know what's going on with you," Eden said, eyes narrowing. "I can tell you're in a relationship where you find yourself . . . on a precipice. You've been asked to take a chisel to yourself, to your identity. Stop for a moment and really think about it. What do you think this is going to feel like in five years? Ten years?"

I closed my eyes, as if I could block out Eden's words. I imagined giving Noah the life he wanted. Four children, my career on the backburner. I flashed back to Penny's sallow face and lumpy body. Her perennial exhaustion. It was a life that threatened to swallow me whole, that left no room for the electric tide of creating to which Eden and Cora had reintroduced me. How had Penny put it? *I used to write twenty-page papers on Klimt. On Van Gogh. Now I don't have the brain power—let alone the time—to read more than a headline in a tabloid.*

I felt nauseous.

"You don't have to say yes, you know," Cora said. "Some girls just aren't cut out for The Sisterhood. Most aren't."

"She's right," Eden said. "After high school, Avery decided she didn't want to swear into The Sisterhood for real. She wasn't willing to make the commitment, and we were completely understanding."

So The Sisterhood had ended up scaring Avery off. It didn't surprise me, given their extreme requirements.

Eden's eyes settled back on me. "So what's it going to be, Liv? Forgo marriage and kids, and lead a life of creative fulfillment? Or have a family, and lose yourself?"

My mouth was bone-dry. It took a couple of moments to formulate words. "I don't get it," I managed to whisper at last. "Why does it have to be one or the other?"

It was the first time Eden had turned away from me all night. "I don't make the rules, Liv. If you're a woman? Those are your two options."

Every rational shred of my mind ordered me to stand up and march out of that pink house forever. But this was the closest I'd come to forging new ground on Sam's disappearance. Eden and Cora had already been cleared by the police; with their powers of persuasion, it was going to take a hell of a lot more to implicate them than a measly description of The Sisterhood's requirements. Besides, it was all so ludicrous coming from the owners of a bridal boutique—no romantic partners, no marriage!—I doubted the police would even believe me. No, if I was going to pin Sam's disappearance on The Sisterhood for real, I had to stick close and find absolutely damning evidence. An incriminating text message. A weapon. *Something.*

"She'll make the right choice," said Cora, and I wasn't sure if she had indeed spoken once more, or if my mind was merely playing back her words like the snatch of a melody. *Or maybe she won't.*

An anemic flicker of hope: How would they even know I was still with Noah? They wouldn't be able to tell if I was still texting him. Plus, he didn't even live in Guilford. I almost laughed aloud with relief; the solution was so obvious.

I flipped my eyes open to the dark room and to Cora and Eden staring back at me. Took another breath.

"I choose you," I said.

"Great!" Cora chirped. She handed me my phone. "Now prove it."

Her words knocked the spirit from my body.

Eden put a hand to her collarbone as if affronted. "No offense, Liv, but you just expect us to take your word for it? This is a big deal. We need to make sure you're committed."

"You can't—" My voice cracked. "You can't possibly expect me to break up with my partner of eight years on the spot. While you watch."

The girls shrugged at me.

"We tend to have high expectations," Eden admitted.

So they'd called my bluff after all. I sat immobilized in the chair, the wicker biting into my lower back.

"Maybe this will help," Eden said. She placed a hand on my shoulder.

Her touch jolted me into the alcoves of my own mind. I saw my own body, as if I were floating along the ceiling, Noah beside me. The Liv standing on the ground—main character Liv—loosened something on her finger. My engagement ring? She handed it to Noah and turned away as he raked his hands through his hair in distress. Main character Liv's eyes were empty of emotion. She strode away from Noah with confidence—straight into the waiting arms of seventeen-year-old Sam. She was wearing the same ripped fishnets and braid she'd worn on the first day of school.

Suddenly, I was back in the bedroom with the guttering candle. My face was wet.

"How are you feeling?" Eden inquired softly.

I touched a fingertip to my tears and scanned my body for those hulking emotions I'd expect after witnessing the breakup of my own engagement. Disbelief. Horror. Pain.

Instead, I felt only a bone-deep relief, spreading warmth through me like a cup of tea through rain-soaked limbs.

I snatched my phone from Eden and sat back down. I wouldn't really call Noah's number, of course, but I made a convincing show of calling up my Favorite contacts. I'd saved our go-to pizza place as three pink hearts: an inside joke, as Noah often accused me of loving their mozzarella sticks more than him. What irony—but it did allow me to flash my phone screen at Eden and Cora, the trio of hearts perched above the line Calling Mobile.

It rang three times, as it always did during the dinner rush.

"No answer," I told the girls.

Eden shrugged. "Then leave a voicemail."

I bit down on my bottom lip. This would be an interesting voicemail for the restaurant to unearth tomorrow morning.

After a breezy male greeting, the tone sounded.

"Hi, it's me. I . . . I know we got into it the other day, and I wanted to thank you for giving me some space to think things through. This is so hard to tell you, but I don't think I can marry you, Noah. It's become clear we want such different things in life. I'm so sorry."

I hit End and stared at the lock screen on my phone: a picture of Noah with his arms around me in Hawaii. My throat was clogged with tears, despite knowing that the only person privy to my "breakup" would be a befuddled restaurant worker tomorrow morning.

I was horrified by how easily the words had flowed out of me.

The girls were at my side in an instant.

"I'm proud of you." Cora laid her head on my shoulder.

"You did the right thing," Eden said. She patted my back.

For the first time, I flinched against their touch. If these girls had a hand in Sam's disappearance, I wanted nothing to do with them. Except, of course, that I'd just agreed to join The Sisterhood in the hopes of uncovering dirt on Eden and Cora.

I could feel it in my bones: it was going to be a long night.

Eden stood and clapped her hands together once. "Alright. Let's get you ready for tonight. Hair, makeup, dress . . ."

"Absolutely!" Cora hugged me, smiling into my hair. "Tonight is going to be all about you."

24

THEN

I HOPED EVERETT COULDN'T SEE HOW MY HAND WAS SHAKING
as I fumbled with the lock on the front door. Mom and
Dad had some parents' meeting at the high school, which
meant our house was—for once—blissfully unsupervised.
Though I relished the opportunity to be with Everett outside the confines of his Jeep, it made me jumpy to think of
the possibility of my parents returning home early. What if
the meeting ran short or they got an important phone call
and had to turn around? Even easygoing Mom would have
some choice words to say about finding me home alone
with a boy.

I couldn't bring myself to imagine Dad's reaction.

Everett went immediately to the stairs to the second
floor when I let him in. He found my room easily and started
studying the knickknacks on my dresser. I'd never even
thought to sort through them in order to weed out the most

embarrassing and juvenile. I looked away, feeling flushed and exposed.

"Aw," Everett said. "Wait a second. Is this . . . you?" I didn't even have to look over to know what he was referencing: the clay-faced puppet Mom had crafted for me when I was twelve. She'd shaped the eyes—slightly downturned and blue—and added a ponytail of brown yarn.

"Maybe," I mumbled, looking at the ground.

"Dare I ask why you have a creepy puppet twin?"

"Well. I may or may not have been an aspiring ventriloquist at one point in time."

Everett's eyes went round. "Are you joking?"

"Unfortunately, no."

"Liv. You've been holding out on me." Everett approached me, pressed his lips to my neck and made me shiver. "I swear, with every tidbit of information I learn about you, the more fascinating you get."

I turned to liquid in his arms. This was what I found so intoxicating about Everett—besides his dark eyes and fiendish smirk, that is. Everett was seemingly mesmerized by peeling back the layers of me, by truly seeing me. His twin was wonderful in different ways—her brash nature, the secret softness stowed beneath. But much as I loved Sam, she had a very particular idea of who I was and grew outraged if I exhibited behavior that ran counter to this. Sometime over the course of the school year, I'd grown weary trying to push back against Sam's projection of easygoing, compliant Liv.

The role was getting old.

Everett and I ended up entangled on my bed, such a

luxury after months in the back seat of a truck. I wished I could forget about the looming possibility of Mom and Dad coming home early so I could truly savor the moment: stretching out my body fully for Everett to touch, marveling at his sinewy muscle moving over me.

It seemed Everett was distracted, too. At one point, he rolled off me, and crossed to the other side of the room. With a rattling sound, he spun a picture roughly around so it was facing the wall.

Oh God. The picture of Sam and me in our ice skates.

"It was just staring at me," he said, crossing back to my bed. He twined his fingers in my hair and pulled my face to his, but the energy behind his kiss had shifted. I responded halfheartedly: I knew the mood had been shot the moment Everett spotted that photo. Shame on me—I should've prepared for his visit; I should've known better.

The sudden grinding of tires on gravel made me spring from the bed.

"What now?" Everett groaned.

I peeked out the window down into the driveway, my heart in my throat. Not my parents' car—the mail truck. In went a bundle of mail, the copper flag on our mailbox flipped down.

I turned back to Everett. "Sorry. The mail just came and—I'm supposed to be hearing back from schools any day now."

Everett rolled his eyes and flopped back down on the bed. Since that day in his Jeep when Everett had proposed taking a gap year together, he'd only been strengthening his case, showing me his itinerary as it took form. It wasn't his style to ask me directly, but he'd make playful veiled remarks like, *I wonder what it would be like to have sex in every European city we visit* and *I think you'd look so hot with one of those French haircuts. You know, with the bangs?* I knew he wasn't wild about the idea of me going to RISD with Sam.

I pulled on my clothes and dashed downstairs.

At the mailbox, my hands gripped a pile of junk mail—coupons, credit card applications, and a magazine for ugly, sack-like women's clothing. Disappointment flooded in as I thumbed through. Then, toward the very bottom—a bulky envelope with a seallike insignia. I shoved it under the magazine, almost afraid to look at it for too long, and hurried back to the house.

Wait, I told myself. *Get inside and open it properly.*

Giddy, I ditched the junk mail in the kitchen and pounded up the stairs with the big envelope. Sure enough, it was the RISD insignia, curlicues like treble clefs spreading above and below the acronym. Fragments of the next four years of my life were starting to coalesce into a dazzling mosaic. Rooming with Sam. Purple curtains and a mini fridge. No more science or math classes! Instead: long days of studios and critiques and pounding Red Bull to meet deadlines, all the while doing what I—what we—loved to do.

In the doorway to my bedroom, I brandished the giant envelope like a flag. "Look!" Then I tore into it, before I could even clock Everett's response.

We are delighted to welcome you . . .

I screamed.

"Whoa there." Everett joined me at the doorway.

"I got in! I can't believe I got in! Oh my God, Sam better have gotten in, too . . ."

"Congrats." Everett sauntered back over to the bed and sat down on the edge, swiping a hand through his hair. He looked weary.

Amidst all the excitement, something unsavory turned over in me. Why couldn't Everett be excited about my acceptance? He was practically pouting.

I grabbed my phone. "I need to text Sam. I wonder if the mail truck hits your place before or after mine."

"So you're definitely going," Everett said. He meant it as a question—he had to—but there was no inflection.

"I mean." I contemplated the ragged-ended envelope. I hadn't even read the entire acceptance letter yet, nor all the forms within. There was so much left to savor. "That was the plan. Sam and I wanted to room together."

"I know." Now Everett was reaching for his shirt.

"What? Why are you being so weird?"

"I'm not being weird. I'm just worried you haven't thought this through."

Thought this through? What was there to think about? I'd gotten into my dream school and would—hopefully—be attending with my best friend. We already had our room designed, down to the curtains.

"I just see the way Sam treats you sometimes," Everett said. "She's kind of . . . dominant. And you go along with it, because you have a good heart."

"Oh, come on," I said. "It's not that bad." Even so, dark knowing was spreading through me.

"I mean, only you can be the judge of that. But do you really want this dynamic for the next four years of your life? College is all about spreading your wings, becoming your own person . . ."

My heart dropped. Everett's words took me right back to Mischief Night. Right before our first, electric kiss, I'd looked up to him and spilled my guts. *Sometimes I worry . . . that I'm Sam's little pet.*

These days, most of our time together was frictionless. But every so often, that prickly side of Sam would surface— the same one that manipulated me to throw the egg at Eden's house. Was it just that Sam had her moments? Or was she reacting to those perilous instances in which she felt her control of me slipping away?

A pounding noise thundered downstairs and I nearly leaped out of my skin.

I rushed to the window again. My ribs were a vise around my lungs. If Mom and Dad had just pulled in, I was absolutely screwed. There was no way we'd be able to get Everett out . . .

Sam's green VW bug was parked askew in the driveway.

"Shit." I spun toward Everett. "It's your sister."

I'd never seen Everett's eyes so wild. "Well, get her out of here!"

I practically flew down the staircase, my hair tangling over my face. The pounding on the door was growing louder, more insistent. As I rounded the corner into the kitchen, I saw Sam through the screen door clutching an identical thick white envelope. She wore a T-shirt printed to look like pink-and-green argyle and a thick belt studded with spikes. Though I knew from context clues she must be elated, her face was creased with frustration: I wasn't coming to the door fast enough.

She threw open the door the second she saw me. "We're going to RISD! Holy shit, we did it!"

I grinned over the top of Sam's head as she hugged me.

Sam pulled away from me to read my face. "Did you see the roommate request form?"

"No, I haven't finished going through all the stuff . . ."

"Wait, where's your envelope?" Her eyes scanned the kitchen.

A firework of panic in my chest. I'd been in such a rush to halt Sam's entrance into the house that I'd forgotten my acceptance letter up in my bedroom. The very room that was, at this second, occupied by Sam's half-naked twin.

"I'll show you later," I said, but it was too late—my own eyes had betrayed me, cutting past the living room and to the staircase leading to the second floor.

It was all the invitation Sam needed. She was familiar enough with my house to know what my glance insinuated, and headed in the direction of my bedroom, stomping stair by stair.

I scrambled to stop her. "Wait. Can we just—?"

But there was no viable excuse for why Sam shouldn't go to my room—it was where we hung out every time she came over. It felt like there was a giant splinter lodged in my throat; it hurt to breathe. I wasn't going to be able to stop Sam. Would Everett have the good sense to hide when he heard her footsteps? I prayed he'd at least finished putting on his pants.

To my immense relief, my bedroom was apparently empty when Sam and I entered. Everett must have stowed himself in my closet or the bathroom down the hall. Sam zeroed in on the RISD envelope discarded on my bed and began riffling through.

"Oh my God, Liv." She looked up at me, eyes wide. "You didn't tell me you got a full ride."

Delight flashed through my panic. "I did?"

"Hell yeah! And here's that roommate form I was talking about." She extracted a piece of paper and placed it on the comforter. "By the way, I think we should shoot for East Hall so we can get a suite . . ."

I zoned out, doing a sweep of my room for traces of Everett. Where the hell had he hidden? Sam was so distracted by RISD minutiae that it seemed we'd averted disaster—she'd never think to go look in my closet. But then an ugly thought surfaced. What if Everett was in the bathroom down the hall and she tried to use it? Now that we had my acceptance letter in hand, it was probably best to migrate downstairs . . .

Oh crap. The splinter in my windpipe seemed to double in size. Everett might have taken his pants and shirt, but he'd left his All-Stars overturned by the foot of the bed—unmistakably a boy's size, and almost certainly identifiable by his twin.

"Let's have some ice cream downstairs to celebrate," I blurted. I hadn't absorbed a single word Sam said about her campus housing research, and I was sure my panic was scrawled across my face.

Sure enough, Sam squinted at me. It reminded me of

the way she looked as she'd banged on the front door—
a combination of frustration and confusion.

"What's that?" she said, pointing.

Game over.

Except Sam wasn't moving toward Everett's All-Stars.
She was crossing the room to my dresser, and as she did so,
I kicked her twin's shoes under the bed.

Sam picked up the photo of us in our ice skates—the
same one her brother had manipulated moments earlier.
"Why is this facing the wall?"

Calm down, I coached myself through the moment, *you
can handle this.* "I don't know. My mom must've spun it by
accident."

It was a lame excuse and we both knew it. If Everett
had placed the photo face down, we could have pretended
it'd merely fallen. But to swivel a photo toward the wall took
a more deliberate action; there was no easy way to explain
that. I held my breath as Sam stared at me, fighting the
impulse to gulp.

"What is wrong with you?" she said finally.

"Nothing! I'm just still in shock—"

"No, you're being weird. You're not listening to anything I'm saying and you look guilty as hell." She blinked,
and something inscrutable passed over her face. "You didn't
even text me when you got your letter."

"I was just about to!"

"Be real with me, Liv. Do you not want to go to RISD
together?"

I should have answered in the affirmative immediately.
But, just as my face had betrayed me by looking upstairs

when Sam mentioned the envelope, my body betrayed me now by hesitating. Everett's voice was too fresh in my mind. *College is all about spreading your wings, becoming your own person . . .*

"Then don't," Sam said, tossing my acceptance letter back on the bed.

"I do, Sam. Come on."

She was already striding out of my room, clomping downstairs. My shoulders jumped to my ears when the slam of the front door reverberated through the house.

"Shit," I whispered. I sat down on my bed clutching the pried-apart envelope. Sam had seen more of it than I had.

Everett emerged from the hallway bathroom. He was laughing—out of relief or genuine amusement, I couldn't tell. "Damn. That was quite the spectacle, even for Sam."

He sat close to me on the bed, started kissing my neck again.

Really? After the shitshow of the past ten minutes, he wanted to just resume as if nothing had happened? I hadn't even really been able to process my acceptance to RISD, let alone the blind panic of having to hide Everett from Sam while pretending nothing was wrong.

"I need a minute," I snapped, pulling away. "Between the two of you, I need a fucking breather."

I felt bad as soon as I said it—I never intended my voice to sound so harsh.

Everett scooped his shoes from the ground. He left the room far more quietly than his sister.

25

NOW

I FOLLOWED EDEN AND CORA DOWN THE STEEP STAIRCASE AND
onto the dark first floor. At Eden's behest, I'd dressed in a
black full-length gown with a row of silk buttons that
pressed itchily against my spine. Now, Eden set a shadowy
veil over my face.

"Here," she said, placing a dusky bouquet into my
hands: black roses and the wilted calla lilies from the studio.
My hands shook as I wrapped them around the stems. A
thorn stuck the pad of my ring finger and I gasped, stuffing
it in my mouth.

"Oh!" Cora exclaimed brightly. "The first bloodshed of
the evening."

But before I could find my voice to ask for clarification,
Eden had looped her arm through mine. "It's time to walk,"
she said.

For the first time, the creaking staircase in this Hansel-

and-Gretel house was completely silent. Eden and I glided down, segueing onto a length of black fabric. The ends of my fingers tingled, going numb. Had Cora been serious when she said tonight would be all about me? The thought made me wither, but I clutched the dark flowers, resolute. I was doing this.

For Sam.

Outside the living room, Eden squeezed my arm. "We're so proud of you," she whispered.

We entered the dim living room, flaring with gentle light. Candles lined either side of the dark runner—if I dared to deviate from the "aisle," the flames would surely catch on my dress. Had that been an intentional design feature?

Eden led me to the center of the room, directly in front of the fireplace filled with tiers of lit candles. Then she unhooked herself from my side. Cora handed her a thick leather volume with an elaborate silver-and-blue eye on the front.

I recognized that eye. My skin went cold.

"Sisters." Eden bent her head over the book. "May the night smile upon you."

"And upon you," Cora chorused back.

The hairs lifted on my forearms.

"We gather here tonight for a momentous occasion," Eden went on. "To welcome a third member into our Inner Circle."

I flinched. *Third?* Every flame on every candle had jumped to attention, straightening into dagger-shaped points. Then, slowly, they morphed from yellow to deep indigo, the same shade as the eye on the front of Eden's book.

Eden cracked open the thick volume. It was audible—the creak of an ancient spine splitting in two. "In preparation for Liv to be inducted into our midst, we must remember the woman who started it all: Harriett Wythers."

My memory stirred. That name sounded so familiar . . .

Eden didn't even have to look down at the pages before her; it was clear they were embedded in her memory. "In 1657, Harriett and her husband Oliver arrived in Guilford. And we know from Harriett's prolific diary entries that Oliver was a monster. He tortured Harriett in every way a man can—with physical, emotional, and sexual abuse—relentlessly attempting to impregnate her, despite her desire to abstain from having children. Fortunately, however, Harriett remained 'barren,' and by 1660, Oliver was dead." Eden put a finger to her bottom lip. "Harriett never did mention in her diary how this came about, but, ladies, we're all capable of using our imagination, aren't we?"

Memory jarred me: Harriett was the woman our docent had told us about on the tour of the Wythers House, so many years ago.

"In her diary, Harriett implored women to 'open their eyes to the realities of this world.' And that is just what we seek to do today. For Harriett, and for all the women who need just a little extra help seeing clearly."

Eden looked up from the book. "Liv," she said, with a beautiful smile. At her intonation, the candle flames turned from indigo to blood red.

I gulped behind my veil.

"Please give me your hand."

I willed my hand to relinquish the bouquet, but I remained a statue. Cora giggled as Eden lifted the dark flowers from me and took my hand in her own icy one. Then she closed the ancient book and settled my palm over the cover. I felt the raised outline of that silver-and-blue eye against my skin.

"Liv," Eden intoned again, looking directly into my eyes, "it's time for you to take your vows. Are you ready?"

I squeezed my eyes shut. What the hell had I gotten myself into? What would happen if I changed my mind, told Eden no? For a moment, the words sat on the edge of my tongue: *I can't do this.* My blood pounded as I held back the syllables like an avalanche. But if I declined the offer, Eden said I wouldn't be able to speak with them anymore. And then I'd never stand a chance of figuring out what had happened to Sam.

I swallowed down my fear like a stone. "Yes," I said.

"Excellent. Then let's begin. Olivia Daniella Edwards, do you commit yourself—body, mind, and soul—to this Sisterhood?"

Hearing Eden say my full name like that made the back of my neck prickle.

"Yes," I said.

Eden's eyes crinkled. "*I do,*" she corrected.

I tried not to think of Noah. "I do."

"Do you vow to forsake all committed relationships—boyfriends, girlfriends, partners in life and in marriage—in favor of your Sisters, who stand before you tonight?"

My heart felt as if it were splintering in my chest. I tried to speak the words, but they stuck in my dry lips like staples.

"Pardon?" Eden said, not unkindly.

Shit. Could I really do this? For a moment, I dug in my heels, resolved to shuck off my veil and call it a night. But I couldn't get the vision of Sam out of my mind, with that dark braid slung over one shoulder. She'd been so ready to throw her arms around me again . . .

"I do," I said.

Eden went on. "Do you vow to choose creativity, passion, and unapologetic self-fulfillment over the martyrdom of wife- and motherhood? And to actively choose these ideals, over and over again, all the days of your life?"

"I do." This time, my words came out from behind gritted teeth. My resolve had flagged somewhat; the repetition of the vows was starting to weigh on me now. When was this going to be over?

"And do you vow to dedicate your life to helping other women see the truth?"

"Yes. I do."

"Wonderful." Eden pulled the book out from under my hand and set it down on the coffee table. "Then we're ready to commence the three trials of commitment. Cora?"

My heart was a metronome cranked to full speed. *Trials of commitment?* Eden hadn't mentioned anything about those, only a "swearing in" that Avery had opted out of. But I'd just taken my vows. Weren't we done here?

Cora disappeared from the living room for a second, only to reappear carrying a high-backed wooden chair. She carried it across the living room and deposited it beside me. I glanced down, every drop of saliva draining from my mouth.

Dangling from each armrest was a length of silk.

I staggered backward, brimming over with panic. "I'm not—"

But Cora pushed me firmly into the chair and held me there. Eden bent over me to tie the cords around my wrists. She tightened them until the material bit into my skin and I cried out in pain.

Eden continued to speak as she worked. "The trials of commitment are critical. It is one thing to recite vows, and quite another to internalize them. This is one of the many problems with wedding ceremonies, isn't it?" For a moment, she seemed to break from her script, her voice becoming almost flippant. "All this blah-blah-blah about *soulmates* and *forever* and *I promise to give you foot rubs every day for the rest of our lives.* All of it, bullshit." Then she looked down at me, catching my eye, and spoke to me in that intimate, honeyed tone that made the rest of the room fade away. "Words are cheap, and time erodes all promises that aren't sound. You must feel the weight of those vows, Liv. You need to truly understand—intellectually, emotionally, and physically— what it means to be a Sister."

I was so terrified my teeth were chattering in my jaw. I thought frantically of Avery in the woods with her bared stomach. Everett and I had run away before we'd seen what Eden had done to her. No wonder she'd decided not to join The Sisterhood for real.

The candle flames around the room shot into points again, shifting now from red to green.

Eden bent to retrieve the book from the coffee table and opened it to a new page. "In her diary, Harriett Wythers wrote, 'We have been conditioned to believe that the key to happiness is pouring ourselves into others, through marriage and children and caretaking and servitude. We must expunge those ideals. In their place, we must welcome creativity, passion, and unapologetic self-fulfillment into our lives. We must absorb these new cornerstones into our essence, into the very marrow of our bones.'"

Something was crawling out of the pages of Eden's book. I recoiled, knocking my head against the wooden back of the chair. Another one of those goddamn black beetles, with the same marking on its back as the one that adorned the book in Eden's hands.

Eden tenderly touched the white-and-blue circle on the insect's back before lifting it into her palm. "You've probably seen these beauties before," she said, cradling the hideous creature. "Not only are they a true encapsulation of all The Sisterhood stands for, they're also loyal servants. The very best little messengers. After all, we have them to thank for bringing you into our midst."

These bugs worked for The Sisterhood? My mind flashed to the first time I'd seen one of those beetles: in the outhouse of the Wythers House. Had The Sisterhood planted it there for me to see? To entice me, somehow, into this house?

Then Eden did something truly horrifying: she set the beetle against my cheek. I flinched as the little feet with its sticky spines tapped right above my mouth.

Cora restrained me as I reflexively jerked to throw the insect off my face.

"These beetles have been tasked with bringing you to us. It is your task to welcome it now—and all it represents—into your essence. Just as Harriett described."

The beetle nudged my bottom lip. Revulsion exploded within me.

No, no, no. Oh my God, no.

I was transported back to my nightmare. The only difference was, in my dream, I'd calmly welcomed that beetle into my mouth. *How?* Cora held me as I bucked against the back of the chair.

"The moment you accept it," Eden said, "your first trial will be complete."

Accept it? A beetle the size of a Ping-Pong ball was trying to force its way inside my mouth. How was I supposed to just let that happen? I snapped my head to one side and the beetle slipped a few inches. Its miniature spines gripped my skin as it sought to regain purchase, and I whimpered.

Cora gripped my shoulder. "Liv," she whispered urgently. "The sooner you stop struggling, the sooner this will be over."

I couldn't; I couldn't do this. The beetle had one leg wedged between my lips.

I spat it out.

Cora squeezed me harder. "You can do this. I know you can."

The kindness in her voice made tears skate down my cheeks. The wetness didn't deter the beetle, though, who had reappeared at my mouth and was directing its pointed head inside.

I tried to imagine what the full insect would feel like inside my mouth, on my tongue, and bile rushed up to burn my throat.

"Easy," Cora said, as I coughed and spluttered. "You're almost there."

I squeezed my eyes shut. I had to get this thing off my face, had to end this torture. I dared to part shaking lips. At the first opportunity, the beetle pushed into my mouth. Its body felt like warm licorice. Just like my dream.

I could feel its weight on my tongue. That rounded shell against the insides of my cheeks. I gagged, but managed to keep my mouth shut.

"Just a few seconds more," Cora said.

Oh God. I was going to vomit. I could feel the tiny barbs on the bug's feet pulling at my taste buds.

Another tear squeezed out of my screwed-up eyes. I had to believe Cora when she said it would only be a few seconds more. But what was a few? Two? Three?

There was a universe of difference between the two.

One Mississippi . . . Two Mississippi . . .

The beetle shifted in my mouth, turning to face my throat.

If that beetle decided to make the descent, I was done.

Three Mississippi . . . Four Mississippi . . .

Suddenly, the weight on my tongue lifted. The beetle had disintegrated into something that felt like freeze-dried ice cream. I dared to part my lips and a black, chalky substance spilled out onto my lap.

Cora squeezed my shoulder triumphantly.

"Congratulations, Liv," Eden said. "You've completed your first trial."

• • •

THEY WERE GRACIOUS ENOUGH TO let me take a break after that. Cora untied my wrist restraints and brought me a goblet of ice water, which I promptly chugged. Feeling the ice cubes slide against the inside of my mouth made me shudder. Would I ever eat an ice cube—let alone a piece of licorice—without flashing back to this night? I held the ice water inside my mouth until it went numb.

Eden and Cora disappeared then, leaving me alone in the flickering living room. I stood up from the chair and set the empty goblet on the coffee table. Stretched my tight limbs. Then I rubbed the red marks on my wrists left by the silk cords and peered at my own reflection in the darkened window. I looked gaunt and terrified. The flames on the candles around the room had returned to their normal color.

I closed my eyes and called up the vision of Sam that Eden had gifted me, my seventeen-year-old best friend with her ripped fishnets and adorable, gummy smile. My hands balled into fists with fresh conviction. This had to be one of the most outrageous decisions I'd ever made. But I was doing this.

All too soon, Eden and Cora were gliding back into the room. My stomach twisted into a knot. Eden had spoken of three trials. I couldn't fathom going through another two. What if they got progressively more hideous each time? Nausea burbled up. I wasn't ready.

Eden resumed her position at the front of the room, holding the ancient book. I almost anticipated it this time:

the candle flames leaping into points and turning an angry fuchsia. Almost the exact shade of the sparkler that had guided my exhilarating flight through the forest so many nights ago.

Eden flipped to a new page. "We move now to the second trial. Harriett Wythers wrote, 'After welcoming in a set of new ideals, we must accept that they will fundamentally alter us. Beautiful though they are, they will mold us in ways that are sometimes painful. And we must cherish the pain, because it is an indication of growth and transcendence.'"

Cherish the pain? Hell no.

Cora was redoing the restraints on my chair. I began to flail my legs, but she had already thought of that and bound each ankle to the chair leg with two additional scarves. Sisterhood or not, this whole ordeal was much worse than any sorority hazing I'd heard of.

Once she had finished, Cora advanced on me with a pair of sewing scissors. "Sorry," she said, with a grimace. Then she slit the side of my silk dress. I cried out, bracing myself for the pain I'd been promised.

But instead of cutting into me, Cora set the heavy scissors back down. The air from the room pressed cold against my naked side. I stared down at my heaving ribs, visible on my flank.

Eden drew something narrow out of the spine of her book. A needle as long as my forearm, thick as a pen. Undoubtedly, the same needle I'd seen her wield by the bonfire on Mischief Night. Eden angled it into a candle flame, which shot nearly a foot into the air, as if it knew what came next.

I burrowed into the back of the chair, needing it to swallow my body.

No. Get that away from me.

Eden knelt beside me. It was strange seeing her in such a deferential position. The white part in her hair was by my elbow. It occurred to me, suddenly, how vulnerable that strip of scalp really was. Had my hands been free, I could have reached out and trailed a fingertip down it, feeling Eden's nakedness.

Eden looked up at me. Then she took the blazing end of the needle and pressed it to my bared side.

All I saw was white: a staggering blizzard of pain. Distantly, I heard my own shriek, but it felt disconnected from my body. I floated in the rafters above the chair, watching Eden scratch an oblong symbol into my hip with the fiery needle tip. Then I jolted back into my body and the agony enveloped me. And that *scent*. It was meaty, bringing me back to those Fourth of July barbeques our neighbors had back in Denver. Back to Mischief Night in the woods.

Was I smelling . . . my own flesh burning?

I screamed again, and Cora pinned me to the chair. Eden seemed unaffected by my suffering, a meticulous artist at work. I tried to focus on the part in her hair but my vision was tunneling in and out like a defective kaleidoscope.

I slumped against the chair.

At some point, Eden's voice trickled in through my haze of consciousness. "All done, Liv. It came out perfectly."

A cool hand patted my cheek. Cora. "You're okay. You made it through the second trial. Only one more to go."

I glanced down at my naked side. A round, livid welt

puckered by my hip bone. I squeezed my eyes shut and turned away as the tears burned.

What had they done to me?

"In the spirit of . . . benevolence . . . we will proceed quickly to the third trial," Eden said.

I was mortified to feel saliva drip from my chin onto my lap. I'd been pushed beyond the limits of my physicality, further than I ever had before.

I had to keep going.

God, Sam. I really hope this is worth it in the end.

"And so," Eden went on, "we have demonstrated the importance of embracing The Sisterhood's cornerstone values. Of accepting that becoming a Sister will mean growing and changing, sometimes in painful ways. For the third and final trial, we look to Harriett's statement: 'The most important thing we as women can do, in fact, is immerse ourselves in sisterhood. But it must transcend superficial declarations of commitment! As women, we must bind ourselves indelibly to other women in a bond so complete, so inextricable, that to rip it asunder would ensure a bloody demise.'"

Her fingers touched down, featherlight on my shoulder.

"You may want to close your eyes for this one," Cora whispered.

If not for her words, I may not have looked up. And then I may not have seen Cora and Eden, poised above me, each holding a jeweled dagger. The same wicked blade Eden had used to slice the bottle of wine at dinner, that I'd unabashedly admired. The blue-and-white gemstones studding the hilts of the gorgeous weapons stared at me like miniature eyes. Glinting in the candlelight, they looked as if they were blinking.

"With these blades, we forge an indelible connection to Olivia Daniella Edwards," Eden said.

The Sisters counted to three in unison.

Then, at once, they plunged their pretty daggers into my abdomen.

26

THEN

I**T JUST SO HAPPENED THAT MY BIRTHDAY WAS THE SAME DAY** as our high school graduation party. Sam and I would be headed to Six Flags the following day for an official celebration, so I didn't expect her to bring a gift when she showed up at my house the night before.

"For the birthday girl," she said, handing me a lavender heart-shaped box.

Frankly, I hadn't expected any gift at all—let alone in a cute box in my favorite color.

"Oh my gosh," I said, taking it from her. "This is so cute. Do I save it for tomorrow?"

"No way," she said, striding past me into the living room and settling onto the couch.

I laughed. "Okay." I followed her to the couch and gently opened the purple box. It was filled with little iridescent strips of plastic that made up a rustling, rainbow nest. I gasped happily. Nestled within was a collection of all my favorite things. A bag of nonpareils from the Village Chocolatier. A thick disc of lilac-scented soap wrapped in fancy foil. A cinnamon twist from Bishop's Orchards. An RISD keychain ("I have a matching one," Sam informed me). Of course, we'd long since made up after my disastrous run-in with both twins, and after celebratory sundaes, mailed our acceptance and roommate forms to our future college.

"This is the sweetest present anyone has ever gotten me," I said, and it was the truth. Though I'd had friends in Denver, they'd only ever given me the most generic of presents: gift cards and lotion kits from Bath & Body Works.

Sam grinned. "But wait, there's more."

I rummaged around the shimmery nest. Something cool and smooth was buried below and I drew it out.

I frowned. "An egg?"

"How could you forget?" Another devilish smile. "I had to find a way to commemorate Mischief Night."

I set the egg back in the box, anger tearing through me. Why did Sam have to do this? She was ruining a perfect moment in our friendship by needling me about a night I'd spent the past seven months trying to forget. But that night had ended favorably for her—she'd manipulated me into doing something that had utterly mortified me. Fleetingly, I fantasized about grinding the egg into Sam's face, right there in the living room. Immediately afterward I felt wretched for even entertaining the thought.

My phone buzzed on the coffee table. I picked it up before Sam could see it. Of course, I'd renamed Everett's contact in my phone—just "E"—but I always felt a flash of danger whenever I saw his contact come up in Sam's presence.

Matt and I were thinking of heading over to Kitty's around 7

Sam must have interpreted my guilty silence as anger over the egg. "Oh, lighten up," she groaned, jumping to her feet. She stretched her arms high over her head. It made her shoulder pop, and the sound was like a gunshot in the quiet living room, goading me to snap. "Come on. Let's get changed for the party."

THE GRADUATION PARTY WAS HELD at Kitty Wallace's, a girl on the fringe of the popular crowd whose parents were in Bermuda for the weekend. She lived in one of those impressive colonials off the Green, with pillars on either side of the front entrance and blood-colored decoration around each window and door. I could hear the thump of the bassline before we even walked inside.

Sam rapped on the door. The music went on; no one came to get us. I looked down at my wedge sandals. It was a uniquely awful feeling to be shut out of a party that you could feel reverberating through your bones. Was it possible Kitty had seen us through the window and decided she didn't want Sam and me here? We weren't pariahs by any stretch of the imagination, but nor were we the caliber of person with whom Kitty customarily surrounded herself.

Clomping heels on stone made the two of us spin. It was Eden Holloway, clad in a black knit minidress and a choker with a red gemstone nestled in the hollow of her throat. Avery and Cora followed behind her, their eyes fastened resolutely on the door to Kitty's house. I startled—I hadn't realized The Sisterhood went to events as pedestrian as house parties. Word was they'd blown off senior prom to scour crystal shops and secondhand clothing stores in the city. Back at school, they sat in their white gazebo passing around baubles that I couldn't quite make out, much as I tried.

"Hey," Eden said, and I couldn't tell if she was addressing me, Sam, or both of us. (*Which was it?* I was suddenly desperate to know.) No sooner had Eden reached for the doorknob than the front door swung open from the inside.

Sam and I slid into the house behind The Sisterhood. I was so relieved to be absorbed into the thick of the party that I didn't even feel guilty for following in on their metaphorical coattails.

Sam excused herself to the bathroom. Alone now in the kitchen, I stared at an island cluttered with handles of vodka and mixers. Clumps and huddles of my classmates were everywhere, their backs to me. I felt, once again, as I had that first day of school, before Sam had offered to give me the tour.

Fortunately, this party had one thing GHS did not: alcohol.

I poured myself some vodka with orange juice and forced it down, gulp by fiery gulp. Then I checked the time—Everett would be arriving any minute. The alcohol dulled my anxiety about commingling with Sam and her twin. We were fairly used to regarding each other coolly in

Sam's presence, but it took a lot of restraint. I always had to be "on."

After Sam's egg gift, I didn't feel like expending so much mental energy on her behalf.

Sam was taking forever in the bathroom. By my second drink, a kid from my social studies class had floated over. We laughed together about our teacher with the yellow pit-stains that yawned each time he wrote on the whiteboard, and I wondered why I didn't do this more. By the third drink, I was bold enough to start exploring Kitty's house. I walked into the living room, past a group of kids sprawled on the couches, and skated a hand over slick piano keys. A couple of girls noticed me and waved from across the room; I waved back. The few parties I'd attended in Guilford, I'd clung to Sam's side like a burr. But maybe that had been unnecessary. There was something immensely freeing about wandering around the periphery of the party on my own.

A guy from my physics class bounded down the stair-case. He lifted his chin at me. "The bathroom up on the third floor—*sick*."

It was all the invitation I needed.

I wound up multiple sets of stairs. Somewhere along the way, I missed the turn to the bathroom, and ended up instead in a sumptuous master bedroom with a gorgeous four-poster bed and a balcony overlooking the lawn. From my vantage point, I could just make out a square of quiet twilit street. By now, the dogwood trees were bursting into bloom. Somehow, I'd made it through an entire revolution of seasons here in Guilford. Soon it would be back to the drowsy, simmering summer that had greeted me—the summer of moving boxes and that horrific tour of the Wythers House—just in time to leave again.

I turned away from the window and ran a hand over the cream comforter on the bed.

"Whoa."

The voice made my Solo cup dip in my hand; I righted it just before my drink spilled onto the bedspread.

Everett stood on the threshold between the bedroom and the balcony. His hair looked windswept. "You found me," he said.

Warmth sifted through my body, as it often did in those excruciating moments before touching Everett. That Sam was somewhere in this very house added a layer of danger. "What're you doing up here?"

He shrugged. "Got bored. Wanted to scout out the digs." He narrowed his eyes. "Did you come with Sam?"

"Obviously." Sometimes Everett asked questions like this and I had to fight not to roll my eyes. *Of course I did. She's my best friend.* It made me realize how little he considered his sister in this big mess of whatever we were doing, when Sam's implicit horror always seemed to hang over my head like a dark specter.

Predictably, my response rolled right off him. Everett tilted his head at me. "Come here."

"Everett." It was drawn out, a warning, but a smile flashed through my trepidation despite my best efforts.

Instead of waiting for me to comply, Everett joined me by the bed. Then he began to trace the V of my sweater with one finger. My skin leaped under his touch.

"You know, it's not too late to change your mind about RISD," he said quietly.

I swallowed down a laugh. "Yeah, right."

Everett tipped my chin up to him. In the moment before his lips descended to mine, I was jolted back to Mischief Night. Leaves and woodsmoke and the feel of Everett's soft mouth. Though we'd kissed—and more—plenty of times since then, there was something about that memory that made me clutch it close like a piece of treasure, despite the months that had passed since.

And yet, kissing Everett was still like entering a riptide. Our clandestine meetups meant we weren't ever able to get our fill. Too, I expended so much mental energy trying to conceal my relationship with Everett—coming up with creative meeting spots, generating excuses for Sam—that when I finally tripped into Everett's arms, I was too exhausted to do anything but surrender.

But tonight felt different. I broke away, breathing hard. "We really shouldn't."

"Why not?"

"What if someone comes in here?"

Everett cast a scornful look at the door. "I *dare* them."

I stifled a giggle. Everett was right—I'd spent nearly an entire semester trying to cover our tracks. We'd graduated; the school year was over. I was done worrying.

I went up on my tiptoes and kissed Everett, hard. In response, his hands tangled in my hair, then slipped under my sweater. I pressed against him, dizzy with need.

"Christ," Everett said, breaking away for a second. His eyes drank me in. "You are something else."

I pulled him on top of me on the bed, taking the back of his neck in my hands. The ferocity of sensation tearing through me was slightly terrifying. I wanted to climb into his skin; I wanted to devour him.

Everett straddled me on the mattress, stripping off my too-hot sweater. He pressed his mouth into my neck, his stubble biting.

"Imagine," he said between kisses, "a whole year of this."

Even I had to admit the prospect was thrilling. To be able to access Everett freely, without the demands of high school or the Sam-specter looming over me? I gasped a little as Everett undid my fly, and I watched him as his mouth trailed down. "Screw a year," he said against me, "I don't think I'll ever get tired of this."

I threw my head back, gripping a fistful of comforter in each hand. Everett was really pushing the gap year agenda today, which would have been irritating if he weren't making up for it in other ways.

A metallic *clunk* registered faintly in the back of my consciousness. But my body was starting to climb and that was all I could attend to in the moment. I grabbed a handful of Everett's hair. That's when I saw his eyes strain away from me, revealing bloodshot white. He was looking in the direction of the door to the bedroom, where, I realized with a lurch of my heart, a new figure now stood.

Sam.

27

NOW

I WOKE TO THE SMELL OF PANCAKES.

"Morning, sleepyhead."

I opened my eyes. Eden's face was millimeters from mine.

I bolted upright. "What are you doing here?" That's when I realized it wasn't only muss-haired Eden in bed with me. Cora was also packed in, laughing and making the mattress springs squeal.

Eden's lips turned downward in an exaggerated pout. "What do you mean, what am I doing here? It's my house. And now—" she bared her teeth in an aggressive smile, "it's yours, too."

Images from the night before rained down on me: being tied to that high-backed chair. The beetle marching down my face and eventually my tastebuds as I fought down

vomit. And then: blinding pain. A giant needle on my hip.
The night had ended with the girls poised above me with
those beautiful, glittering daggers . . .

I ripped the sheet off. Someone had shucked the silk
gown from me and dressed me in a cotton men's undershirt.
I scrabbled at the hem to assess my abdomen. To my shock,
it was smooth and unmarred—except for a small, dark
scabbing at my hip bone.

"What the hell?" Eden and Cora had plunged two daggers into my abdomen—and there was absolutely no sign
of that. I ran a tentative finger over the oblong wound at my
hip bone and hissed through my teeth in pain.

Cora bent over to look, her long hair brushing my
stomach. "Ooh, it came out so pretty! Just like mine." She
lifted her own T-shirt off her hip, exposing a white scar in
the shape of an eye.

"You know what that means." Eden crossed her legs on
the bed. "There's no turning back now."

"Geez, Eden. No need to sound so scary about it!"
Cora set a wooden tray in my lap. "Here." On it was a stack
of pancakes dotted with berries and a melting pat of butter,
a tureen of syrup, and a tiny vase holding two dark purple
buds. "I made this just for you. After last night, I'm sure
you've worked up an appetite."

I gripped the sides of the tray, even though I had no
intention of eating the food upon it.

"You were a rock star," Eden said, leaning over to rummage for something off the side of the bed.

Cora nodded vehemently.

"Unlike this one here," Eden added, indicating Cora.

And just like that, the light behind Cora's eyes extinguished.

"Oh, come on, Cora." Eden jabbed her in the ribs with an elbow before turning back to me. "The Seeing Beetle made her throw up all over Harriett's book. Some of the pages are permanently stained as a result."

Cora's voice was almost inaudible. "It's not my fault I have a weak stomach."

"Here." Eden handed me what she'd been holding: a shallow box inlaid with panels of wood in different shades. The wood was butter-smooth. "Open it," she urged.

I did. The inside of the box was lined with red silk. And nestled in the center was a gleaming dagger studded with eyelike jewels.

"Aren't you going to take it out?"

But the box had already fallen to the mattress, the dagger sliding out onto the sheets. Was this some kind of sick joke?

"Hey," said Eden. "What's the matter? I thought you liked our daggers and would be excited to get one of your own."

I couldn't spit the words out. *It's what you stabbed me with last night.*

"Oh, Liv." Eden rolled her eyes with a smile. "Are you upset because of how we used the daggers during your Initiation? That was a metaphor. We would never stab a Sister for real."

"Not unless she's done something to piss us off," Cora added, in her characteristic sing-song.

My stomach plunged to the floor. Every moment I spent with Eden and Cora seemed to reinforce my suspicion that they were involved in Sam's disappearance. The sheer barbarism of last night's Initiation made it clear they didn't shy away from blood and mutilation. My mouth grew suddenly dry.

Oh, Sam, what did they do to you?

As my mind whirred, Eden was busy packing the dagger gently into the wooden case. I noticed she was studying my face avidly, and I flinched when we made eye contact.

"Cora," Eden said, not looking away, "can you give Liv and me a minute alone?"

Cora blinked down at the bed. She looked as if she was going to say something. Then, in one swift motion, she cleared my untouched breakfast away and swept out of the room. I could hear the cutlery clattering angrily down the hall.

Now it was just Eden and me in perfect silence. My body went rigid.

Eden rolled over onto her side facing me. Her smirk brought a single dimple to the side of her face—an unexpectedly girlish detail on such an imposing face. "Hey, chickadee. I wanted to check in. See how you were feeling about all this."

I clenched my jaw. "I'm fine."

"Are you?" Eden reached out and touched the side of my face gently. "You seem . . . tense."

"Nope. I'm good."

"Hmm." Eden regarded me intently with her face cradled in one palm. I tried to focus on the ceiling, taking shallow sips of air to calm myself. Could Eden read the betrayal on my face? Could she sense the way my guts were twisting inside me, the way my brain was screaming that I'd just made the most dangerous mistake of my life?

If Eden and Cora had hurt Sam for betraying The Sisterhood, how the hell was I going to get out of this unscathed?

Eden reached out then and turned over my left index finger. That permanent welt stared back at both of us. "You going to tell me what this is about?" she whispered.

I ripped my hand away and stuffed it under the sheets.

"Come on, Liv." Eden scooted closer to me. "You can trust me. We're Sisters now."

"I don't really want to talk about it."

"Hmm." Eden's black-cherry nails marched slowly over the comforter toward me. Then she slid a hand under the sheet—ostensibly, searching for the bruised finger I'd hidden.

My body stiffened once again.

Eden's fingertips skimmed up my inner arm. "I know it can feel scary, but you need to learn to let go. These parts of yourself that you despise? They're inextricably linked to what makes you so powerful. You can't have one without the other. Losing control," she murmured, "doesn't have to be a bad thing."

God, how did she do that—weasel right into the corners of my brain I'd barricaded off from the world? I bit the inside of my cheek. Then I wrenched away. I'd been determined not to give Eden any more leverage than she already had, but the words shot out of me unchecked. "When you've spent your childhood watching your father 'lose control' and almost land your mom in the emergency room . . . yeah, actually, it does have to be a bad thing."

Realization dawned in Eden's eyes. "Ah," she said slowly, "thanks for connecting the dots for me." To my horror, she drew closer, leaning her head on my shoulder as I'd seen her do with Cora. Though she barely breathed the words, they filled my head like an echo in a cavern: "It seems you and I have a lot in common, don't we?"

THE MOMENT EDEN VACATED THE room, I texted Mom letting her know I was okay and that I'd be back home sometime that evening. There was a cake tasting scheduled at Beloved for later that morning and I wanted to take advantage of the event—of Cora and Eden being preoccupied—to see what evidence I could scrounge up connecting The Sisterhood to Sam's disappearance.

The couple arrived at eleven sharp, the bride with a ballerina's build and a burst of corkscrew curls tied high up on her head; the groom hulking, with a distinctive purplish beauty mark at the edge of one eye. Cora had prepared another antique platter full of samples, slicing slivers of white cake layered with buttercream frosting and jam with a wood-handled knife. She seated the clients and gave them the rundown on the different flavors spread out before them. Olive oil–lemon, carrot and marble, jasmine green tea ganache . . .

"And in addition to all this," Eden cut in, "Liv here made the brooch you requested. I have a feeling you're going to love how it turned out."

Sam *and I made the brooch,* I corrected her silently. I hadn't done it alone and it seemed an important distinction.

Eden nodded at me and I opened the jewelry box I'd been clutching, exposing the elaborate pin. It glittered against the crushed velvet.

The bride's eyes widened. "Oh my God." She ripped the box out of my hand. "This is stunning. Exactly what I imagined." She tore the brooch out and began jabbing the needle through the silk of her top.

Eden glanced at me with a secret kind of smile.

I looked down at my feet.

"Oh!" In her excitement, the bride had caught the end of the thick, spear-like pin under a fingernail.

Laughing, the groom covered his eyes. "Am I not supposed to see this? Won't it be bad luck?"

"There aren't any superstitions about seeing the bride's jewelry before the wedding," Cora assured him.

"At least," Eden added, "none that we're aware of."

I took advantage of the excitement to murmur something about having a headache and slipped out of the boutique. Then, feeling daring, I walked quickly to the back door and let myself out. Coldness pricked in through the gaps in my sweater. With Cora and Eden occupied in the main house, it was a critical opportunity for me to search the detached workshop to see if I could uncover any evidence about Sam. In a missing person's case, I simply didn't have the luxury of time.

I snatched at the bronze face on the doorknob. This time, the door resisted, as if it could sense my intentions.

"Screw you," I muttered, twisting the knob harder and shoving against the door with my hip.

Grudgingly, it opened. The sweet, homey smell of the workshop enveloped me, and it took all my restraint not to sink into it, to slink behind Sam's workbench and cede myself to that hypnotizing work again. I commanded myself to focus on my mission. *Evidence on Sam. Dirt on The Sisterhood. Go.*

I started by investigating Eden's workspace. This made me shaky with nerves—it was an intimate space, after all, and if I failed to replace everything exactly as it had been, Eden was sure to notice. Delicately, I poked around the scraps of fabric she'd been arranging, flipped through the open sketch pad beside them. In it, Eden's pencil strokes were long and graceful. She seemed to be trying to refine lacy cap sleeves on a gown through iterations of sketches. In each rendering, the lithe figure of the bride was elongated and wispy, almost insect-like. Under Eden's workbench was a set of drawers, and I began sliding them open one by one. Thimbles rattled in response. Chalk. A couple of transparent rulers and a studded pincushion shaped like an artichoke.

Nothing incriminating at all.

Frustrated, I turned to the closet at the far end of the room. It was stuffed, as I expected, with supplies: additional bolts of fabric, massive plastic bins filled with spools of thread and buttons. Toward the back of the closet, my fingers closed over something that felt like a painting. I dragged it to the front so I could study it.

A giant photo portrait of a smiling young woman stared back at me. What the hell was this? I rummaged in the closet and drew out a stack of similar photo canvases, laid them out on the floorboards. The sun streaming through the studio windows played over them and a prickling unease uncurled in the pit of my stomach. Each one of the canvases featured a blown-up photograph of a different woman. They were all posed photos, the women with natural light hitting their hair just so, angling their faces over their shoulders at the camera. I frowned, taking them in. Did they have a photo of Sam in here? And if so, what could that mean?

No Sam—but I found the smiling face of the curly-haired bride currently tasting cake in the boutique. It looked almost like an engagement photo with her groom cropped out. A chill shot down my spine. There could be a benign explanation for this. It would make sense, for instance, that Cora and Eden would like to keep track of their clients by keeping their engagement photos, allowing them to match faces with names. But wouldn't a simple list have sufficed? Why the giant photographs? Blown up to this size, the bride's eyes—paired with her clenched smile—were two voids.

Shivering, I gathered the canvases off the floor and shoved them back in the closet. Eden and Cora were likely to start wondering where I'd gone—if they hadn't already.

THE BRIDAL BOUTIQUE WAS PLUSH with silence when I entered. Midday sun streamed in through the windows, casting a bar of light over the vase of gardenias on the table. In the entryway, my legs filled with pins and needles. I shifted from one foot to the other.

"Cora?" I called.

Silence echoed back at me. I turned the corner to peer at the bakery side of the boutique: empty, save for an abandoned table of drained champagne glasses and a frosting-smeared silver tray. I couldn't have been in the studio for more than twenty minutes—was it really possible the bride and groom had finished with their appointment during that time?

"Eden?" I rounded into the hallway with the powder room accessible to clients. There, my toe caught on something and I stumbled.

A giant man was curled on his side. His face was gray, mouth open slightly and crushed against the floor.

I stumbled back.

What the hell?

Trembling, I dared to bend closer. It was— unmistakably—the groom from the cake-tasting appointment, that distinctive birthmark smeared by his left eye. Only then did I register the black-red blood pooling from his neck. My heart launched into the back of my throat. His throat had been slit, the skin around the wound ruffled and vivid. In another context, it might have even looked beautiful, like a flower or an exotic sea creature. The bloody implement lay against the man's crisp white shirt and had brushed red upon it. How was this even possible? My stomach turned, imagining the force with which this weapon must have been deployed. It was an intricate, pearl-studded brooch that my hands knew all too intimately.

Just before my knees gave way, I saw the flicker of a familiar patent-leather-like carapace slither out from the groom's gaping mouth and scuttle off down the hallway.

28

THEN

"OH MY GOD." SAM'S HANDS WERE IN HER HAIR. SHE TURNED around, back toward the hallway, as if to erase what she'd just seen.

Everett scrambled upright; I flew off the edge of the bed and zipped my jeans, catching a bit of my left hand in the process. Pain zinged through me.

"Jesus Christ," Everett said again, but it wasn't the reverent exhalation of moments earlier. The blood vessels lacing his eyes were all I could see.

I was praying that Sam would back into the hallway to leave us to compose ourselves, but evidently, she had no such intention. Instead, Sam strode into the room. Her eyes sought out mine. "Liv. What the fuck."

I felt a start of indignation. Why *my* name? It took two to tango.

"Sam—" Everett started.

"No," Sam snarled. "God, this is so twisted, I can't even look at you. Either of you. Seriously, Everett, get out of here."

Everett swiped a hand through his hair. I felt a pang of need for him to stay, to defend me from his sister's wrath. For an instant, I was sure that he would.

But then Everett threw on his shirt and stormed out of the room.

Sam's eyes were still trained on me. "How long has this been going on for?" I'd never heard her speak like this, her words grainy and severe.

I contemplated lying. Would she believe me if I told her Everett and I had just hooked up for the first time, emboldened by the alcohol downstairs? But a second thought emerged: Why should I have to apologize for this? For the entirety of our friendship, I'd bowed to Sam's whims. I was allowed to have needs of my own.

I met her gaze straight-on. "Seven months," I said.

Sam's mouth fell open, and her shock stoked a tiny thrill in me.

"How did you pull *that* off?"

Why did the way she said that sound . . . so insulting? As if she couldn't even imagine my having the ability to interest her brother and sustain that interest for so long. Or was it my craftiness she was questioning? The way I'd hidden it from her—from everyone? I crunched down on the bed, maneuvering into my shirt. If Sam was escalating things, I was going to need every shred of dignity I could muster. "Well," I said, swinging my legs over the side of the bed and picking up my abandoned drink. "We hooked up on Mischief Night and . . ."—I couldn't stop the smirk that jumped to my lips—"just kept doing it."

It wasn't the answer she wanted. Sam advanced on me and smacked the Solo cup out of my hand. "Don't you dare make this into a joke."

I shrank away from her, feeling the first billow of genuine fear. I'd never seen my best friend lash out physically before. "Hey," I said. "I'm not trying to make light of this. I just don't get why you're so upset."

"It's because you don't listen to me, Liv." Rage made Sam's upper lip roll under itself, disappearing almost entirely. It exaggerated her yellowed overbite, the same one Everett had taunted her about at the fair's rabbit exhibit. "I told you not to waste your time on my brother. You have no idea how he treats girls. He uses them and then . . . fucking disposes of them. You're no exception. I'm embarrassed for you, and for what's coming. Honestly, I am."

Now my hackles were rising. "I don't need you feeling embarrassed for me, Sam."

"I'm your best friend! Of course I'm going to feel that way!"

How dare she make it sound like such a charitable reaction. I kicked the cup she'd knocked out of my hands; it went rolling under the bed. "You have no idea what's coming," I said, in a low voice.

Sam snickered. "What's that supposed to mean? You guys planning the wedding already?"

"No." Defiant heat surged under my skin. Everett was right—so what if we'd already mailed in our acceptances to RISD? It wasn't too late for me to change my mind. And if

Sam was going to treat me like this, I didn't want to be her roommate. I didn't want to decorate a dorm room with her, and I definitely didn't want to condemn myself to four years of being her little pet.

Most urgently, though, in that moment, I just wanted to hurt her.

"I'm taking a gap year with Everett."

Something about the set of Sam's mouth changed. "No, you're not. We have RISD in the fall."

But I saw it—the way my response had thrown her. It was the perfect barb, just as I'd suspected. I straightened my spine. "I was going to tell you tomorrow, after my birthday, but I might as well do it now. I changed my mind about RISD. Everett and I are going to spend the year exploring Europe together."

To my shock, Sam let out a snort. "Sure you are."

That pissed me off even more. "What, you want to see the plane tickets as proof?" They didn't exist yet, of course, but Sam didn't need to know that part. "We're leaving next month. Flying into Prague."

"Next month?" Now Sam's eyes were huge. "Move-in is September tenth."

"I told you, Sam. I'm not going to RISD with you."

"Shut up." Sam's voice was soft. "You're not giving up a full ride to art school. Not for him."

This was, of course, the part I'd been wrestling with. To hear Sam speak it aloud made me squirmy. I crossed my arms over my chest. "I am. It's decided. Sometimes we have to make tough decisions in life, and this is just one of those times."

"Liv." The pitying note in her voice made me bristle. "Come on. You don't know what you're saying. You hardly know him."

My hands curled into fists at my side. For seven months, I'd drank up Everett Mendez greedily. Sometimes, when we were cuddling after sex, he'd touch my body and tell me stories about growing up. None of them involved Sam. Her statement put me on the defensive, though. For all the contortions I'd put myself through to know Everett, at the end of the day, Sam was his twin. By default, thanks to straight-up genetics, she knew him better.

Even if she didn't appreciate him like I did.

"I do," I insisted.

Sam stared at me, hard. Then, unexpectedly, she threw her head back and laughed. "Oh," she said, resurfacing from her mirth. "I get it now. I see what's going on here."

I stared back at her. *By all means, Sam. Enlighten me.*

"That first time you told me about your parents fighting. When we were at Jacob's Beach."

I couldn't believe she was bringing up such a vulnerable moment at a time like this. Weaponizing it. "Shut up, Sam," I said quietly.

"Why? Have I hit a nerve or something?" The dynamics in the room had shifted. Sam, knocked off-kilter by anger minutes earlier, had regained her composure. Now she was almost swaggering. She sauntered out onto the balcony, as if to cool off from the heat of our fight.

I looked on, trembling.

"You have to admit it, though," Sam went on. "It's pretty messed up. There you were, complaining about how your mom gave up everything for your dad. And now look at you."

I pressed my lips together, painfully. I couldn't believe she'd taken it this far.

Sam cocked her head to one side. When she spoke next, it was a whisper. "You're doing *the exact same thing.* Imagine that! After all the pain that your dad put your family through, all the suffering your mom experienced . . . you have learned absolutely nothing." Sam barked out a crisp, cruel laugh. "I can see it now. You're going to grow up to be just like her. You've already gotten a head start! Giving up everything to please a guy who will only treat you like shit. You're well on your way to finding a husband who smacks you around for years and then walks out on you."

I'd never told Sam explicitly about Dad throwing Mom across the kitchen, but she must have connected the dots somehow. To think that she must have held on to this revelation, only to whip it out now to humiliate me—it was enraging. I blinked and my vision turned black-red. Something dark reared inside me, a force that had been latent for too long. A second was all it took to subsume me, like thunderous water. There was a strange kind of relief in being swallowed. It meant I could finally stop pretending this wasn't part of me.

Before I'd registered it, my hands were on Sam's shoulders, shoving her roughly against the balustrade.

Sam's eyes were blank with shock. It satisfied me to see that I had, in fact, defied her expectations.

I was so intent on slamming Sam's back into the hard lip of the balustrade, repeatedly, that I didn't hear the telltale crack of the foundation. I shoved Sam against the ledge and this time, there was a curious give. For a perilous second, I realized what was happening, poised at the edge of catastrophe. The next, my best friend was sailing in slow-motion to the patio stones three stories below.

A hand flew to my mouth, teeth clashing into my rings. Sam's body plummeted gracelessly. That was perhaps one of the cruelest details of the night. In another context, it might have looked even comical, the way her limbs flipped back behind her, arms pinwheeling. My own body felt stitched together with dread, waiting for the inevitable impact. And then it came: a wet-sounding smack giving way to a grotesque contortion of limbs.

I jerked into a paralysis of my own. I could only stare down at Sam's ruined body as a sick dread pumped through me. The diaphanous balcony curtains curled malevolently in the night air.

A moment later, I dared to swing my gaze to the bedroom door, breathing hard. It was ajar. A slit of face was peering at me without expression—that unmistakable dark slash of a brow, pale blond hair, red jewel at her throat—before it disappeared from view.

29

NOW

"Liv?"

It was Cora, shaking my shoulder gently.

I blinked up at her from where I sat on the polished hardwood of the boutique hallway, clutching my knees to my chest. At some point, my body must have slumped against the wall and slid, down and down.

"Eden called the police," Cora said. "Want to wait for them together in the living room?"

Time had collapsed around me since finding the groom with his torn-open neck outside the powder room. My scream had summoned Eden and Cora within seconds. Apparently, they'd stepped out of the boutique to give the bride and groom some privacy to decide on a wedding cake flavor. Cora said she'd heard a low moan through the door, but had chalked it up to the groom's appreciation for her culinary prowess.

"Liv?" Cora shook my shoulder again, more insistently this time.

I was rocking back and forth, my chin pressed to my left knee cap.

Cora slid her hands under my arms and pulled me to standing. "Come on," she said. "I think we'll all be more comfortable waiting in the other room."

Eden's bright hair was fanned out over the top of the living room couch, her knee-high suede boots crossed on the coffee table. She scrolled her phone in one hand; in the other, she swigged from a crystal decanter of electric blue.

"Here." She held the decanter out to me.

I balked at her. I'd just seen a dead person for the first time in my life; there was no way I was keeping alcohol down.

"I think Liv is in shock," Cora said, helping me onto the couch beside Eden.

Eden tossed her phone aside. "That's understandable."

I stared at a seam in the couch cushion between us. It puckered slightly at the corner, bringing to mind the way the groom's skin had puckered around his wound.

Finally, I found my voice. "How is this happening?"

A sly look passed between Cora and Eden. Then they sidled closer to me on the couch.

"Let's do a toast," Eden said. She lifted the blue decanter, took a sip, and passed it to Cora. "To The Sisterhood."

Cora took a swig. "And our beautiful new chemistry. Here." She passed me the alcohol and the living room floor promptly tilted to one side.

"Hey, chickadee." Eden's shoulder pressed against mine; I smelled the flower on her breath. "I really think you should try having a drink."

I squeezed my eyes shut and reopened them. "Eden. Someone was murdered in this house."

She pulled away from me then, lifted her long hair off the back of the couch.

"You're so right," she said.

I couldn't bring myself to say it aloud. But the sentiment rose just as swiftly as the bile in my throat: *Then why the hell are you smiling?*

"And we're proud of you," Eden added.

"*So* proud," Cora echoed.

"Me?"

"Yes, you! Don't be modest. You're the one who made that brooch. To give our bride the courage to do something about her rotten fiancé. And, well . . ."

My body stiffened. What Eden was suggesting was impossible. It was a piece of wedding jewelry, for God's sake. There was no way my brooch had prompted a bride to—what? Fly into a psychotic rage and murder her partner?

"I had nothing to do with this."

Eden recrossed her ankles on the coffee table. "I mean," she said, "tell yourself whatever you need to be able to sleep at night. But this was all you."

I refused to believe it. But even as I choked off the possibility, Eden's words filtered back through my memory. *I've seen how you infuse your jewelry with intention . . . That bracelet you wore back in high school that calmed your nerves when you needed it.*

The ring you're wearing right now that pulls you from your own . . . darkness.

"I don't know, Eden." Cora's lips pressed into a pretty pout. "I'd like to think of it as a team effort."

I lurched to my feet where I swayed for a moment. "I'm going to be sick."

"Well, please don't do it here." Any warmth had drained from Eden's voice by now. "That rug is an antique."

I stood paralyzed in the center of the living room. Now was the time to make a run for it—but my muscles were locked up like a set of jammed gears.

Presently, Eden joined me on her feet and slipped a cool hand under the hem of my dress. I flinched. What was she doing? Then, I realized: her fingertips were feeling for the "eye" on my hip. When her thumb found it, she stroked the dried blood a couple of times, almost affectionately. Then, without warning, Eden dug her thumbnail into my scab.

I gasped in pain.

"I suggest you go splash some cold water on your face and pull yourself together," Eden said, in that low voice of hers. "Then maybe we can have a civilized conversation about all this."

At the last possible moment, my muscles sparked to life. I bolted upstairs to the safety of the bathroom, slamming and locking the door behind me.

AFTER EMPTYING MY STOMACH INTO the toilet, I pressed my forehead to the bathroom tile. Reality was scrambling and rewriting itself in my short-circuiting brain. Was it really possible I'd made a brooch that compelled a woman to kill her fiancé? Just like I'd felt compelled to push my best friend off a third-story balcony? I thought of the darkness that had reared up in me on Kitty's balcony like thunderous water. Despite my best efforts, it was still with me all these years later—and somehow, it had leaked into my jewelry.

What the hell was wrong with me? As much as Eden liked to crow about my "power," I knew what it really was: that mealy, rotten part of me that I just couldn't seem to shake.

As for Sam, that reality was swiftly coalescing. Brendan was right—there had been somebody controlling in Sam's life: two somebodies, in fact. I held my breath; the girls' laughter tinkled a floor below. They were laughing about a murder. They'd told me they were proud.

I was willing to stake my life on it: Eden and Cora had done something to hurt Sam.

I fumbled for my phone and dialed Patterson. Thank God I'd had the foresight to program in his number from his business card. The call went straight to voicemail.

"Hi, this is Liv Edwards. I need you to come to 128 Whitfield Street now. I have something important to tell you about Sam's roommates and—please come now. Thanks."

After hanging up, I stared at the dial pad as my heart thudded urgently. *Eden called the police*, Cora had told me. But judging from Eden's smug toast in the living room, this must have been a lie. She didn't want anyone to find the groom's body; she saw today as a success. And if Patterson wasn't answering his phone, I couldn't rely on him to get here fast enough. My thumb stabbed at the numbers: 9-1—

A knock on the door made me jump.

"Liv? You alright in there?"

Eden.

Panicked, I canceled the call.

"Fine," I said through the door.

"Are you ready to talk now? Cora is sending up some ginger ale to settle your stomach."

"Almost."

Silence. "I'll wait."

A sharp pain zinged in my side. I looked down: my eye-shaped wound had started to bleed into the fabric of my dress. How hard had Eden dug her fingernail in there?

Silence thrummed on the other side of the door: Eden really wasn't going anywhere. I tore off some toilet paper and blotted at my side. Then, heart pounding, I stepped out into the hallway.

"I think your soda has arrived." Eden reached for what I had always assumed was part of the built-in cabinetry in the hallway, opening the door to a plate of water crackers and a glass of ginger ale, complete with a thick striped straw. She cracked a smile at my incredulous look. "I guess we never showed you the dumbwaiter, did we?"

I gripped my phone.

"Come on," Eden said. She took the provisions and led me into Sam's bedroom.

I stood frozen in the doorway.

"You trust me, Liv, don't you?"

How, exactly, was I supposed to answer that question?

"I mean," Eden went on, "you trust your Sister, right? To look out for your best interests. To love and protect you."

She handed me the ginger ale with the pretty straw.

"I know you're scared," Eden continued. She settled on the edge of the bed and placed the plate of crackers on the bedspread beside her. "But you need to trust us, Liv. That man was bad news. Remember I told you about our extensive interview process? We knew all about the ins and outs of that relationship, and specifically selected this bride so we could intervene. We're looking out for our fellow women. It's our job to make sure they don't sink their lives into bad marriages. We're saving them, Liv."

I gripped the cold glass of soda, too terrified to take a sip.

"What's bothering you?" Eden asked gently.

"The blood," I admitted, in a hoarse voice. "The mess of his body. I still can't believe—"

"You're reacting to human suffering," Eden said. "As any empathic human being would. But to be a Sister, Liv, you need to push yourself past that. You need to suspend your reflexive reactions to act for the good of our Sisterhood and women at large. You saw the groom suffering today because it was necessary to keep his bride from a lifetime of suffering. Does that make sense?"

I thought suddenly of my own mother sailing across our kitchen and cracking the back of her head on the edge of a cabinet. "What about the bride?" I managed. "Do you know where she ran off to?"

"Nope," Eden said cheerfully. Then, almost as an afterthought: "Godspeed to her, though."

I glanced again at my phone. What the hell was taking Patterson so long?

Eden jumped off the bed. "Okay. I'm calling an emergency meeting. Come on." She offered her hand.

But with the untouched ginger ale in one hand and my phone in the other, I didn't have any free hands to accept hers. Eden's eyes slid over my body and I felt myself turn to petrified wood.

"Why are you bleeding?" she asked softly.

I did a double take. The small patch of blood I'd glimpsed in the bathroom had ballooned to triple the size, dark as lipstick. Panicked, I dropped my phone and the glass of soda, which shattered against the wood floor, soaking my feet. But it barely registered—I was too concerned with lifting my dress to investigate the blood. Then I gasped aloud. This was far worse than any damage Eden's fingernail could have inflicted: the entire area around my "eye" wound had caved in on itself, forming a bloody chasm.

What had Eden said during my Initiation? *As women, we must bind ourselves indelibly to other women in a bond so complete, so inextricable, that to rip it asunder would ensure a bloody demise.*

Was it possible her words were coming true? That my betrayal—calling Patterson and attempting to dial 9-1-1—was turning my body inside out for all to see?

"Why would you turn on us?" Eden whispered. "We haven't done anything wrong."

I stared back at her, mute.

The next instant, Eden's nails were burrowing into the soft flesh of my upper arms. She was startlingly strong, wrestling me to my knees on the ground. I managed to press into the floor and gain some leverage, but just as soon, Eden brought me slamming down, crushing my widening wound. I screamed in pain.

"You need to stop struggling," Eden said, still in that low, intimate register of hers. "You're going to bleed out."

Pain juddered through my shoulder, through my bones, as Eden shoved me against the floorboards again. But then—there was a curious squealing sound beneath me. The corner of the floorboard opposite my shoulder had popped open. Like a seesaw, it puckered now a full two inches above the rest of the floor.

"What the—?"

I scrabbled at the edge of the floorboard; Eden stomped it back down.

"Leave it," she snarled.

But a dark thought persisted: there was something here. I shoved Eden aside and took advantage of the free moment to grab ahold of the edge of the floorboard and pry it up. Groaning, cracking wood. Then, a sound like a seal breaking, and the full plank popped up, exposing humid blackness below.

That familiar scent of warm tin—the same one that had permeated the attic oasis Eden had created—hit my face. There was an alcove beneath the planks, stuffed with something lumpy, like a rolled tarp. Two dark holes stared back at me. It took me a horrid couple of seconds to register what they were, and then bile flooded my mouth, making me gag.

Human eye sockets, filled with congealed blood. A face sagging with rotting flesh. Tendons standing out on the neck, losing their protective cover of skin. The corpse wore the same silk black dress I'd been put in for my Initiation. But the material was entirely soaked through: a crusted blossom of blood bursting from the midsection. Sam's distinctive dark waves were the only recognizable detail remaining.

The Sisterhood had removed her eyes.

I vomited again onto the floor by my elbow. For all the nights I'd slept in this room, Sam's corpse had lain directly at my feet. My eyes fell on the broad floorboard I'd ripped up and tossed upside down. There were streaks of gouge marks on the underside. Claw marks. With a lurch, I remembered the mouse scrabbling in the wall that had woken me weeks ago.

Tiska-tisk-tisk.

Except it hadn't been a mouse.

Eden knelt beside me, her brow creased with concern. "Maybe we should talk about it?"

Rage churned like a machine coming sluggishly to life within my chest. For a second, my vision began to evaporate; I clutched my hemorrhaging side.

"It's just, you look like you're experiencing a lot of feelings," Eden added.

Her silky tone set the churning in my chest into high gear. I staggered to my feet. "How could you do this to her?"

The hallway light spilled onto Eden's face at an angle that intensified her starkness. Her concern had fallen away like a mask. "*I* didn't do anything. Sam took vows, just like the rest of us. And she broke them."

"What do you mean? Because she had a boyfriend?"

"Liv." Eden shook her head, looking disappointed. "This is about so much more than just a boyfriend. Yes, Sam started dating Brendan behind our backs. She probably filled out that restraining order as a way to throw us off, once we caught wind of it. But that was only the tip of the iceberg; Sam had already turned against The Sisterhood."

"How?"

"I mean, it started small, with little disagreements about the brides Beloved would take on—understandable, given Sam's personality. But then it turned into something far more severe. That boyfriend of hers turned her delusional— she suddenly thought all these doomed relationships could be saved, that she could save them! Sam started going behind our backs. Sending flowers secretly, as if from one of our grooms. Writing stupid love notes. Anything to resuscitate these toxic partnerships that should have been ended."

I never would have pictured Sam making such an effort in the name of love. Still, it wasn't adding up. "So? She sent some flowers, wrote some love notes . . . and that was grounds for murder?"

Eden uttered a dry, frustrated laugh. "You're vastly oversimplifying things, Liv. Sam broke the sacred oath. She undermined everything our Sisterhood stands for. And if there's one thing I cannot stand"—she gritted those perfect teeth of hers—"it's when people make promises they cannot keep."

Goosebumps prickled along my thighs, remembering my walk in the woods with her. The way Eden had spoken about her father. *He made an ironclad promise to her: they were in this together.*

"And as for 'murder,'" Eden was—somehow—still talking, "we barely had to lift a finger. Those ceremonial daggers from your Initiation? They're primed to recognize betrayal and they're no joke. Sam's body responded in turn . . . just like yours is, right now."

I pressed my hand to my bleeding side. "You ripped her *eyes* out, Eden."

Eden sniffed. "What does it matter? She'd already been blinded."

"You— You buried her alive! I saw the claw marks!"

"We punished Sam, yes, but what were we supposed to do? We couldn't very well dispose of one of our Sisters until we found a replacement."

My stomach plunged. *A replacement.*

Me.

"We needed to keep Sam alive as long as possible, to ensure you actually worked out. We'd seen your jewelry and had a feeling you had the same gift that Sam did, but there are never any guarantees. It's critical that we maintain the threesome. Always."

Oh God. What had they done to drag out Sam's death? Frantically, I ran through timelines in my head. "If Sam was still alive the night I met you . . ."

Eden nodded. "We had her locked in the hallway closet when you came over for dinner, yes. At that point, she was barely hanging on, but Cora had managed to whip up some special mints to sustain her for just long enough."

The smell of my own vomit on the floorboards swept through me. I thought back to the intoxicating night I'd flown to Whitfield Street through the serpentine back roads. That very night, The Sisterhood had held Sam captive in the closet, hemorrhaging from her eye sockets, as they wooed me with mushroom soup and pomegranate salad one floor below. Later that night, I'd practically slept beside her. Now, my body undulated, jockeying to empty itself again. "Why . . . why didn't I smell her body under there?"

"We have enchantments to deal with that."

Right—the warm tin scent I smelled up in the attic. I leaned forward, bracing my hands on my thighs. Any moment, I prayed, this horrific nightmare would have to crush to a close and I'd be waking in a sun-soaked bed. Safe.

"I almost feel bad," Eden added, looking down at Sam's corpse under the floorboards. Then she gave me a weighty look. "Given everything that Sam had been through."

I stared at her, shell-shocked. After all the time we'd spent working and dining and drinking together, Eden had finally spoken the truth aloud. It dangled in the air between us, threatening to detonate.

Eden clucked. "You're acting like this is a surprise. Like you conveniently forgot you flung your best friend off a third-story balcony."

There it was. Her words were acid, confirming my worst suspicion: Eden had seen me that night at Kitty's, after all. For the past couple of weeks, I'd studied Eden's face incessantly, trying to puzzle out how much she knew. Like tearing petals from a flower and agonizing: *She knows, she knows not.*

Turns out, I hadn't imagined that dark brow in the doorway.

Not a day passed that I didn't feel guilty. I'd made the ultimate betrayal by choosing Sam's twin over her. A hypothetical gap year in Europe—which hadn't even been booked yet—over a full-ride scholarship to art school with my best friend. And all just to lash out at Sam, too. To hurt her. What was my problem? Despite her prickly moments, Sam had encouraged and supported me. She'd come to my rescue when I'd been alone and suffering. Why couldn't I have recognized that, back at Kitty Wallace's house years ago?

To add insult to injury, the ripples from my lashing-out seemed never to end. When our freshman class was moving into their dorms, Sam was in a hospital bed with a shattered femur. Even after that had healed, she needed another year of rehabilitation to regain her ability to walk. Because of me, Sam had to forfeit her RISD acceptance. Because of me, Everett hadn't been able to go to Europe, and had to stay home instead to help care for his sister. Because of me, Sam's parents had to take out a second mortgage on their home to pay for medical expenses. And because of Sam's concussion, there were memories that she'd never access again.

How convenient for me.

"Why didn't you ever turn me in?" I whispered. "If you'd seen what I'd done—"

Eden shrugged. "What good would that do me? Besides, I had a feeling you'd be back."

I hung my head. Eden had let me get away with a felony, let me blubber out my lies to the police when they'd questioned me that night, and all for what? Potential leverage down the road? It was part of the reason I hadn't wanted to anger Eden, why I'd worked so hard to stay in her good graces. Yes, of course, I wanted to ensure I stayed looped in on Sam's investigation. But if I was being honest? This entire mess had probably always been more about myself. About absolving my own guilt.

Saving my own ass.

I brimmed over with self-loathing. The suffering Eden and I had caused Sam was unfathomable.

"What about Everett? His hospitalization. You did that, didn't you? You knew about his peanut allergy from high school."

Eden opened her mouth, then closed it. "*I'm* not the one who bakes," she said finally.

I flashed back to the plates of baked goods on Everett's counter, tinfoil peeled away. Of course: Cora. "Why?"

"Because the two of you were talking about Sam. Poking around. I didn't want any more of that going on." Eden stared at me for a minute, her gaze sharp as tacks. "Let me guess," she said. "You're going to try to leave now. Just like your bestie."

Would my body spontaneously turn inside-out in a bloody torrent if I admitted it aloud?

Eden took a couple of steps toward me. "You've made a huge mistake, Liv."

My body was certainly indicating as much. I pressed the heel of my hand into the blood, sucking air in through my mouth.

"We saw such promise in you. Such power. And now, look at you. About to throw it all away to—what? Run back to your boyfriend and become some pathetic housewife? Ask any wife, any mother." She'd come within inches of me now. "You *will* lose yourself."

I ground my teeth, working up the strength to run.

"Remember what it felt like with us, in the workshop?" Eden pointed toward the back of the house. "Well, you won't get that anymore! You won't get to immerse yourself in anything, because your life will be crammed. Full. Of other people's. Shit." Eden let out a single, bitter laugh. "Actually, there's something even worse than all this." Her voice dropped into an even lower register, forcing me to grasp at her words, even though they revolted me. "Do you know why Sam joined our Sisterhood? What motivated her to make such a difficult commitment in the first place?"

I looked at her with horror.

Eden reached out to tuck a damp lock of hair behind my ear. The brush of her hand made my skin crawl. "She told me her greatest fear was ending up like you and your mom."

My hands were around her throat in a second. Eden emitted a startled sound, and it just made me squeeze harder, pressing my thumbs into her delicate webbing of muscle. Because of the pain and blood loss, I was weaker than usual, but Eden's soft throat against my hands kicked the hunger inside me into a frenzy.

She struggled, admirably. But then, suddenly, there was a pounding on the staircase. Cora flew into the room and wrestled me to the ground.

There were two of them against me now, and it was a losing battle. Someone bound my hands; that familiar blindfold slipped down over my eyes. A sweet, grainy substance was painted gently onto my lips. It called to mind the hollow, sugared eggs Mom used to get me at Easter, the ones that doubled as little dioramas of woodland creatures.

Then the world fell away.

30

NOW

MY EYES BLINKED OPEN TO THE LAVENDER BRIDAL SALON. An oily, knowing feeling slid down between my shoulder blades. Hesitantly, I attempted to raise a hand.

A familiar silk scarf bit into my wrist.

Eden's hand pressed down on my shoulder, against a gathered satin neckline. I'd been dressed in the same black gown I'd worn to my Initiation, with the line of itchy buttons down my spine.

No.

"May the night smile upon you."

"And upon you," Cora chorused back. The cadence of the girls' voices brought back flashes of my Initiation, and I broke out in a cold sweat.

Why had I been brought here? What the hell were Eden and Cora going to do to me now?

"Tonight we celebrate another successful mission," Eden said. "Another bride's eyes have been opened."

Their attention was directed to a large covered easel on the other of side of Eden—the same easel, doubtless, I'd glimpsed when spying on The Sisterhood through the window.

Eden lifted the drop cloth, revealing a photograph of that afternoon's bride, corkscrew curls free and rampant. The same photo I'd found in the studio closet earlier that day. After Cora passed her a single candle from a three-branched candelabra, Eden touched the red flame to the corner of the canvas. I stifled a gasp. The fire leaped through the material, audibly eating away at the photo of the bride, crackling and angry.

As the flame tore through the canvas, it left brittle black material in its wake. But the image was blackening in an unnatural way: narrowing, tunnel-like, around the bride's eyes. First her hair, then her jaw and cheeks . . . the fire crept steadily inward. Finally, when only the bride's eyes remained, the flames extinguished themselves.

Eden tapped the candle against the canvas. The blackened areas shuddered into dust and fell to the floor in a heap. Eden's hand shot out and plucked the bride's eyes just before they fell. Then, gently, Eden rolled the canvas eyes into a tiny scroll and slid them inside a small tin box proffered by Cora.

"May our bride have the insight and courage to chart the rest of her life with her eyes wide open," she said.

"May the night smile upon her," Cora intoned.

Eden took a step away from the easel. The candle flames shifted to chemical green. Cora approached with a broom and a dustbin and swiftly swept up the ashes.

"Unfortunately," Eden said, "we have some less pleasant business to deal with now."

My teeth began to chatter again. The fear I had felt during my Initiation was unmatched by the explosive terror I felt in this moment.

Now, it was me Eden addressed directly. This was so much worse than her prior incantation. "Liv, you showed such promise when you were initiated into our Sisterhood. Power. Creative prowess. But unfortunately—and it pains me to say this—you broke your vows. Just like Sam. And as you know, we cannot abide such behavior. We cannot stand by our Sister when she begins to rot from the inside."

Eden's fingertips danced along my shoulder and I squeezed my eyes shut, vibrating with dread. Each breath in was laborious, rattling my ribs. The agony had crept steadily from my hip down the entire left side of my body. When I opened my eyes and looked down at my restrained forearms, I bit back a cry. The veins beneath my skin had jumped into brown-black relief. And there were so, so many of them: vivid arteries branching into hundreds of grasping tributaries, devouring the surface area of my body. I was rotting in real time, just as Eden had said.

I gritted my teeth and looked away.

Breathe. It isn't real.

But as for the stabbing pain in my side, there was nothing artificial about that. Around me, the candle flames turned dagger-sharp, a silvery shade now. Eden headed toward the far wall of the salon. Surreptitiously, I strained against the silk restraints. They were only silk—surely, they were breakable? But to do so would require a burst of strength that the girls would see.

A single, mournful tone shot through the house.

The doorbell!

Eden and Cora exchanged a look.

"I'll get it," Cora said.

"No," Eden said. "Best if I do." She squeezed my shoulder once before gliding out of the bridal salon. Was it possible that Patterson had gotten my voicemail and finally made it over here? I clenched every muscle in my body with hope, so hard my bones hurt.

Please, Patterson. Whoever you are. Get me out of here.

The boutique remained deathly quiet. I focused on the vase of gardenias in the front of the room until my eyes watered. Then—the creak of the front door opening. Strains of Eden's voice, rising and falling in that polished way she spoke to bridal clients.

I screamed. "Help!"

Come on, Patterson. I'm right back here. All you have to do is ask to come in.

Mocking silence rang back at me. I tried to catch Cora's eye, to appeal to her. She'd always been the warmer of the two, the one bringing me food and drinks and Band-Aids. If I stood any chance of being freed, it would be with her.

"Please, Cora," I whispered.

Finally, she made eye contact with me. She gave me a tiny smile and sidled up to my chair.

"Liv," she said, in a voice like spun sugar.

Then she slapped me across the face.

I cried out, doubly wounded.

Cora turned away, as if the very sight of me repulsed her. "I'll never fucking understand what Eden saw in you."

I closed my own eyes into the sting, the accompanying explosion of stars. I was rocked by Cora's lashing out; I'd never even heard her curse before. But of course, on some level, I'd sensed her growing resentment. I'd just been too enchanted by Eden's attention and my own burgeoning power to care.

Finally—the groan of the front door again. Footsteps— two pairs of them—approaching the salon.

I felt woozy with relief. Any minute now, I'd see Patterson's silvered head emerge in the doorway, putting an end to this nightmare.

"Here we are," came Eden's voice.

But there was something wrong with this—she was still using the same formal tone she took with her clients. That she'd taken with Noah and me, during our interview.

Patterson stepped into the bridal salon.

I had to seize my opportunity. "Help!"

He scanned the room—the gowned mannequins, flowers, and flickering candles—and looked directly at me, tied to that wicker chair.

Even from a distance, I could see his eyes were bone-white.

"See?" Eden said, pleasantly. "Like I said. No one here."

I thought I might throw up for a third time.

"Hey!" I yelled, louder this time. "Patterson! I'm right here! And there are two dead bodies—"

But it was useless. To him, I was a ghost.

Patterson trained his white eyes back on Eden. "Glad everything is okay. I'll leave you ladies to it."

"Thanks, Detective. I'll show you out."

I wanted to scream. How was this happening? I couldn't fathom it—my last opportunity for rescue, dashed before my very eyes.

Too soon, Eden was back beside me. "Where was I?"

If she saw Cora's red handprint on my face, she didn't acknowledge it. Cora nodded at the vase of gardenias. Eden lifted them off the table, exposing a faint rectangular outline in the wall. This she prodded with her fingertips and the drywall came away with a dull *thuck*, revealing a dark recess.

Balling my hands up, I yanked at the scarves again. Something snagged in the material and I looked down in surprise. My bird's nest ring had caught in the fabric.

Eden reached into the hole in the wall. Then, gingerly, she lifted out a dark object. It was about the size and shape of a cantaloupe, and its very surface seemed to be alive. Writhing.

My shoulders slammed against the back of the chair. It was a mass of madly scrambling beetles—I'd never seen so many of them in one place. Several fell away and scampered into the corners of the room. Only two beetles remained perfectly still, poised at the front of the ball to create the illusion of two unblinking, blue eyes.

Eden made no reaction as one beetle scurried up her

arm to rest in the hollow below her throat. She continued to regard the ball of writhing insects with exaggerated reverence. "Do you know what this is, Liv?"

I looked closer—sure enough, the cantaloupe-like item coalesced into the form of a human head: square mandible, eye sockets filled with those two unmoving beetles.

"No, of course you don't," Eden answered her own question. "This is the skull of Oliver Wythers, Harriett's husband. After years of systematically abusing his wife, Oliver died from mysterious stomach complications. He was buried in the tract of land behind his home, not far from where we stand."

It was a familiar story, of course. I'd heard it during my tour of the Wythers House as a teenager, and Eden had alluded to Oliver's death during my Initiation. Suddenly, Everett's voice rang in my memory: *There was this one time I showed up early at Eden's house. Her friends were still there . . . They were all huddled around . . . a piece of bone . . .*

Had Eden dug up this skull as a teenager? Stolen it from her workplace? How the hell had she kept it hidden, all this time?

"And this is where our beloved Seeing Beetles took up residence," Eden went on, "nestling right into the corpse of this hideous man and consuming his flesh. They were drawn there and continued to multiply for years. Such an important reminder that beauty and hope can blossom out of ugliness. Out of indescribable darkness."

I jumped at a slight tearing sensation in the scarf. I'd succeeded in maneuvering my ring against it and opening a slice in the fabric. But I couldn't be obvious about the tearing. I'd have to do it little by little, while Eden was still speaking.

A singular beetle clambered into the palm of Eden's free hand; she passed it gently to Cora, who took it, giggling. "Isn't it so cute how they've evolved to wear The Sisterhood's eye on their backs?" Cora had reverted back to her normal saccharine tone, as if she'd never cursed me out, never slapped me across the face. "They live in the insulation and framework of the house now, eating . . . what, Eden? Mostly pollen and ants?"

I felt the sting of sweat on my upper lip. The wound in my side seared. I'd already had to put one of those vile bugs in my mouth—what the hell were the girls going to subject me to now?

Eden studied the writhing skull in her hands. "Mostly. But you know that after poor Oliver, their tastes evolved a bit."

It took a few, jerky moments for me to connect the dots, and then horror exploded in my heart. The Seeing Beetles had eaten Oliver's flesh so many years ago. And I'd just seen Sam's body under the floorboards—it couldn't have decomposed to that extent in only a week. Had Eden and Cora unleashed these beetles on her when they found out she'd broken her oath?

Eden must have read my mind, for the millionth time. "Liv," she said, "it's your turn to take this now." And she set the beetle-covered skull in my lap.

At first, I could only stare down at the squirming mass on top of me, those patent-leather-like, clicking carapaces sliding over one another. Mean heads narrowing to a point, needle-like palpi bracketing each hungry mouth. The two motionless beetles stared up at me as eyes in the sockets of Oliver's skull. I could just feel the prickle of insect feet through the fabric of my dress and repulsion roiled through me.

I screamed, thrashing about in the chair.

The beetles fanned out along my stomach. They trailed in lines up my every limb. A couple nuzzled into my throat and clavicle, finding welcoming grooves in the hollows against my bones.

Then the bites began, so fiery they felt electric. I gasped as the shocks of pain radiated down my legs. When the beetles began biting me in the sensitive skin beneath my jaw and my arms, I thought I might pass out from the agony.

A beetle clambered over the back of my hand and sank its fangs into the skin between my index and middle fingers. I was unprepared for how intense the pain would be, in this forgotten area of my body. I used the bird's nest ring like a machete, slashing at the gauzy scarf as the torturous bites raged on. At last, my right hand ripped free, and I began tearing at the knot on my left wrist. Slowly, the beetles were eating away at the satin of my dress, opening holes along my thighs. The exposed skin of my upper arms was already mottled with shiny red abrasions. How long before they started to bleed? Before the beetles started ripping flesh from my bone?

Finally, my left hand flew free; I swiped the skull out of my lap and began scrabbling to undo the scarves at my ankles.

It took Cora a few moments to notice. She dove to restrain me, but by then I'd already succeeded in freeing myself. I hefted the ancient wooden chair and slammed it crosswise against her body; she crumpled with a scream, crashing into the floral display and dashing broken glass and flowerheads across the floor.

Eden was on me in an instant. Somehow, the beetles still clung to me, despite my frantic movements. Eden grabbed at me, her hand catching on my spiny ring. She recoiled with a yelp, then snatched at me again, causing my ring to go clattering onto the floor. It gave me the opening I needed to wrench out of Eden's grip and shoot across the room, toward the frosting-smeared plates left by the bride and groom.

Eden lunged at me, grasping for my shoulder, but I managed to grab the wood-handled knife from the table and drove it into her face. I'd been expecting to come up against a wall of bone, but the end of the blade pierced something softer, with the initial rubbery tension and subsequent give of a grape.

Eden screamed, clutching at her eye.

I shot through the double doors of the bridal salon and scrambled to lock it behind me, shaking the last of the insects from my body. As Eden and Cora clamored behind it, I staggered into the heart of the pink Victorian, through the living and dining rooms toward the front door. My mind whirred fast as a machine, plotting my escape. I had no phone and no car—I'd have to rely on some good Samaritan to bring me to the hospital. Once outside the house, the closest neighbor was about fifty yards to my right. If I could just get them to answer the door before Eden and Cora broke down the one to the bridal salon . . .

At the front door, I slammed down the lever on the black, spade-shaped handle.

Nothing happened.

I felt over the lever and the door, searching for a button or bolt to release. Nothing. Ugly realization dawned: after seeing Patterson out, Eden must have locked the front door from the inside.

This house was going to be the death of me.

A cracking, splintering sound—Eden and Cora had succeeded in breaking down the salon door. Panicked, I did the only thing I could think to do next: I fled upstairs. I looked around wildly. I'd have to hide somewhere, but the only ideas that occurred to me seemed like the most obvious prospects: closets, behind shower curtains, under beds.

You'll have to do better than that. Think!

Breathing hard, I took in the second-floor hallway. Then, at the far end—the rectangular outline of the dumbwaiter Eden and Cora had shown me, about the size of a small nightstand. Would I even fit in there?

Footfalls sounded at the base of the staircase.

I threw open the door to the dumbwaiter and wedged myself inside. It took a couple of tries before I was able to close the door on myself. Crushed into the dark cubbyhole, I grimaced, tried to rearrange my limbs so they wouldn't shove the door back open.

I held my breath.

Footsteps on the landing, on the second floor now.

Eden's voice: "Check the bedrooms."

Then—the whine of hinges opening and closing. Bedroom and closet doors flung wide. I forced myself to pull in a shaky breath. Inside the dumbwaiter, it smelled like damp wood. The rough woodgrain tore at my scalp as I pressed myself against the wall. I thought for sure the girls would be able to hear the pounding of my heart through the door. I thought for sure I'd chosen a terrible hiding spot. What was stopping them from flinging open the door to the dumb-waiter? Was it that inconceivable for me to have shoved my body in here?

"Cora." Eden's voice had to be inches from my face. I bit back a gasp, digging my nails into my palms to steel my-self. "I need you to check the attic."

Breathless, I listened to the squeal of the rickety ladder being pulled from the ceiling. Had the door to the dumb-waiter been open, I could have reached out and touched them.

A sudden, scorching sensation along the tender scoop of my underarm, and my body went hot and then cold. *Shit.* There was still a beetle nestled in the lining of my dress— I could feel it clambering along the curve of my rib cage. The very thought made me want to retch right there in the dumbwaiter. A scream coiled inside of me; I longed to swipe that damn bug off me and crush it to a pulp under my heel. But any movement would reveal myself to Eden and Cora, and then my escape from the bridal salon would be in vain.

I sank my teeth into my fist to quell my disgust.

Just get through this.

The attic ladder screamed and shuddered under Cora as she climbed. Presently, her steps sounded directly over my head as she made a sweep of the attic space. The beetle paused above my right hip bone, and I tensed, preparing for another fiery bite.

"Nothing," Cora called back down.

How hadn't they thought to look in the dumbwaiter? When would it occur to them to open the door to the crawl-space directly in front of their faces?

Eden's voice was so cold it made my chest seize. Because of my positioning, crouching there in the cubbyhole facing the hallway, it felt as if she were speaking directly to me. "Check under the pillows on the daybed."

"I did."

A piercing in my side. I clamped my own teeth over a knuckle to silence a whimper.

Eden spoke under her breath: "We'll just have to wait her out downstairs."

I waited until the girls' footsteps on the stairs had faded. My entire body was quaking—from revulsion, from pain, from the sheer tension of having wedged myself nearly in half to fit inside the dumbwaiter. Slowly, I eased the door open, one tiny slice of empty hallway revealing itself to me after the next. Finally, when I was sure it was clear, I spilled out into the hallway. Then I ripped the beetle from inside my dress, flinging it to the ground and grinding it with my heel until it was a shiny black smear in the grain of the floorboards.

Panting, I assessed my options. The girls knew I was somewhere in the house and certainly wouldn't be leaving any of the exits unattended. Hysteria built in me again, vibrating through my bones as if they were tuning forks.

I was screwed.

The dangling chain to the attic stairs shivered above me. I'd been out on the widow's walk before—was it at all possible to get down from there? I tried to remember the night of the shooting stars, if there were any hedges or pipes that would aid in my descent.

No, that was absurd. I had a gaping wound in my side that was starting to make me loopy with pain. I wasn't about to walk onto a third-story balcony and try to shimmy down the side of a house.

A nasty voice threaded through my mind: *Got any better ideas?*

Gritting my teeth, I pulled the chain to the attic stairs as gently, as quietly, as possible. The wooden steps unfolded like an accordion. On the third stair, I doubled over in pain and lost my footing, nearly crumpling to the bottom once again.

Pull yourself together.

I struggled up the last of the stairs and into the attic. The fainting couch had been upended, its pillows scattered on the floor. Were the girls still tearing the house apart looking for me? Grimacing, I pulled up the attic stairs and went straight to the window leading to the widow's walk. Hefted it open and maneuvered my body outside. For a moment, my side caught on the sill, and the pain was so intense it left me seeing white.

Focus. Just get out of here.

The wind was violent up on the widow's walk. I peered down at the scallops of the house, a swath of ivy covering one pink face. It must have taken years for the leaves to wind themselves around that wooden latticework. But thank God the trellis was there, because it was my only chance at escaping.

As I placed one shaking foot on the first wooden slat, it occurred to me how fitting it would be if I died this way. I'd thrown my best friend off a third-story balcony; wouldn't it be perfect karmic retribution for me to die in a similar fashion? I slotted my second foot onto the trellis and the entire structure flapped perilously beneath me. What thoughts had burst into Sam's mind as she sailed down the side of Kitty's house? Had she even had time to be afraid? Or had her brain fast-forwarded straight to acceptance? *I'm falling. I might die.*

Another step down the trellis and this time, it shuddered so gravely I cried out. One spot of rot and I'd be screwed. It was likely to happen on such an old structure— I only hoped it would happen far enough down the side of the house that the injury would be minimal, that I'd still be able to drag myself the fifty yards or so to safety. A splinter jammed itself into the heel of my hand and I blinked past the pain. It was nothing compared to the agony tearing open my side, streaking dark blood along the ivy.

Another couple of feet lower. My arms and calves trembled with exertion. I had to think about my descent in bite-sized pieces; otherwise, I'd never make it. One slat lower. One more handhold.

Then, it happened—my foot broke through a rotted wooden slat. I flailed against the side of the house, wildly seeking purchase somewhere, anywhere else. In my panic, my right hand slipped from its hold and my entire body slid down the trellis, scraping splinters down my throat and chest.

I crashed into a hedge at the base of the house, waxy needles against my scalp. Had I broken anything? My entire body blazed with agony; it was impossible to tell. At this point, the only thing that mattered was dragging myself onto the porch of the only visible neighbor.

I began to stagger down the drive, toward the beckoning gray clapboards.

I made it about ten yards before sinking to my knees. The pain was too intense; blood soaked my side, reminding me of the widening wound in my flank. I probed it with a finger: it had gotten even worse. My vision narrowed to a tunnel. Furiously, I channeled Eden's rebuke: *Pull yourself together!*

Finally, through the foliage, the neighbor's house emerged. I lurched toward the front porch, throwing myself upon it. Felt around in the dark for a doorbell. I couldn't tell if it was my vision fading or if it was really that dark. After years in Boston, I'd forgotten what true darkness felt like. Suddenly, a porch light flicked on above my head. Had someone in the house heard me? Were they coming outside now?

Please, please. Come get me.

"Liv."

I whirled.

Eden stood, panting, on the first porch stair, one eye socket flooded with bloody pulp.

How the hell could she see? I started banging frantically on the plate glass of the neighbor's door. "Help!"

"Stop." She was inches from me now, that bite of white teeth blinding in the porch light. "I promise not to hurt you, okay? We made a mistake; we want you back. Don't you want to be one of us, to keep helping our brides?"

I shrank away from her bloodied eye socket. "You aren't helping anyone."

Eden recoiled as if I'd struck her. "How could you say that? Everything we do is to free our brides."

"From *what?*"

Eden's hand slid up to my neck and began to squeeze. "From the world closing in on them, of course. Tell me if this sounds familiar." She adopted a jeering tone. " 'Find a husband; you're no one without a man. Have babies; you're not a real woman until you have kids. Nope, one isn't enough. Won't your first child be lonely? God, woman, you're so fucking *selfish.*' "

Golden sparklers burst against my eyelids.

Then, all at once, she released her grip.

I gasped for air. It was so cold and glorious, I thought I'd never tire of gulping it.

Eden watched me, smiling. Her bloodied eye socket, so close now, made me shudder. "Feels good, doesn't it?" she said quietly. "To be able to breathe?"

My own hand migrated to my throat, pulsing and raw. I didn't know if my voice would even function after all that crushing pressure. "You're not freeing your brides, Eden. You're just trapping them in a different way."

Where the hell was whoever had flipped on the porch light? Then a horrifying thought crested: it could have been motion-activated.

I didn't care. I had to hold on to hope. I returned to banging on the door with all my might.

"Hey," Eden chided, pulling my hands into hers.

I shoved her away. "I don't want this."

When Eden righted herself, her face was poisonous. "You've already turned your back on Sam. On your girl-friends in Boston. Don't you dare make the same mistake again." She paused. "Are you honestly telling me you don't want sisterhood? You don't want power?"

I kept pounding at the door, determined to block out her words.

"You're choosing family, then? You're choosing endless sacrifice and creative death instead?"

"Stop saying it has to be one or the other!"

"Why? It's the truth."

I wouldn't make eye contact with her. "I refuse to be-lieve that."

Eden laughed a little, smoothed hair away from my face. "Oh, chickadee. Then you have a very harsh reality check coming."

Accordingly, there tore such pain in my side that the neighbor's porch flashed in my field of vision like a photo-graph negative. Was Eden bewitching me again, or was this reality? Was I really dying? I gasped, feeling hot blood gush forth in a torrent—through the satin of my dress and onto the slats of the porch by my feet with a grotesque splattering sound.

Here it was: my rejected body bleeding out, just as I'd been promised.

The wood under my hand pressed forward. I didn't

even register the face at the door, just the silhouette. With my last reserves of strength, I pushed inside the neighbor's house, slammed and deadbolted the door behind me. Then, at last, I collapsed onto the cold tile floor as Eden's grandmotherly neighbor looked on in horror.

"Don't open the door," I begged through my tears. "Don't let her touch you. Whatever you do, don't let her touch you."

31

NOW

WHOEVER DESIGNED MY HOSPITAL ROOM MUST HAVE had a thing for seafoam green. The shade was everywhere: on the walls, the nurses' scrubs, even in the inoffensive framed print of a girl walking along a canal holding a green umbrella. There was also a window, which painted a square of buttery light on my bed at the right hour. I enjoyed that window up until the day one of the nurses pointed out a black-and-gray bird flickering past.

"Oh!" she'd said. "I think a little chickadee has come to visit."

Remembering Eden's nickname for me, iciness streaked down my spine. I asked to close the curtain for the remainder of the day.

I couldn't recall arriving at the hospital. I must have lost consciousness shortly after collapsing on the neighbor's floor. What I did remember was blinking awake in my hospital room, clutching at the fleeting tendrils of a dream. Mom and Penny were sitting by my bed and jumped to summon the nurse.

"Thank God," Penny kept saying, stroking the back of my hand. "Thank God."

Mom comforted me as well, but her eyes kept filling with tears, and then she'd have to look away.

My voice emerged as a croak. "Where are the twins?"

"With Carter," Penny said, sounding impatient. "They're fine. Everyone's fine. Thank God."

Of course, they wanted to know what had happened. I stammered my way through a feeble excuse about falling from a friend's attic window. What else was I supposed to do? Mom and Penny would never believe the truth. Besides, I wasn't sure how I wanted to proceed regarding implicating The Sisterhood; I had to speak with Detective Patterson first. But Mom and Penny grew increasingly frustrated with my evasion, to the point where the nurse had to interject.

"Her memories are probably still scrambled from her accident," she told them. "What's important now is that she's able to focus on recovering."

I shot her a grateful look. She winked back at me.

When Mom and Penny stepped out to get something from the vending machine, I snuck a look under the sheets. I'd been told the wound in my side had been cleaned and stitched up, but now it was covered by a length of gauze and adhesive that made it impossible for me to gauge how dire

332 K. L. CERRA

it really was. Later, when I asked the nurse how deep it had been, she shrugged.

"Pretty deep."

"Like, life-threatening deep?"

"It could have been."

I was haunted by memories of that night's atrocities: standing on the neighbor's porch, having Eden touch my hair. Then my side opening up, spilling my blood onto the planks. It drove me wild that I couldn't determine if this was real or not. Had I really been on the brink of death? Or had that been Eden, messing with me yet again?

Next to surface were memories of Sam's body under the floorboards. They dug under my ribs like a dull blade: visions of that congealed blood in her eye sockets, that same black dress I'd worn for my own Initiation. That night— and many nights to follow—I would gasp awake from nightmares of Sam's body staring back at me from the gloom.

I asked the nurse to contact Patterson for me. She nodded, but she didn't look like she approved of the request.

Noah visited me that first evening in the hospital, after my mother and sister had left. His eyes looked wide and hollow when they fell over me; I'd never seen him look so spooked.

"I'm fine!" I insisted, batting away his concern. "Just a few stitches. Geez, Noah."

He dragged the plastic chair an awkward distance from my bed—too close for a polite acquaintance, too far away for a loved one. I could tell he was trying to figure out whether or not to touch me.

"It really freaked me out to get that call from your sister," Noah said. "After Ben . . ."

I hadn't even connected the dots like that. Sympathy welled within me. "Oh God. I'm sorry."

"Don't apologize. You're the one in the hospital." He shifted in his chair, looked over at the print of the green umbrella. "Your mom told me you fell out of . . . an attic?"

I nodded. "Yeah." I could tell he was hoping for more information, but I wasn't going to give it to him.

Noah bent forward in his chair and tenderly touched the back of my hand. "I miss you."

Longing shot through me, laced with something like frustration. "I know."

Noah sighed. He sounded exhausted. "Honestly, Liv, I haven't been doing so hot since I left Guilford. I don't like how we left things."

"I know."

"Can we talk? Clear this up, once and for all? Maybe once you're feeling better."

I squeezed my eyes shut against the threat of tears. "I don't know how talking will fix anything." Maybe it was unfair of me to keep running from a necessary conversation. I would never be like Noah, facing confrontation head-on. But didn't he realize the pain on the other side of this was going to be debilitating?

Noah's voice cracked. "That's not what I wanted to hear."

A single tear slipped down my face. More than anything he'd said to me so far, it was that involuntary rip in his voice that did me in. "I don't know what to say," I whispered.

"Say you'll come home with me."

Tell me I'll get what I want.

I shook my head.

Another sigh, this one less anguished, more frustrated. "You know, I've been thinking. And if you're dead set on going back to work after we have children, we can look into how much daycare would cost."

"But you still want four kids?"

A beat of silence. "Yes."

"I don't know, Noah. Even with daycare, I just . . . don't want my life to be consumed like that."

"Well, I really do. It's important to me."

Now it was my turn to brim with frustration. How could I possibly convey to Noah that—if the world around me was any indication—any consuming of *his* life post-kids would pale in comparison to mine?

A couple more tears burned their way down my face. I caught a glimpse of myself in the window reflection, just as my mouth contorted hideously.

"There has to be a rational way of working this out," Noah said. He was using the same assured tone I heard him use on work calls, but it sounded like a front, like he was fighting to keep his voice from cracking open again. He put his hand on mine, beseeching. "Couples therapy. Something."

Ugly, unspeakable thoughts filled my mind. *This is all your brother's fault. Why did Ben have to die and make you change your mind about everything? We had everything figured out. We could have been happy.*

"You want a big family, Noah. I don't."

"But can't we figure out some kind of middle ground?"

I hesitated. "Honestly, I'm starting to wonder if I want any kids at all."

Noah's face went red, eyes rolled to the ceiling. Then, with one fist, he hit the foot of the bed. "God-fucking-dammit!"

How is this fair? I thought, as we both shook with silent tears. The door to my hospital room was open, letting in the sounds of the mundane: the squeak of rubber on the linoleum, the clatter of empty plates on a cafeteria cart. Outside this room, it was business as usual, which seemed a cruel juxtaposition to the fact that my own eight-year relationship was detonating before my eyes.

I reached for Noah's hand. He looked at me finally, and seeing his tears and bloodshot eyes made me feel as if I were being gutted alive. Then I slid my engagement ring off my finger—since my spined ring had been lost in the fray of the bridal boutique, it meant my hands were now bare. Gently, I uncurled Noah's fingers and laid the ring in his palm, pressing the warm cage of his hand back around the diamond. It didn't feel anything like that staggering wave of relief I'd experienced seeing Eden's vision before Initiation. She'd sold me a lie: despite my certainty I was doing the right thing, I just felt hollow.

. . .

THAT NIGHT, AFTER MY NIGHTMARE about Sam, my coursing anxiety and the relentless beeping of the machines kept me awake. I was worried about meeting Patterson. Without a phone, I couldn't get my news alerts about Sam to see what the media was saying. Would the nurse even indulge my need to meet with the detective? My stomach writhed at the thought of facing him after the showdown at 128 Whitfield. The last time I'd seen him, his deadened eyes had swept right over me. What had Eden made him see? How deeply had she gotten her talons into him?

The detective arrived early the next morning, before I'd even had the chance to wipe the sleep from my tear ducts. He carried a steaming paper cup, which he set on the table beside my bed, along with a tiny lollipop in a question mark–spangled wrapper.

"What's this?"

"Coffee and a Dum-Dum. I thought you liked that flavor. I saw you take one from the station a while back."

I twirled the lollipop between two fingers. As much as the gesture warmed me, Patterson was so very wrong.

"You probably haven't heard the news," he said, settling into the same chair Noah had filled yesterday.

My heart accelerated. "What news?"

"I'm confident we'll be closing Sam's case soon. Her roommates received a postcard from Ireland the other day and our experts confirmed the handwriting was a perfect match."

I stared at Patterson, my blood a battering ram in my chest. A *postcard*? That was something Eden could have easily fabricated. I could just imagine her slipping into the police station, laying her fingertips on Patterson's forearm as she pulled out the card . . .

"I—" The crushing panic was overtaking me again. What about Sam's body under the floorboards? Was that just going to be left to rot away in that wicked house, never to be returned to her family? And speaking of her family, did this mean they would be clutching to false hope for years, waiting indefinitely for their dead daughter to come home?

I thought I might pass out. "Are you sure?"

"Absolutely."

"But what if she never comes back from Ireland? Did you ever really comb Sam's room? Under the floor? I—"

"Liv," Patterson cut me off. He gave a little chuckle. "Everything turned out for the best."

Furious tears built behind my eyes. I turned away from Patterson, studying the sharp corners of that rectangle of sun at the base of my bed. It was hopeless: Patterson had fallen under Eden's spell. Besides, even if I told him about Sam's body, The Sisterhood was sure to have removed it by now. No matter how hard I tried, they would always be one step ahead. I wanted to take the steaming coffee Patterson had brought me and hurl it against the wall.

Patterson was studying my face with a cautious smile. "It's okay to feel relieved, you know."

I clenched my fists under the sheets.

"Hell, sometimes it's even okay to be happy."

I stared at him. *Happy?* How could I be happy after finding Sam under the floorboards? After learning that her family would never know the truth? Besides, it was never happiness I'd come to Guilford to chase. Absolution, maybe. And later, after being tempted by The Sisterhood, the intoxication of creative power and female comradery. But happiness? I wasn't sure that was even something I deserved.

Patterson nodded encouragingly.

Excruciating as it was, I forced the ends of my lips to curl upward into a grotesque parody of a smile.

AFTER PATTERSON'S VISIT, I GOT permission from a nurse to use the restroom down the hall: I didn't relish the idea of using the foldaway toilet in my hospital room. Besides, I'd healed enough that Mom and Penny were coming to pick me up in an hour.

The nurse in her seafoam scrubs escorted me down the hallway, Crocs squeaking against the floor. We passed nursing stations and rows of curtained partitions.

The door to the women's room flew open, gusting a puff of antiseptic-scented air against my cheek.

Eden stood before me in a ribbed turtleneck and jeans. Her captivating face was unmarred, except for the eye I'd gouged, whose remains had—inexplicably—turned milky white.

A cascade of shivers ran up and down each vertebrae, accompanied by a stab of pain in my side that made my vision darken momentarily. I crumpled backward into the nurse's arms.

"Whoa!" the nurse exclaimed, breaking my fall. "Easy."

Eden's face was blank of emotion. Her eyes drifted to the bandage taped to my side, which had suddenly begun flowering red. As she swept past me, her gravelly voice was nearly inaudible.

"You're bleeding."

EIGHT YEARS LATER

M Y DAUGHTER WAS STANDING TOO CLOSE TO THE TRAIN
tracks.

"Careful!" I yanked her back and her little rose-
bud of a mouth squinched together with displeasure, the
same way her father's often did.

"Ouch, Mommy!"

"See this yellow stripe? It's not safe to walk on the yellow. We need to stay on the gray," I said to her. "Sorry," I
muttered into my phone.

My realtor laughed warmly on the other end. "I thought
I heard your little Mini-Me in the background."

We were finalizing the offer on a storefront in Stony
Creek, Connecticut. Over the past year, I'd finally built up
the inventory—and the courage—to expand my jewelry
business to a brick-and-mortar location, thanks in large part
to my husband's encouragement. Blake and I had met when

I was just starting the craft fair circuit and still felt like a wobbly imposter. He'd picked up one of the mermaid's purses I'd placed on the table alongside the sea glass earrings—my little nod to Sam.

"Mermaid sac?"

The misnomer—combined with his earnest expression—had cracked me up. Nowadays, Blake swung by my craft fair booth with little Hope in tow; he'd encouraged me to hire a graphic designer for my website and helped me find the storefront in Stony Creek. His relentless support was heartwarming and sometimes intimidating. It meant I didn't have the luxury of giving up.

On the train, I wrapped up the conversation with our realtor and gathered Hope onto my lap. She squirmed as I planted a kiss on her plump cheek. Sometimes, when I was lucky, she still emitted traces of that milky-sweet scent from infanthood. I remembered putting my lips to her downy head and breathing it in, slightly terrified by the ferocity of my love. Hope had Blake's pert little pout and my own downturned blue eyes. She'd been delighted to see her own features mirrored on the puppet at Grandma's house, squealing when Blake animated her. *Hi, Hope. I'm Hope, too!*

Out of habit, I pulled the heart-shaped piece of notebook paper from my pocket, its edges feathered with age. Hope tried to pry it out of my fingers.

"Open," she commanded. She'd been doing this ever since I told her it was a letter from an old friend.

I shook my head, slipping it back into its pocket. "Not today, honey."

Now that Blake and I lived in Stony Creek, I occasionally met Sam's stepmother for lunch. She'd been the one to give me the stack of heart-shaped notes in Sam's jewelry box: notes I'd written Sam back in high school. I'd unearthed a couple Sam had given me in my closet in Guilford and carried at least one around with me at all times like a good luck charm. The one in my pocket now was the note in which Sam had mentioned buying purple curtains for our future RISD dorm room. Remembering the line gave me a deep pang, even while making me smile.

Sam's case remained cold. I still regularly woke to nightmares of finding her body. For years I continued calling the police station, urging them to look under the floorboards at 128 Whitfield Street, even though I knew it was far too late for them to find anything. Shortly after Patterson came to talk to me in the hospital, The Sisterhood relocated to New Mexico, leaving the pink house barren.

Some nights, when Hope and Blake were both asleep, I stalked them online. Unsurprisingly, they'd rebuilt a following in New Mexico and were still advertising their wedding services. Sometimes they posted videos of sliced cakes and couture gowns before speaking directly to the camera. Then their luminous faces filled my phone screen, mouths bracketed now with fine lines. Eden didn't shy away from showcasing her whitened eye. It seemed a point of pride. Three months after our showdown at the house, a new girl had joined their ranks. She had a face like a beautiful alien and my first reaction, ridiculously, had been a lash of envy.

Eight years later, I felt The Sisterhood's aliveness like a phantom limb. I thought of them whenever I heard about an engagement or a wedding. Sometimes I'd wake in the dead of night, heart stuttering, certain they'd arrived on my doorstep to kill me once and for all. Although I'd managed to escape physically from 128 Whitfield Street, Eden was right—I'd always be tethered to them. It was something I wrestled with. I'd never be a part of that world again, and while that should have been a comfort, there was a kernel of me that grieved the fact they'd turned out to be who they were. After all, I had The Sisterhood to thank for opening my eyes to my power, and also them to blame.

I'd be lying if I said getting married and having a child hadn't given me pause. Truthfully, I'd always had my reservations, and Eden and Cora had only amplified them. Was it really an either/or situation for women? If I chose to have a family, did that have to mean sacrificing my selfhood? I decided to throw caution to the wind and find out. Blake and I had a courthouse wedding, which lessened my anxiety somewhat (though for a week before tying the knot, I'd had nightmares of spotting Eden and Cora in the audience while taking my vows). And in the end, though I still don't consider myself especially nurturing or maternal, I did succumb to the pang of wanting to create something— someone—meaningful with Blake.

On days when I feel like I'm crushing this motherhood thing, I imagine flinging it in Eden's face. *Told you I could have it all!* Other times, I worry Eden might have hit on some irrevocable truth, and it chills me to the bone. Because for all the times I feel like I'm pulling off the impossible, there are the days I flail.

Take the hellish week or so when baby Hope started feeding every hour and a half. Nauseous with exhaustion at three A.M., I'd looked down at her screaming in her bassinet, and the thought had ripped through me: *Why did I do this?*

And the afternoon I'd turned away from Hope on the playground to draft an email to a client and looked up to find her shrieking with a skinned knee. I'd felt so guilty I didn't touch my phone until Hope had gone to bed that night. I couldn't stop thinking about the way the other moms on the playground had looked at me, their doe-like eyes telegraphing pity and its subtext: *Thank God it wasn't me who screwed up this time.*

"So she fell," Blake had said, when I told him what was bothering me. "Kids skin their knees all the time. You can't be expected to shield her from everything."

My mouth had twisted up. I didn't know how to tell him the moms at the playground wouldn't have looked at Blake the same way, had *he* been the one supervising Hope.

It took me until I was undressing for bed that night to realize the scar on my hip had started to bleed. Since our wedding, this had been happening with some regularity. The bleeding was never severe, but enough to stain the waistband of whatever I was wearing. I'd gotten into the habit of wearing a Band-Aid every day just in case. The scar itself was neat and unassuming: a tiny white eye. Yet on some level, I was always bracing for it to rupture, just as my vows had threatened.

As the train doors clacked shut, I twirled my engagement ring on my left hand. It was a yellow sapphire; far more modest than the flashy diamond I'd returned to Noah. After losing my spined ring on the floor of the bridal salon, I'd never made a replacement. Now, I studied my naked right hand. Maybe it was time to start thinking about a new ring, and the intention I'd bury within it.

Hope wormed around in my lap, stabbing a finger at my phone screen to bring it to life.

I deadened the screen. Much as Blake rolled his eyes, I was determined to minimize her exposure to screens for as long as possible. "Let's play a game instead. I spy with my little eye, something . . . blue!"

Hope's bright lips drew together with concentration as her eyes flitted around the train. Suddenly, her finger shot out to point directly across the aisle. "That lady's ugly dress?"

I managed to stifle a guffaw just in time, pushing my daughter's pointer finger away from the sack-like number. Hope could be vicious in that unfiltered way kids often were, but I had to hand it to my daughter: her taste was spot-on. "Don't point, honey. Keep looking."

Hope's eyes continued to rove around the car. I was waiting for her to spot the cobalt wings of a butterfly pin on a nearby messenger bag, but maybe I'd chosen something too discrete.

Sudden coldness slithered along my forearms. Out of the corner of my eye—something blue. Or, more accurately, white-and-blue: a perfect painted eye on the back of a black beetle, scurrying across one grimy windowpane.

Terror spiked in me. The next second, I blinked, and the blue-and-white pattern disappeared. It was just a roach, clambering along the smudged glass.

I touched a hand to my breastbone as if to quiet the hammering of my heart beneath it.

"Mommy," Hope said. Her eyes were urgent.

"What, honey?"

She pointed to my side. "Your boo-boo."

I looked down and gasped. Hope was right: my scar had started bleeding—and far worse than I'd seen it in years, painting my blouse with a crimson sunburst.

I dug frantically in my bag for a Band-Aid, but came away with only handfuls of Hope supplies: pouches of applesauce and goldfish crackers and her raggedy-eared stuffed rabbit. I took a couple of tissues and pressed them under my shirt. I could only pray they'd be enough to stanch the blood before we made it to my in-laws'.

Hope was still staring at the spreading blood. "It hurt?"

It did, in fact, feel like a hot knife twisting in my side. But I forced my grimace into a smile. I'd do anything to keep my daughter from understanding this particular brand of pain. At least, for as long as I could.

"No," I said, smoothing down her hair. Straight and dark, just like mine. "Mommy's okay. Promise."

ACKNOWLEDGMENTS

Jenny Chen, I am so very grateful for you and your enthusiasm for *Under Her Spell*. When we met for the first time on a video call and you asked me about a second book, I blurted what felt like an absolutely absurd idea and worried I'd scared you off. I wasn't prepared for the way your eyes lit up—and, later, all the grueling work you'd pour into shaping both the novel and me as a writer. Thank you, from the bottom of my heart.

Chelsey Emmelhainz, what did I do to deserve you?! You are the best champion a writer could ask for—warm, encouraging, and oh-so-wise. It's a privilege—and a massive relief—to have you in my corner.

Mae Martinez, it's been an absolute joy working alongside you. In fact, some of my favorite memories surrounding this book include the brainstorming calls with you,

Jenny, and Chelsey. I'm sure all that crackling creative energy would've made The Sisterhood proud.

Thank you, Scott Biel, for the breathtaking cover: the perfect combination of spooky and beautiful. A big thanks goes to Katie Horn, Sarah Breivogel, Meghan O'Leary, Emma Thomasch, Jocelyn Kiker, Susan Turner, and the rest of the spectacular team at Random House who played a part in making this book come to life.

Thanks to Mom, Dad, and Sara for providing comfort during the inevitable ups and downs of publishing a sophomore novel. And, of course, a huge thank-you to Andy—for so many things, but mainly for serving as the model for a generous, loving, and supportive spouse. You make me so happy, and I'm beyond excited for our next adventure.

© KOMAN PHOTOGRAPHY

K. L. CERRA uses her writing to explore the complexities—and the darker sides—of relationships. When not writing or seeing clients as a marriage and family therapist, Cerra is likely walking her Boston terrier or exploring the local botanical gardens. She lives with her husband in a small beach town outside of Los Angeles.

klcerra.com
X: @kl_cerra

ABOUT THE TYPE

This book was set in Baskerville, a typeface designed by John Baskerville (1706–75), an amateur printer and typefounder, and cut for him by John Handy in 1750. The type became popular again when the Lanston Monotype Corporation of London revived the classic roman face in 1923. The Mergenthaler Linotype Company in England and the United States cut a version of Baskerville in 1931, making it one of the most widely used typefaces today.